WIND-UP

A Peter Marklin Mystery

WIND-UP

NEVILLE STEED

St. Martin's Press
New York

mys
F
STE

Library of Congress Cataloging-in-Publication Data
Steed, Neville.
    Wind-up / Neville Steed.
        p.   cm.
    ISBN 0-312-05998-1
    I. Title.
    PR6069.T387W5   1991
    823′.914—dc20   90-21948
                                                                          CIP

First published in Great Britain by George Weidenfeld and Nicolson
Limited.

First U.S. Edition: May 1991
10 9 8 7 6 5 4 3 2 1

For my family

WIND-UP

One

The incline proved too steep for the tank. It slithered backwards, its gun turret swivelling loosely around in its mount. Before I could react, it hit the jeep parked on the level ground and overturned.

With fear and trepidation, I looked down on the scene. Then after a surreptitious glance over my shoulder towards the street, I reached out and picked up the jeep. To my relief, the slide of the tank had not scratched its military paintwork. For post-war Dinky jeeps in truly mint condition are a bit hard to come by these days and, thus, a scratch or chip can knock some twenty or thirty pounds off its value.

The same manufacturer's Medium Tank was already slightly playworn, so one chip more was neither here nor there. But on quick inspection, no further damage had been inflicted. I picked it up and placed it on a less steep section of the moulded Diorama, where its metal-link tracks could still find some grip.

By then, I must admit, I was starting to regret my first real foray into window-dressing – something slightly more ambitious than my usual arrays of neat toy boxes with contents removed and displayed on their lids. But having acquired the Diorama from a war-games freak, who tossed it in with a collection of military toys I had bought from him, I had decided to put it to some use. And, I must say, by the time I had finished dressing it with a selection of Dinky, Corgi, Britains and Solido tanks, transporters, armoured cars, reconnaissance cars, jeeps and Bren gun carriers, the window of my Toy Emporium did look a mite more attractive, even though the differing scales of the vehicles displayed did not exactly lend dramatic realism. And what's more, I doubted whether it would really trigger any more punters to ding my doorbell and shell out (military shells, of course) their shekels on my vintage toys. For your average toy collector, in my experience, is often a deadly serious customer with an almost Calvinist suspicion of anything that smacks of showmanship.

So why did I bother with the Diorama at all? Good question. Well, I suppose, because it would otherwise have just lain there in my shop, gathering dust rather than customers. Secondly, dressing the window had given me something to do that trade-slack morning, other than worry about my overdraft with the bank, that is. And thirdly, I had felt for some time that my dear old shop, from the outside, looked about as inviting as an undertakers during the Great Plague or, even worse, a VAT office.

The early June sun suddenly melted the mist that had been drifting round Studland Bay since before dawn and its shafts soon laser-beamed my window area into a good imitation of a Hotpoint oven at regulo five. So I finished off the Diorama at a rate of knots, before I was done to a turn, then had the perfect excuse for going out into the late spring air to appraise my handiwork from the punter's viewpoint.

The effect of my efforts was, somehow, disappointing. After a minute or two's appraisal, I analyzed the problem down to two causes. One, the Diorama was sitting too low in the window to dominate the display, and thus needed raising nearer to eye-level. Two, it was totally at variance with the rest of the offerings on show.

The next half-hour, therefore, saw me sweating it out in the fenestered furnace, building up a base for the Diorama and then arranging serried ranks of toys each side of it, so that the whole took on a pyramid shape, like some Aztec temple designed by a short-sighted priest before the Spanish introduced the concept of spectacles.

It was as I was setting the last building block in place – a pre-war Schuco Telesteering Car 3000, in its original box and with its original piano-wire steering control – that I heard a real car slow and swish to a stop outside. Now, had the car thumped, ground and shrieked its way to a halt, I would have known immediately that it was the dreaded Gus, my neighbourhood sometime-fisherman-and-all-time-angler-after-free-Heinekens friend. After all, it was daylight and thus well within Gus's prescribed hours for morning drinking. But the svelte swish and the costly clunk of the car's door spoke of new Rovers and Jaguars, rather than forty-year-old Ford Populars.

Now, rather embarrassed at being caught sweating like the proverbial pig in my window by what I imagined, with my rose-tinted brain, to be a well-off customer, I started to sidle out past the display, without looking back towards the street. But I had only managed to get one foot down on the floor when I heard a sharp rapping of knuckles and not on the door, curse it, but on the window.

Now I had to look round. But instantly, I wished I hadn't. For, though I had been quite right about the style of car – it was a Rover, the 800 series – it bore a red slash down the entire length of its whiter than white paintwork. And the knuckles belonged to the pinker than pink, freckled and carrot-topped copper of the Bournemouth branch of the Dorset constabulary – one Inspector Digby 'Keep out of my hair, Marklin' Whetstone.

'Taken to playing with your toys in full public view, have you now?'

The Inspector smiled patronizingly as I mopped my brow with a handkerchief.

I have long since learnt not to rise to every taunt from the dear officer's lips, otherwise my hackles would never have been in the retracted position in his company.

So I countered with, 'You've got me stumped, Inspector, this time.'

He puckered the freckles on his forehead. 'Stumped? You? I can't believe what I'm hearing.' He leaned forward on my counter. 'I thought very little could ever beat your powers of perception and analysis.'

I looked into the slits of his eyes to try and read his mind. But too many hard years in the force had glazed them into ice-cold nuggets that gave nothing away. So I was forced into the full-frontal question.

'May I enquire why you are sparing time out of your no doubt hectically busy schedule to visit my humble Toy Emporium?'

Whetstone pulled up the stool I keep for my customers and unfolded his weight on to it. 'Can't you guess, Mr Marklin?'

I raised my eyebrows to the ceiling and sighed. 'Okay, Inspector. You win, all hands down. No, I can't guess why you are here. After all, I've done nothing to be in your bad books for months. Promise. Not since the murder* of that poor teacher at

*_Clockwork_, Weidenfeld & Nicolson, 1989.

9

Manners School. What's more, I'm up to date with every parking-ticket fine. I haven't been caught speeding or driving dangerously. (Notice how carefully those last comments were constructed.) I haven't obstructed the highway, covered the countryside with litter, grown marijuana in my window-box, exposed myself to anybody who doesn't reckon it, raped a policewoman or pumped sewage or sileage into Studland Bay. Least, on that latter point, no more than you have, I suspect . . .'

I stopped, not because I had run out of heinous crimes, but because Whetstone's face was now verging on the vermillion.

'All right, Mr Marklin,' he seethed. 'Now you've had your little bit of fun, perhaps I can answer your question.'

I gestured for him to go ahead.

'I asked you to guess why I am here, Mr Marklin, because I thought a man like you might well keep himself abreast of events in the locality. Especially, as your . . . friend, Miss Trench, works for the media too.'

'My friend, as you call Arabella, has a few days' holiday and is up in Shropshire visiting her parents. She won't be back until tonight. And I'm sorry to disappoint you, but I very rarely listen to local radio. I've nothing against it. I guess I'm just too lazy to switch over from long wave and Radio Four.' I paused to mop the last few beads of sweat from my forehead. 'Anyway, Inspector, bring me up to date. What has been happening in this neck of the woods that I don't know about?'

Digby Whetstone slowly filled up his lungs, so I knew I was in for either a longish spiel or an event of mind-blowing drama.

'Murder, Mr Marklin.' He exhaled, then went on, 'Murder. That's what has been happening in this little neck of the woods.'

I did not react for quite a few moments, as I tried both to digest the news, and more crucially, fathom the Inspector's motives for involving yours truly in any way with the killing. If precedent were anything to go by, the dear Inspector was as keen to hear my views on police matters, as a rattlesnake to heed the pleadings of a jack-rabbit. So, if Digby wasn't shopping for advice, what other reason could he possibly have for. . . ? At that point, my whole being froze solid. And Digby obviously heard the cracking of the ice.

'What's wrong, Mr Marklin?' He leaned further forward across the counter, his moustache twitching like a rodent's whiskers at the scent of fear. 'You been kidding me about not knowing about poor Mr Maitland?'

I shook myself free of my iceberg and surfaced with, 'No, no, I promise you I've heard nothing at all about any murder.'

He followed up instantly with, 'But you *have* heard about Mr Maitland?'

His look said I must have done, but try as I might, my memory bank flashed up a big negative. Not only had I never heard of a local Maitland but I had never actually met anyone at all called Maitland in my life.

Digby tried again. 'Maurice Maitland?'

I shook my head. 'No, I've never even heard the name bandied about. Now perhaps you would like to tell me why you think I *should* have heard of the poor man.'

The Inspector blinked his eyes with slow deliberation, then equally deliberately, said, 'Well, in my humble way, I just thought that a vintage toy-dealer like yourself would have heard of a man whose attic is stacked from end to end and from floor to rafters with old toys. That's all.'

We were now in my sitting-room, some ten minutes or so later. Minutes that seemed like hours, as I tried to convince Digby Whetstone that, as far as I knew, no vintage toy-dealer in the whole of the south west had ever heard of a man called Maurice Maitland, with a hoard of old toys that sounded worthy of a Junior Aladdin's cave.

'Toy collectors don't usually keep their obsession to themselves,' I explained. 'Let alone when they've amassed a collection of the size you are indicating. Besides, where on earth would he have come by all these toys, if not from us dealers. So we should have heard of him, shouldn't we? Unless, of course, he only moved to Dorset recently and built up his collection hundreds of miles from here. Say, up north or even abroad . . .'

'Forget that,' Digby interrupted. 'It would seem Mr Maitland has lived in the Purbeck area all his life. From what we've been able to gather so far from his poor wife, he doesn't sound like a globe-trotter. Far from it. Mr Maitland seems to have been a most sober man. His business partner describes him as a model of self-restraint, cautious and careful with his money. Certainly, his home, though comfortable, you understand, by no stretch of the imagination could be called luxurious.' A thin smile flickered

11

across his face. 'Quite unlike his partner's house. But then, that's quite another story.'

'What's the main story, Inspector?' I asked, anxious now to get down to exactly why Digby had called round. I could hardly believe it was simply to check whether I had heard of the murder victim's rather amazing hoard.

'Story? What do you mean, story?'

Impatiently I rose from my chair. 'Look, Digby, you wouldn't have come round here without a damned good reason. And I'd like to know what it is.'

Digby sighed. And when I heard his full reply, I knew the reason.

'I have come round to ask you to accompany me to the Maitlands' house . . .' I swallowed hard. '. . . so that you can give me a rough assessment of the value of the toys that appear to have been stolen last night.'

I swallowed more gently, then looked round at him. 'Maitland was murdered trying to protect his precious collection?'

'It would seem so, Mr Marklin, yes.'

I thought for a moment. 'So someone in Dorset had heard of it.'

Digby shrugged. 'Quite a few of Mr Maitland's intimates must have known, of course.'

'Like his wife?' I tried.

'His wife, his business partner, Savage, and no doubt, some personal friends. Naturally I have my men checking up on how many were aware of his obsession right now.'

'May I ask when all this happened?'

'We know precisely. Soon after midnight. Twelve forty-five, to be exact.'

'How can you be so sure of the time?'

'Mrs Maitland woke up when she heard a crashing noise from downstairs. This, we assume, must have been her husband's body falling back against the dresser in the kitchen. She looked at the clock, then got up and went into her husband's bedroom . . .'

He caught my look.

'. . . Yes, Mr Marklin, they apparently preferred to sleep in separate bedrooms, as Mr Maitland had a habit of snoring. Anyway, she went down and into the kitchen and was immediately set upon by the thief himself. Got some very nasty bruises and abrasions has Mrs Maitland, I'm afraid.'

'So she saw her husband's murderer?'

12

'Only for a split second, before she fainted away with the shock of it all. And do you blame her?'

'But she's managed to give you his description?'

The characteristic thin smile returned. 'A description. But too vague to tell us whether it was Pretty Polly, Kayser, Aristoc, St Michael, or even Tesco's own.'

This time I sighed. 'So he wore a stocking over his head?'

He nodded. 'Don't they all these days? Stocking manufacturers must owe the criminal fraternity a great deal. A fact they carefully avoid to mention in their company reports, no doubt.'

'May I ask what the murder weapon was?'

'You may. Indeed, it's somewhat in your line of country.'

My mind boggled. 'He was killed by a *toy*?'

Digby laughed and shook his head. 'Not a toy, exactly. But a model all the same. A bronze model that was apparently Mr Maitland's pride and joy. I'm told it's a sculpture of a Benz racing car, made around 1920, probably as a presentation piece. Anyway, the thief certainly presented it to Mr Maitland's skull last night with shattering effect.'

Digby looked at his oversized and overgilded watch, then unfolded from the chair. 'However, I'm afraid I have already spent too long here answering your questions. If you don't mind, Mr Marklin, perhaps we can now go over to the Maitlands' where you can begin to answer some of mine.'

And so it came to pass . . .

We went in separate cars, as I had no wish to be away from my Toy Emporium for longer than necessary. For this particular spring had not, up to now, sprung a rate of income that kept much in advance of outgoings; and that was without having a closed shop policy enforced for a morning by one Digby Whetstone.

The Maitlands' residence proved to be a cottage just outside the stone and slate village of Corfe that lies within the protective shadow of its ruined castle. Although it was over a mile from the village, on the Church Knowle road, the tip of the tallest of the castle's remaining ramparts could be seen from the small but immaculately tonsured garden.

The house itself lay some way back from the road, where two police cars were parked like white uniformed guards, one each side of the drive's gate-posts. Like its garden, the cottage was compact, but neat to a fault, its whitewashed walls reflecting the sun and contrasting with the shiny fresh green paint of the window frames and doors.

After Digby had muttered a few words that I couldn't catch to the men in the patrol cars, he indicated that I should follow him up the stone-flagged path to the front door.

As I obeyed, he whispered across to me, 'See what I mean about the house? And yet, if your prices are anything to go by, his toys must be worth a fortune.'

I made no comment. Firstly, because the house, though small, possessed more than a smidgin of charm. And secondly, it was certainly quite large enough for two people – that is, if those two people were unlike Digby, and did not equate quality with size and ostentation. I've never set eyes on the Inspector's own 'Dunroamin' – and hope to keep it that way – but I suspect his mortgage is stretched as thin as a condom over the maximum square footage feasible. Never mind the quality, count the bedrooms.

The door was opened by the squarest-set constable I have ever seen and then I was wafted speedily through the tiny hall and into the sitting-room – but not so fast that I did not spot the activity still going on in what I took to be the kitchen and scene of the murder.

'If you don't mind, Mr Marklin,' Digby instructed, 'we'd like you to restrict your movements to this room and, of course, the attic area, where most of the toys are.'

I nodded assent, then commented, 'If you want me to value what's stolen, then it would help if there was an inventory . . .'

Whetstone reached into an inside pocket and took out a folded sheet of paper and handed it to me. On inspection, it proved to be a handwritten list of around twenty or so toys.

'Are these the toys that are missing?'

'As far as Mrs Maitland can tell right now, yes. But she is still suffering considerably from the shock of it all and there could well be more she may remember later.'

'So Mrs Maitland knew her husband's collection well, then?'

Digby shrugged. 'I suppose so. You can't really live with someone for years without getting to know more or less what they possess, now can you?'

I looked back at the list and read it carefully. One thing struck me immediately. All the items bar one were small die-cast models

of the forties and fifties, including the complete 40 series from
Dinky – Austin Devon, Standard Vanguard, Hillman Minx, Riley
and Triumph 1800 and the like – and an almost complete 100
series from the same manufacturer – M.G. Midget, Sunbeam
Alpine, Triumph TR2, Austin Healey, and so on.

The one exception to the die-cast rule was a Minic Green Line
bus. But there was no indication as to whether it was of pre-war
or post-war manufacture. (The models are more or less identical,
except for their present-day values.)

'Well?' Digby asked.

'Their approximate value?'

He nodded.

'Well, if they are all boxed and in mint condition, the nineteen
die-casts could be worth fifteen hundred pounds plus. The Minic
bus about another hundred. Maybe more.'

'So we could be talking almost two thousand pounds.'

'On a good day.'

Digby pursed his lips so that blue veins showed. 'Not too bad a
haul for a burglar.'

I frowned. 'But worth murdering for?'

'Oh, he didn't murder for the toys, Mr Marklin. He struck out
because he had been caught in the act.'

He took the list back from me.

'Anyway, thanks for valuing the list.'

'Not at all,' I smiled, then added hopefully, 'Anything more
you would like me to do?'

For I was more than a little curious about the rest of the goodies
in the attic, and it would have been a pity to have visited
Aladdin's cave and not caught a glimpse of the treasure.

At first, his reply disappointed me. 'I'd like your comments on
the list. Might give us a clue as to the kind of criminal we're
dealing with.'

I paused for a minute, which gave me time to dream up both a
reply and a ploy.

'Well,' I replied eventually, 'the items stolen certainly point to a
die-cast rather than a tin-plate collector. But that conclusion could
be totally misleading.'

'How do you mean?'

'Could be that ninety-nine per cent of Maitland's collection is
composed of die-casts. Or the intruder was interrupted before he

could lay his hands on any more toys. May I ask whether these were stolen from the attic or are there cabinets full of. . . ?'

'No cabinets,' Digby interrupted. 'Mrs Maitland told me the house is only just big enough for the normal furniture, let alone toy cabinets as well. So the collection has always been kept in the attic, which apparently Mr Maitland had specially converted into one big room to accommodate it.'

'How do you get up to the attic? By loft-ladder?'

'No. They've had a separate spiral staircase made that runs up an old disused chimney in the kitchen. You know, where the open range must have been years ago. Goes straight up and into the loft. Cramped but convenient, I suppose. I find it dark and eerie myself. Mrs Maitland says she has always hated going up there herself.'

I took my opportunity. 'Well, if you would like me to, Inspector, I'll willing to take my chances in the chimney, and go and have a look at the rest of the collection. After all, what burglars leave behind must sometimes be as significant as what they take.'

He eyed me for a second, then started for the door. 'Wait here a moment, Marklin and I'll see if our boys have finished up there yet.' And with that, he was gone.

For the first time, I had a chance to look round the room. Somehow, it was not quite as neat as I had been expecting. Perhaps 'neat' is the wrong word. 'Ordered' might be a better one. Though everything that could shine, shone with polish and there was not a speck of dust to be seen, even on the exposed timbering of the walls and ceiling (dust traps in old cottages and often neglected), there was not the same sense of orderliness about the arrangement of the furniture – the chintz-covered easychairs, the sofa, even the grandfather clock in the corner – that the garden, for instance, displayed.

Over by the mullioned window, I spotted a framed photgraph, the only one in the room, standing on a compact nest of tables. It seemed to depict a couple. Curious as a cat, I went over and inspected it. The two figures looking out at me, I assumed, must be the late Mr Maitland and his wife; the husband with a rather proprietorial arm around his spouse. Their expressions gave nothing away, as they were both beaming back at the camera lens in that glazed way only saying 'cheese' can produce. He, tallish but rather stooped, somewhere in his forties, with dark hair matt and dead enough to be dyed, contrasting sharply with his pale, almost chalklike, complexion. All in all, poor Mr Maitland, if such he was, did not look a million laughs.

She, too, had dark hair, but with some natural life and colour still left in it. Which, I suppose, was not too surprising, as she looked about ten to fifteen years younger than her companion – say thirty-five or so. An age gap heightened by her considerable tan that spoke of as many hours under the rays of sun or lamp, as her companion had obviously spent indoors in smoke-filled rooms, trying, no doubt, to earn the odd crust.

It was as I was about to replace the frame on the table that Digby Whetstone popped his head round the door.

'This Mr and Mrs Maitland?' I asked, indicating the photograph.

His eyes shut down to even narrower slits as he peered my way. 'Looks like it from here,' he muttered, then beckoned with his finger. 'But if you're going up the chimney, Santa Claus, you had better come right away.'

I put down the photograph and followed him.

I instantly saw what he meant about the staircase. There being no windows, it was rather like going up a very narrow version of the leaning tower of Pisa wearing a blindfold. Anyone with claustrophobia would have had the screaming ab-dabs.

Once in the attic, however, there was sufficient light from a fluorescent strip screwed to the rafters to illuminate what I had climbed to examine. And the sight took away what little breath the staircase had left.

'My God . . .' I whispered to myself in amazement.

'What's wrong?' came Digby's voice from behind.

'Wrong?' I half-laughed. 'There's nothing wrong. I guess Aladdin must have come out with the Persian equivalent of "My God!" after Sesame had opened up the treasure cave.'

Digby puffed up beside me. 'I take it you think it's a pretty fair collection.'

'Pretty fair. That's a bit like saying the Queen has a pretty fair collection of jewellery or the Saatchis of paintings. And that's just from a first glance around all this stuff.'

I stooped and picked up the nearest box to me. 'See this?'

The Inspector screwed up his eyes to peer at the label.

'Meccano Motor-Car Constructor Outfit No. 2.'

'Know roughly how much this is worth?'

I lifted the lid and the red and blue car parts were exactly as new and still tied into their positions with the original string.

He shrugged.

'Well, it would raise enough to buy a second-hand real car like a Mini.'

I pointed down towards a small stack of similar boxes. 'Seems he's got quite a few of these Constructor kits, too.'

Digby did not seem to be all that impressed. 'What about the rest of it?'

I walked slowly round the stacks of boxes, between which Mr Maitland had conveniently left narrow walkways; and I quickly realized I needed far more time than I would obviously be allowed that morning to really assess their quality and worth. But what did quickly become evident was that Mr Maitland seemed to have had a penchant for acquiring in bulk. For there was rarely only one item of any type. Most were in threes or fours, the rest at least in pairs. For instance, of the hundred or so boxed Minic clockwork vehicles that I found stacked in a corner, there seemed to be only around a dozen different types, mostly buses and lorries and, curiously, caravans. Of the equal quantity of Schuco tinplate vehicles, again only ten to fifteen types. In this case, mainly 'Studio' racers, 'Examinico' sports cars, 'Radio' cars (with tinny musical boxes standing in for radios), and the slug-like 'Kommando Anno 2000' streamliners that stop and start through a breath operated shutter in their grilled roofs.

Naturally, there were stacks of boxed Dinkys, Corgis and Spot-On die-casts, mainly from the fifties and, once more, most types seemed duplicated or triplicated. I counted at least ten Dinky De Sotos and, would you believe, fifteen Spot-On Rolls-Royce Phantom Vs – one of the most sought after models in the range, complete with tiny figures of the Queen and Prince Philip seated in state in the rear, a rug over their knees.

As if that wasn't enough, the next two stacks of boxes put everything I had seen so far completely in the shade. And proved to be the pièces de résistance of this extraordinary attic hoard. I just did not believe my eyes. For the first stack was completely composed of those incredibly wonderful tinplate cars, taxis and light commercial vehicles produced in the twenties and thirties by the car manufacturer, Citroen. Originally created, no doubt, as publicity for their full-size vehicles, their quality and accuracy

18

are so superb that they have become the crème de la crème for the tinplate toy collector and have for years now commanded four-figure prices at auction. And Mr Maitland had four Citroen taxis, four 'Torpedo' open cars in different colours, three tipper trucks, two saloons in brown . . . need I go on?

But the second stack was, if anything, even more breath-taking. A collection of legendary Marklin (no, no relation) tinplates made in Germany in the twenties and thirties. They ranged from their very fine Motor-Car Constructor Kits (in my opinion, considerably superior to those made in Britain by Meccano), to the superb Junkers 52 Trimotor Aircraft Kit, to, undoubtedly, the most valuable items in the whole attic – three large Marklin tinplate ships, a battle-cruiser and two liners, any one of which at auction could raise enough to buy a small house or pay off a mortgage.

I had hardly recovered from the shock of the last discovery, when I heard Digby mutter impatiently, 'Come on, Mr Marklin, what do you think? I really can't waste any more time up here, while you . . .'

'. . . .salivate,' I interrupted.

'Okay. So you find the collection impressive. That doesn't really surprise me. But what I want to know right now is roughly how much you think the whole lot might be worth. And two, whether what the murderer took and what he left behind gives you any ideas as to his likely character.'

I took a deep breath and then cast my eye once again over the whole collection.

'Answer to first question. At least half a million. On a good day, maybe three quarters or even more. All I can advise is that when poor Mrs Maitland comes to sell all this – that is, if she ever does – she doesn't sell it all at once, at one auction. She'll get more if she spreads it out a bit over . . .'

Digby waved his hand. 'Okay, okay. Tell that to Mrs Maitland, when she's recovered, not to me.'

'By the way, where is she right now?' I asked. 'Still at the station?'

He shook his head. 'No. A friend of hers is looking after her. Woman called Cartwright. She lives the other side of Corfe. But I would advise you not to contact Mrs Maitland for quite some time. She's very distressed. Anyway, on to my second question. About the murderer. . . ?'

'Oh, yes. The murderer. Well, look at it this way. He took goodies worth two thousand and left at least half a million pounds' worth behind.'

'So? He was obviously caught in the act, before he could take any more.' Digby pointed to the piles of die-cast toys. 'After all, the Dinkys are nearest the top of the staircase.'

'And anyway,' I added, 'you can't carry much at a time down that spiral horror.'

'Right. And some of those other boxes are pretty big. At least most of what he took he could have stuffed into his pockets. Any more clues about him?'

I shrugged. 'Not really. What fascinates me is how he might have heard of Maitland's hoard in the first place.'

Digby smirked. 'Maybe one of you old toy merchants blabbed.'

I looked back at the skyscraper stacks.

'If I had to guess right now, none of this was bought recently or from any "old toy merchants", as you call us.'

'Really? So how did Mr Maitland come by all this stuff, do you imagine?'

'I reckon he bought these toys many years ago, when they had little or no value. Probably as job lots at closing-down sales. You know how many small toy shops and confectioners have gone out of business since the initial post-war boom. At least it would explain why there are precious few single items in the whole collection. Most are in lots of three, four, five or more.'

Digby fingered his moustache. 'So you think Maitland may have got most of it for next to nothing?'

'Maybe. It would also explain why I've never heard of him and I doubt if my colleagues have, otherwise I'd have picked something up on the grapevine.'

'The murderer must have had a grapevine of his own,' the Inspector muttered, then suddenly grasped my arm. 'Thank you, Mr Marklin, for coming. And for your comments. I will check out your theory about how the poor man came by all this stuff, when Mrs Maitland has had a chance to pull herself round a bit. Meantime . . .' His fingers tightened their grip on my arm. '. . . meantime, Mr Marklin, on no account interpret my invitation of today as an opening for you to get involved with this case.' His voice hardened. 'In any way whatsoever. Do you understand?'

'Message understood, Inspector. Roger and out.'

'And stay out,' he couldn't resist adding, as he turned and beckoned me towards the spiral calamity.

Two

I refreshed Arabella's glass from my anonymous bottle of Muscadet – won in a raffle at our local, not by me but by Gus. He exchanged it for a four-pack of Heineken – and went over and switched on the lights. For the evening sun had by now definitely dunked itself in Studland Bay.

'I just don't believe it,' she reiterated, stretching her long legs out in front of her.

I laughed. 'I would never have dreamt Digby would ever ask for my help either.'

'No, it's not just that, Peter. Think of it. Here am I, a reporter on the local rag, and a rotten murder just would happen at the exact time I'm taking a few days' holiday. What's more, it's all connected with vintage toys and just who exactly am I daft enough to live with – a blasted dealer in old toys, that's who.'

She threw up the only hand free of a glass. 'Wowee! Talk about sod's law, sub-section, timing. Arabella Trench, you must have written that statute from start to finish.'

I settled into a chair opposite her and raised my own glass. 'Me Lud, may I intercede for a second? To welcome you back to this modest Studland circuit and I think I'm speaking for the whole court here,' I glanced down at Bing, curled up on the carpet, but still cocking a blue, Siamese eye in Arabella's direction, 'when I say, we have missed your happy, smiling presence whilst you've been away in Salop, administering to your mater and pater, who, I trust, are both in fine fettle . . .'

'I've never seen their fettle in better shape,' she smiled, then raised her own glass. 'Missed you too. I mean . . . you two, and you, comma, too.'

'Point taken,' I grinned.

'No. A point is a full stop, isn't it?'

I blew a kiss. What other answer can you give, when conversation had really come to a full stop.

We both sipped our wine for a bit, then Arabella suddenly put her glass down and looked at me with her big, Liza Minelli eyes.

'But, joking aside, it's really awful, isn't it? I mean, being murdered for a handful of toys. Who the hell would do such a dreadful thing? I know you've told me enough stories of the lengths collectors will sometimes go to get the toy they want, but . . .'

'I've never mentioned murder,' I interrupted, but then added, 'But don't forget last night's intruder did not go expressly to murder Maitland, I would imagine. Just to go up to his attic and help himself to the toys. But he probably woke Maitland going up that awful flight of stairs, then, when he heard someone coming, rushed down again to the kitchen, picked up that bronze trophy, waited, say, behind the kitchen door, then when Maitland came in . . . crash. Down with the Benz racer on his head.'

Arabella closed her eyes and ran her hand through her short hair. It sprang back through her fingers like pile on the most fabulous of carpets.

'Oh, God, don't go on. I can see a very similar scene playing out in your Toy Emporium, if you're not careful. Especially now we know there's some crazed collector on the loose round here, who's not averse to stoving a few heads in to get a handful of the little toys he lusts after.'

She grabbed her drink and emptied it in one. 'Hell, here am I imagining how I would feel if anything like that happened to you. Think of how Mrs Maitland must feel right now, wherever she is. Her husband lying in some morgue or being cut up on a post-mortem slab, all because he had a childish fascination for playthings that she probably did not value at all.'

'She may have liked them too. Who knows?'

'If she liked them, he wouldn't have kept them all stashed away in the attic, would he? I mean, you'd have thought they'd have had at least a few dotted about the house. But, you say you didn't see any.'

'Maybe they were afraid of burglars . . .' I stopped abruptly, as I realized the ironic significance of what I had just said.

'So should *you* be, from now on.' Arabella's eyes flashed their concern. 'I don't know when you last valued the stuff in your shop, but it must be worth a considerable amount too.'

'Not nearly as much as Maitland's. Besides, I borrow money to buy some of my stock.'

'But you know what I'm getting at.'

'I know. But short of fitting locks worthy of Fort Knox and a burglar-alarm system as big as a Buick, what can I do?'

I rose and dribbled the last of the Muscadet into her glass.

Neither of us spoke for a while and then Arabella remarked, 'I wonder if Mrs Maitland realizes the value of that atticful. I mean, if you're right and he's had them for donkey's years, maybe she just regards them as her husband's harmless hobby and not as a potential goldmine.'

'Could be. I've heard of quite a few collectors who are afraid to tell their wives the true worth of their hoards. Just in case their better halves get assinine and irresponsible ideas about cashing them in for a bigger house for the family or a cruise round the world, a holiday home on the dreaded Costa Brava or private education for the kids . . .'

Arabella grinned. 'Women can be so damned selfish, can't they just? I wonder you men can put up with us for a second.'

Putting down my glass, I got up and went over to her. 'Look, that's enough of the poor Maitlands. I don't want to spend your first night back raking over other people's tragedies, however terrible.'

She looked up at me. 'Got something else in mind to rake over?'

I grasped her hand and pulled her up out of the chair. She didn't resist.

'Yes, you, my love. After four days of enforced celibacy, I can't stand, or rather sit, looking across at your mini-skirted legs any longer.'

She moulded herself to my, not as lithe as it used to be, front. 'So don't look at them.'

'That an order?'

'Until I give my next one.'

'Dare I ask what that's going to be?'

She shrugged, as much as our embrace would allow. 'Don't see why not. One Peter Marklin, sunny side up, to be served in my room in five minutes flat.'

'That's funny,' I smiled. 'I always thought your preference was "well done and over".'

It was great having Arabella around for the next few days. For

23

running toy emporia can be a pretty limiting, lonely experience if punters don't call in to buy or, at least, exchange a little gossip or maybe a precious toy or two. And as I have already indicated, that spring had hardly been the success of the century for either sales or interesting or profitable acquisitions. And I was really far too heavily reliant on my mail-order business to keep the wolf from the door. Luckily, that side had held up fairly well and most days' post included an enquiry, if not always a firm order, for items from the latest stock lists I send out regularly to my comprehensive list of past customers.

So it proved the next morning, a Tuesday. Through my letter-box dropped an enquiry about a boxed Heinkel III bomber, a rather fine small tinplate made by Lehmann of Germany just before the war, complete with leaflet depicting Hitler watching a fly-past of said bombers, which I had advertised for sale at a hundred and thirty-five pounds; and a firm order for a post-war tinplate Hudson car by Tipp & Company, also of Germany, accompanied by the necessary cheque for ninety-five pounds.

This last, the cheque I mean, not the car, Arabella offered to bank for me, as well as doing some shopping for us all and posting the Hudson, whilst I opened up shop and waited for things, or rather punters, to happen.

Well, nothing happened for the first hour, I'm afraid to say. Unless you call Bing spending twenty minutes shut-eye across my knees 'something' – which I guess *he* does. And I'm even more afraid to say what happened ten minutes into the second hour. Squeal, skid, rattle, bang, should give you a clue. It was Gus, as usual making the exact reverse of a svelte and smooth arrival in his upright Ford Popular.

But if the style (?) of his coming was only too familiar, his appearance as he clod-hopped into the shop was certainly not.

'Good God, Gus, what's got into you this morning?'

I stared with amazement at his shirt (I've never seen him wear one. Only a sweater. Season in. Season out.), open at the neck to reveal a cravat (I wouldn't have dreamt he'd ever heard of them, let alone that I'd see him with one). Lowering my eyes, I took in his trousers with equal astonishment. Instead of baggy and patched jeans (I'll swear his are still war-surplus), or nondescript flannels that must, at one time long ago, have been grey, but were now any and every colour under the sun, paint spots, egg stains, oil smears and you name it, I'd rather not, he was wearing a pair of corduroys in dark blue, that could actually pass for near new.

'Correction, Gus. Perhaps I should have said, "What's got on to you this morning?"'

He looked down at himself rather sheepishly. ' 'Ere, don't you go casting nasturtiums at what I'm ruddy wearing. Took a lot of trouble, I did, this morning.'

He pulled up my counter stool and sat down gingerly, as if any sudden movement might crack his crisp ensemble.

'I'm not casting anything, Gus.' Again I gave him the once-over, then added, 'But I would like to ask why we have not had the benefit of eyeing all these gladrags before. Nice as your usual sweater and pants aren't – except for Bing, who loves a sniff through the threads in case a sprat has got caught in them – this kind of gear is as much an advance over them, as a fax machine over a long-distance runner with a bad susceptibility for blisters.'

By this time, Gus had closed both his eyes and his mind to my mean meanderings. And rightly so.

'Finished?' he asked.

'Sorry, Gus, but you can't change the habit of a lifetime and expect no one to take a blind bit of notice.'

I leaned forward across the counter. 'Besides, you wouldn't really want that, would you, Gus?'

He looked up, his bluff old forehead deep ploughed by a frown. 'What yer getting at, old son?'

I grinned. 'Gus, it's what you're getting at that intrigues me. Or rather, *who* you're getting at.'

He looked away, swinging his rock-like frame round on the stool. If he hadn't been a six-foot something, sixty-plus-something even larger, hunk of a fisherman from way back, I'd have taken him right then for a blush-ridden teenager.

'Oh, come on, Gus. Tell me her name. After all, she must be an exceptional lady to get you to jettison your vintage fisherman's clobber for . . .'

'I've jettisoned nothing,' he snapped. 'Be back in 'em this afternoon. Be ruddy glad too.'

He ran a thick digit between his neck and the edge of his cravat, like a cook runs a knife around a cake before turning it out of its tin. 'Feel a right poof in all this.'

I laughed. 'Gus, believe me, even if you wore a dress and

25

lipstick as thick as a whore's brain, you could no more look a poof than . . . well . . . fly.'

He looked somewhat reassured. 'You're not just . . .'

'No, I'm not just . . . Gus. Straight up. What's more, it's nice to see you for a change in some decen . . . different gear. Suits you.'

I came out from behind the counter. 'Now, tell me who this special lady is and why you've got to get all dressed up this morning.'

He straightened his back and I could hear the stool creak. 'Going to me first art class, aren't I?'

I swallowed. 'Pardon?'

'Art class,' he repeated more loudly. 'You know what they are, don't you? Hold 'em down at the Memorial Hall in Swanage.'

I nodded. 'They hold them in other places too. But what on earth are you. . . ?'

He held a great thumb up at arm's length and shut one eye like a comedian imitating a great artist.

'Going to learn all about water-colours, aren't I? Milly's got me paints and brushes, 'cos she knows all about that kind of thing.'

I smiled. 'So she's a Milly, eh? Are you going to tell me Milly who?'

'All right,' he shrugged. 'Her name's Milly Milligan. *Mrs* Milly Milligan.'

I repressed a grin. 'Is there a Mr Milligan?'

He reversed the direction of his thumb. 'Was. Been dead ten years or more now.'

I walked round his stool. 'So your metamorphosis is all because Mrs Milligan would rather you turned up amongst her mates at the class with a clean bib and tucker.'

Another furrowing frown. I guess over my third word but it would have been too much of a hassle to explain.

'Well, I wish you luck, Gus. Who knows, you might turn out to be a Grandfather Moses or another Lowry or. . . ?'

I'd lost him. So I ran back. 'A great painter, Gus. It's never too late to find out you've got talent.'

He sniffed. 'Only going to please her, really. Said it'd be a chance to meet some of her friends. Don't suppose I'll enjoy the rest one bit.'

'I'm sure you will, once you get into it. By the way, do you know yet what you will be painting?'

'Something called Still Life, Milly says.'

'Suits you,' I laughed. 'Anything to do with stills.'

He double, or by the length of time, probably treble took, then grinned himself.

'Rather draw a pint of beer.'

'That a hint, Gus?'

He shrugged. I looked at my watch. It was more than a mite early – even for Gus – but I felt he might need some Dutch courage before he braved the new world of the water-colourist.

I pointed back into the house. 'You know where to find them. I'd better not leave the shop untended. Especially after . . .'

But he'd upped and gone before I could get into the 'afters'.

I'll swear Gus's gullet must be a dead ringer for a bath plug-hole. For that first Heineken had almost disappeared by the time he resumed his seat on the stool.

In a break for a breather, he wiped the froth off his lips with his hand and muttered, ' 'Ere, heard about the murder, then? Over near Corfe. 'Eard it on the wireless, I did.'

I nodded, but no more. I wanted to hear what Gus had to impart first.

'Poor sod. Seems he must have caught the ruddy burglar in the act. Then wham! Skull crushed by one of his own trophies. Cor, I don't know what it's all coming to.' Then Gus leaned towards me. 'And did you hear what the burglar was after? Eh? Did y'hear?'

I nodded again.

'That's really why, old son, I came round on my way to this ruddy water-colour class. See if you'd heard. 'Ere, you'd better be a bit careful yourself.' He pointed a great finger round the shop. 'With all this 'ere on public view. Wireless said he only got away with a few hundreds' worth of toys. But seems there was a whole atticful he left behind. That poor widow woman had better keep her eyes and ears peeled 'case the feller comes back again for the rest.'

He, very pointedly, downed the last of his lager. For the moment, I ignored it. With a shrug, he went on, 'Heard of him, have you, this chap? Must have, I suppose. Big collector like him. What was his name again?'

So I told him – Maitland. And went on to tell him all the rest, right from Digby Whetstone's tap on the window. For once in his life, Gus did not interrupt. Not even with an expletive. But the last mentioned, naturally, formed the overture for his reaction.

'Bugger me, old son. Old Digby! Asking for your help? Cor, loveaduck. Oh dearie me, pull the other leg, it's got bells on. Oh, dearie, dearie me. Cor . . .'

I touched his arm. 'Gus, I've got the point. You're surprised, right? Right. Well, so was I. But it happened. So I went. And saw. And did what he asked of me. Valued the toys.'

'More than half a bloody million, you say?'

'Yep. Could be nearer a million.'

'Why anybody should keep hundreds of thousands of pounds tied up in old toys is well beyond me, old son. Don't mean to be rude and all that, but really . . .'

He looked deep into his empty glass. '. . . you could buy a ruddy brewery for that, you could.'

I took another Heineken out of the six-pack he had so kindly brought from my kitchen fridge into the shop and pushed it across the counter.

As he pulled at its loop, I said, 'From her photograph, Mrs Maitland doesn't look the brewery-buying type.'

Gus raised his can in salute. 'So Digby showed you her photograph, eh? Why was that, then?'

'No, Digby didn't show it to me. I caught a glimpse of it on a table in their house.'

'Suppose she's in hospital, is she? Wireless said she'd got knocked about a bit too.'

'Mrs Maitland is back, and staying with a neighbour, so Digby said.'

A few more gurgles down the bath plug-hole and then Gus surfaced to comment, 'Wonder who'd do a thing like that? You know, break in and murder the husband and beat up the wife, just for a few old toys. Must be a bloody maniac. Not nice thinking of people like that roaming round the countryside. Not nice at all. Especially for people like you, trading in what he seems to be after.'

Gus wagged a finger at me. 'Bet you when they find him, he'll turn out to be some weirdo. Know what I mean? You've often told me quite a few of the people who drop in here are a bit strange. Met one or two, I have, when you've asked me to mind the store. Come to think of it, could be one of your customers, now, couldn't it? Did you say that to the Inspector?'

'No, of course I didn't, Gus,' I said sharply. 'There's a helluva difference between being eccentric and being crazed enough to

28

kill somebody. Besides, I doubt if any of my customers have ever heard of Maitland's little hoard of toys. I don't think any of us dealers know about it, so why should any of them?'

I took it from Gus's sniff that I'd got him there. A couple of glugs later, he said, 'So, old lad, that's the end of it for you, is it? I mean, you don't think Digby will be back?'

'Doubt it. Surprising he came once.' I looked at my watch. 'Hey, I don't want to worry you, Gus, but there's not much point putting on your gladrags, if you turn up too late for the art class.'

Gus blinked at a rate of knots when he saw the time. 'Oh, my Lord, better be off, then. Wish me luck.' He downed the last of the lager in one, then made for the door. As he opened it, he said, 'Like your new window, old son. With the model hill and the tanks and all. Very arty-crafty you're getting all of a sudden.'

'*I'm* getting arty-crafty,' I exploded, pointing at the new 'poncey' gear his Milly had forced him to wear. But all I got from him was a wink. Sod him. He'd got me going yet again.

After Gus had gone, I brooded for a while over the whole Maitland affair. Then, as I had only had one customer – a beetroot-faced man in a Hawaiian shirt that just about completed his Technicolor image, who, after ten agonizing minutes, decided to buy a die-cast Mercury B50 bomber for fifty-five pounds – I spent a little time on the telephone, ringing around my local vintage-toy trade competitors. But none of them had heard of this Maitland either and were just as surprised at the news of his collection as I had been. But nearly all agreed with my conclusion from inspecting the hoard, that he must have bought his goodies years ago, in job-lots at closing-down sales.

'Would we'd had the foresight ourselves,' we all echoed to a man (and one woman).

My last phone call was not about Maitland, however, but about where Arabella and I were going to eat that evening, by way of a little celebration of her returning to the fold (of my arms, that is). I chose a fairly new restaurant we both liked in Bournemouth, that I'd actually had somewhat of a hand in creating – the rather 'tweely' named Gourmet's Playroom.

'Nice to see it doing so well,' Arabella smiled.

I looked round the room. There was not a spare table.

'It's not the food. It's the toys,' I bragged.

913339

Perhaps I had better explain. The Gourmet's Playroom was so called because the owners, a gay pair called Adrian and Amos, had decided they wanted a 'theme' restaurant. And having chosen vintage toys as their theme, they had come to me both to advise on their choice and in some cases, to supply them. These toys, varying in age and type from tinplates of the thirties to die-casts of the forties and fifties, were arranged in display cabinets around the walls, with the occasional larger toy, like the vintage rocking horse and Victorian doll's pram (neither supplied by me), free standing amongst potted palms and the like. The end result was both attractive and original for a restaurant and certainly had helped publicize and mark out Adrian's and Amos's creation from all the other gourmet establishments in the area.

'Rubbish. It's the food,' Arabella corrected me with a mock frown. 'Anyway, I somehow think dear Adrian and Amos' (in case you're wondering, Amos is black. But Amos isn't his real name. God knows what is, but he only affects the name Amos as a tribute to the late and great character from the 'Amos and Andy' series) 'might be starting to regret their theme, after hearing about that poor man Maitland.'

She pointed to the cabinet full of tinplates just across from us. 'At least you live on your premises. Adrian and Amos live over in Sandbanks, so that our maniac killer could empty this place any night he likes.'

'They are well insured,' I commented, 'but I know what you mean. They'd hardly want to start all over again. Vintage toys get harder to find every day that goes by.' I sipped my wine. 'Still, they've one consolation. If Mr Madman does drop by, they won't be here to be killed.'

She took my point and stretched a hand across the table to mine.

'You ought to get one of those burglar alarms that connects straight to the police station.'

I sighed. 'Yeah, maybe.'

There was a pause, then Arabella remarked, 'I know that look of yours. What are you thinking about?'

'Oh, nothing, really.'

'Come on, out with it.'

I put down my wine. 'Well, it's the Maitland business.'

'Which is none of your business,' she reminded me.

For Arabella, quite understandably, had experienced quite

30

enough worry over my amateur sleuthing activities to last her a lifetime. And so she certainly did not want me to get any further involved with Digby Whetstone's current hot potato.

'Which is none of my business. But it doesn't stop me being curious.'

'Okay. Be curious. But don't forget what happened to that cat.'

'I won't. Promise. All I was going to say is that with all the old toys around that are on public display – like in this restaurant, at my shop and many other shops like mine – don't you think it a trifle funny that a toy-crazy burglar should choose to rob an innocuous private house, where even to get to the collection, you have to mount a hellish staircase in total darkness. And that's ignoring the big question mark that hangs over the whole tragic affair.'

'Which is?' She held up a hand. 'No, let me guess. Ah, yes. How said burglar had got to hear of the Maitland collection in the first place.'

I raised my glass. 'Go to the top of the class.'

She laughed. 'And I didn't even bring you an apple this morning, either.'

'I noticed that. Don't let that happen again, Miss Trench. Or . . .'

'Or what?' she asked, the smile in her eyes now taking on rather too naughty a slant, some might say, for a public place.

'Or my teeth will fall out,' I offered, to try to tone things down a bit. For Arabella and I have too often in the past gulped the last of repasts far too fine to hurry, all because we've so over-indulged in sexual word-play over the table, that the only real solution was to leave town fast and head for home. Tonight, I was determined to get to the sweet trolley, at least, before events got out of control. 'For sweets, darlings, are our real speciality, aren't they, Amos?' as Adrian always gushed, usually adding their standard joke, 'Just because dear Amos is around, don't feel you have to choose something chocolate covered.'

Arabella got my drift and her eyes 'Whitehoused' or as near as they'll ever get to that.

'Could be that the burglar will turn out to be someone who knows the Maitlands,' she picked up. 'I mean, maybe not a friend or anything. But we all know a helluva lot of people that we don't class as friends exactly. Like postmen, milkmen, anyone really who calls at one's house regularly. Or perhaps, workmen, who have been employed on the house or in the garden at some time. Even window cleaners. I've often wondered why more window cleaners don't turn into burglars. After all, they have a chance to suss out almost everything in a house every time they whip out their leathers.'

'Yes, I suppose you're right. And the Maitlands' house is all on its own and up a dark lane. Not like this restaurant, in a well-used and well-lit street. Or my shop, even, where there are other houses around. I guess solitary houses up country lanes are considered much safer bets by the itchy finger brigade.'

'Unless the owner catches them at it.'

'M'mmm. Yes. Poor Maitland. He should have stayed in bed, when he heard the intruder.' I shrugged. 'After all, even vintage toys aren't worth dying for.'

'They're not?' Arabella's eyes popped out of her head. 'Well, I'll remind you of what you've just said, if *we* ever hear a bang in the night.'

'Pardon?' I smiled. I should never have said that. For I got the most crippling indigestion through having to bolt those profiteroles . . .

Three

I must say that over the next days, I was far more meticulous about locking up the house and shop than I had been in the past. I even went so far as to fit extra bolts on the shop door, front door and French windows. For some reason, the back door already hung heavy with metal, chains and all. (Previous owner, not me.)

The Maitland murder, of course, still remained a pretty major talking-point in the area, with both local radio and television programmes featuring it strongly. But in essence, they had little new to report, for whatever progress Digby Whetstone and his boys in blue might or might not be making was kept tightly to their collective chest. But, naturally enough, gossip abounded, for it's not every day that the Purbeck hills ring to the cry of 'Murder!' – praise the Lord and don't pass the ammunition.

The wildest piece of tittle-tattle was something dear old Gus overheard in the local hostelry. And that was that Mrs Maitland had not just been knocked about a bit, but also actually raped by the assailant. But that the police were not disclosing this unsavoury fact because they did not wish to reveal to the murderer that they had a specimen of his semen which, these days, could identify him quite as dramatically as a fingerprint.

'Could be, old son,' Gus had ventured, when he'd told me the story. 'From the photos I've seen of her in the paper and on telly, she's quite a looker, isn't she? With all that tan and that. Must have been a temptation for him, once he'd knocked her down. Especially if she was . . . well . . . in her night stuff, like.'

I expressed my doubts and explained the speculation away by saying that some of the men I had met in that particular hostelry had minds that made even the British sewage system seem squeaky clean.

'Take old George Ponsonby, for a start,' I'd said. 'One day I heard him swear that he knew for a fact that Mrs Thatcher was having it away with one of her chauffeurs. And that Dennis didn't mind too much as long as he got driven to the golf course first. Now, really, Gus . . .'

I think he took my point. But he had been right about the particular pictures that the media had published of Mrs Maitland. For, in their usual salacious way, they had chosen shots taken obviously some years ago, when she was a good deal younger, and one of them depicting the poor lady on Studland beach in a rather tight bikini. It was little wonder men like George Ponsonby salivated over their fantasies as to what might have happened that terrible night.

As far as I was concerned, no further light was thrown on the mystery, until, I think it was the next Friday, Arabella blew home from her first day back at the *Western Gazette* with a rumour she'd picked up in the press room. But unlike the gossip, not about Mrs Maitland, but her late husband.

'Seems toys may not have been the only thing he collected,' she announced, when she had plonked herself down in her chair. 'Or kept secret from everyone else.'

I raised my eyebrows. 'Surprise me,' I invited.

'Heard of toy boys?' she grinned.

'He had a toy girl?'

She nodded. 'So the rumour goes.'

I sat back to digest the news. Somehow, the toy girl speculation was hard to fit with the rather humourless, austere man I had seen in the photograph in the Maitland house.

'Want to hear more?'

'I suppose so.'

'Well, you see, one of the typists has a mother living in Wareham and it's she, apparently, who started this rumour off.'

'The mother?'

'Yes. Seems she helps out in a fancy-dress hire place in Wareham.'

'Yes, I've noticed the shop when I've been stuck in a traffic jam in the High Street.'

'Well, she told her daughter that a man the spitting image of the photos of Maitland in the paper, had taken to visiting the shop quite a few times recently. And the lady owner has always insisted on dealing with him herself, What's more, often in a back room.'

'Must be a secret fancy-dress freak,' I muttered in considerable disbelief.

Arabella laughed. 'I know it sounds a bit weird, but that's what her mother maintains.'

'Does she say what the shop owner is like? I mean, is she young, old, attractive, plain, what? Or is she always so dolled up in her own fancy dress that the mother hasn't the slightest idea and thought she was Charlie Chaplin until last weekend?'

'No, you idiot. She knows all right. The woman's real name is Fiona Fairchild.'

'But she calls herself something else?'

'No. Other people call her something else. Seems she runs one of those thirties-style Morgan sports cars. In camouflage, would you believe? You know, painted in irregular stripes of brown and green. I suppose, like a Battle of Britain fighter. Says it's to advertise her shop. Anyway, because of her car, she's called Morgan Fairchild. Get it?'

'Wish I could,' I grinned. 'She's that stunning blonde actress who willows her way through mini-series and *Dynasty* and so on, isn't she?'

'That's right.'

'Don't tell me the Dorset Morgan Fairchild is as sensational a bombshell.'

Arabella laughed. 'No, I don't think she is. But she is quite young. Around twenty-nine, thirty, the mother reckons. Slim, and not at all bad looking. Men, apparently, like her.'

I raised my eyebrows. 'So it would seem. Is she married?'

'Was. Divorced, as far as I can remember.'

'And your typist's mother reckons she might have been having an affair with Maitland?'

Arabella held up her hands. 'If she hasn't mistaken the man.'

'Do you know if she has gone to the police with her suspicions?'

'No. I wouldn't have thought so. But that doesn't mean to say she hasn't.'

I thought for a moment and then heaved a mighty sigh.

'Yes, I know what you mean, darling,' Arabella said quietly. 'It's bad enough having your husband murdered, without then finding out he's been playing around upstairs with far more than old toys.'

The next day, Saturday, started well enough. The late spring sun had chased all the previous day's clouds away and hat jauntily on head, was beckoning everyone down to the beach for an early tan.

I had to take a raincheck on his invitation, so to speak, until at least lunch-time, as Saturday, especially the morning, is the most promising day of the week for vintage-toy customers and I could not possibly afford to let the gold of the sun replace the gold that might be issuing from their pockets. (The perpetual optimist, me.)

But I did manage to persuade Arabella to accept the sun's kind invitation, on the simple basis that in England you never knew when he would ever issue another. So off she went, loose blouse over G-string and halter, with Beryl Markham's *West with the Night* tucked into her canvas holdall, along with a towel and Ambre Solaire. I promised to join her for an hour or so around one, when I took Bing for a walk. He loves the beach, especially if there's a mastiff or St Bernard to frighten out of its wits.

The morning dragged, even though it was Saturday. For I'm afraid the sun had obviously issued his invitation to toy collectors too. A factor I hadn't really considered, as my customers tend, on the whole, to be a sallow lot, much akin in complexion to professional snooker players and with little outward sign of ever having been outdoors of their own volition.

So by quarter to one, when I shut up shop, I had only had two dings on my doorbell. One a typical G&T (gawper and toucher), who studied everything in the shop with a beady eye and with a view to not buying anything next time either, the other a concrete block of a man, who eventually bought a mint Dinky Armstrong-Siddeley (38 series) for fifty-five pounds.

I'm afraid the idea of taking Bing for a walk was rather blown by the amount of traffic making its way down to the National Trust car-park, just up from the beach. So until we actually reached the sand, I had to carry him in my arms. Which did not exactly impress him and he expressed (in Siamese, of course) his frustration more than once, especially when passing Gus's cottage – which is on the beach lane. For normally, on quieter days, he liked a good rummage around in what Gus laughingly calls a garden, but which is really a pocket-sized nature play-ground, preserved for the nation and posterity simply by utter neglect.

Once on the beach, I let him down on his lead. For whilst cars rather faze him, people don't. And as I have already stated, he

36

thrives on a diet of dogs who all seem terrified of him. (I think their doggy minds can't accommodate the idea of anything being on a lead other than their own species. I wonder if Pavlov would have a comment on this.)

It did not take too long to find my inamorata, despite the rows of bodies, on their backs like fish drying in the sun, or clumped together behind that glorious British invention, the wind-break, like wild west pioneers hiding behind their waggons from marauding Indians. For Arabella always goes where the crowds are thinnest – which is usually just before the naturist section. For the great British public seems to be nervous of public nudity – at least, in the great outdoors. And does not seem to be able to cope with your actual full frontal, except in the comfort of its own copy of the *Sun* or girlie magazine.

Arabella held up an arm when she spotted the blue of Bing's eyes. She couldn't see mine, because I was back-lit by the guy throwing the party. Her first words rather took me aback. 'You're too late, you two.'

I looked around with a frown; I guess, so did Bing.

'Too late? What do you mean? Too late for what?'

'The kerfuffle.'

I thought she must be referring to something over in the 'pardon me for being dressed' section, but all seemed very quiet. Most were spreading their assets to the sun's blatant gaze. And there wasn't a trace of a volley ball, let alone a game going on. And even the ice-cream van in the dunes seemed deserted.

'What kerfuffle?'

Arabella raised herself on one elbow, the light glinting off the delicious down on her arm.

'The boys in blue have been here, haven't they?'

I frowned again. 'What for? You are allowed to be in the altogether on this next section. Oh hell, don't tell me the local council's gone puritan all of a sudden and is clamping down on . . .'

She waved her hand. 'Nobody is clamping anything. No, I take that back. They might be clamping something. Or rather, someone. In gaol, for instance.'

I was starting to get the message. 'You mean the boys in blue came down here to . . . take someone away?' I sat down beside her and released Bing from his lead. 'Tell me more, oh browning one.'

She pointed her browning arm back towards the dunes. 'I was lying here minding my own business with Beryl Markham, when I heard those cars arrive. I looked back over my shoulder and saw that ice-cream van completely surrounded by flashing blue lamps. A moment later, I saw what I took to be the vendor being hustled by two policemen out of his van and into one of the Rovers. Then, in a flash, or rather, a series of flashes, they were gone.'

I looked back towards the van but it was side on to me and I couldn't see whether its shutters were closed or not.

'Any idea what it was all about? I mean, had he been fiddling his VAT forms or selling listeria on the side or touching up the full frontals as he hands them their ninety-nines?'

'No idea.'

I smiled. 'It must have created quite a stir amongst the volley-ball set. I mean, where are they going to get their ice-creams and drinks now to dribble down their wobbly bits?'

'Have to put some clothes on and go up to the kiosk at the sea lane end.'

'They won't like that. It's a bit of a hike, even if you're used to carrying the weight of nasty, silly things like clothes.'

I paused to stop Bing from biting the end of Arabella's toes (he's got a thing about feet, kinky cat), then flashed a finger towards the altogethers.

'Heard any comment about it from anyone else?'

'Not directly. But I overheard one woman say, as she swabbed her boobs down with oil, that she wasn't really surprised he'd been arrested.'

'Say why?'

'Oh, something about his being a dirty young man and always looking where he shouldn't when someone is at his counter.'

'So I gather he's not any age?'

'From here, he looked in his mid-twenties or so. But he could have been older.'

She rolled on to her front and pushed the bottle of Ambre Solaire towards me.

'Anyway, darling, let's forget about him. I've been longing for you to come, so that I can do my back.'

'Oh great,' I smirked. 'So that's why you wanted me to join you. Just to be a massage man with the old cream.'

'Something like that.'

I took the cap off the Ambre Solaire and emptied some into my palm. A Hawk trainer aeroplane just had to take that very moment to perform a sea-skimming run across the bay. The shattering noise from its jet propelled a panic-stricken Bing into my arms and instantly, shock horror, I had a cat whose fur resembled a shag's back after an oil-slick disaster.

As I strolled back, with a now rather slippery Bing (Arabella having opted to skip lunch for a further basinful of sun), I noted that there was still no sign of life at Gus's cottage. But that was no great surprise, as the sun was well over the yardarm and I assumed Gus had ducked into the cooling shade of one of his many pub haunts.

Back home, after swabbing an indignant Bing down with detergent and drying him with a towel, I grabbed a ploughman's and a Heineken from the fridge and refreshed my inner man. That done, I reopened my shop early in the hope of catching the odd fish up from the beach. But none snapped at the bait and it wasn't until past four that the first customers arrived. One was an enquiry for a boxed set of pre-war Dinky warships, that I, unfortunately, did not have in stock, another bought a chipped Minic dust cart for thirty pounds, but it was the last that stopped my Saturday opening being rather a wash-out. It was an elderly lady, who had not come to buy but to sell.

Out of a wicker shopping trolley, she produced item after item, all wrapped carefully in tissue paper that smelt of moth balls.

'It was reading about that poor man who was murdered the other day,' she disclosed confidentially, 'that gave me the idea. You remember, he had a lot of toys in his attic?'

As if I could forget.

'Well,' she went on as she started to unwrap the first object, 'it triggered a memory for me. Years and years ago, I'd put away some of my son's old toys in my own attic – he got killed in the Battle of Britain, poor boy. He was only fifteen. A hit and run raider. Hit his school. Well, anyway, up I went into the attic to see if they were still there. And here they are, for what they're worth. I'm afraid some of them are a bit scratched, but you know what kids are. Still, you might find a home for them. No good me hanging on to them. Besides,' she grimaced, 'I might get that burglar myself, if I'm not careful. Dreadful, dreadful thing, wasn't it?'

Her shaky fingers at last revealed the first little gem – a very early, circa 1934–5 Dinky Town Car, complete with all its headlights and very little playworn. Thereafter followed nearly all the '30' series cars, from a cream Chrysler Airflow to an almost perfect Daimler and then a few more of the much prized '24' series, the best being a Vogue saloon with side mounts and two almost pristine tourers in yellow and blue, and cream and green.

When she had finished placing them on my counter, she asked hesitantly, 'Think anyone would like them?'

'I'm sure thousands would,' I smiled genuinely. 'They are some of the earliest Dinkys made and much sought after.'

Her rheumy eyes brightened. 'So you'll take them?'

I nodded. 'I'd love to. How much do you want for them?'

She thought for a moment, then said quietly, 'Would twenty-five pounds be too much? You see, the bus fare from Wareham is over . . .'

I stopped her right there. 'Hang on a moment whilst I just count the cars.' There were fourteen. Now fourteen times twenty-five is three hundred and fifty pounds. But I just couldn't bring myself to pay her that.

'They are worth a good deal more than you're asking,' I pointed out.

'Oh. Really? How nice,' she blushed. 'Well, perhaps then you might be able to run to . . . say, thirty pounds . . . thirty-five pounds?'

'No. I'll give you fifty pounds.'

She blushed even deeper, so that her liver spots disappeared into the red.

'Well, that's very generous of you, I must say.'

I got out my book and wrote her a cheque. I thought she was going to faint when she read the amount.

'But you've made a . . . terrible mistake . . . you've made it out for seven hundred pounds.'

I reached over and touched her hand reassuringly. 'That's right. Fourteen cars at fifty pounds each *is* seven hundred pounds.'

'No, I meant . . .' she began, but my laughter interceded.

'I guessed you did. But I'd have been robbing you blind if I had only given you fifty pounds for the lot, believe me.'

She probably doesn't believe me to this day. But the expression on her face right then was worth a million times more than I paid her, in anybody's money.

As she finally went shakily to my door, she turned and said, 'Isn't it sad the way life doesn't treat everybody the same?'

'How do you mean?' I asked.

'Well,' she said, 'here I am, with old toys bringing me just about the nicest windfall I've had in my life, whereas for that poor man . . . well, they brought him just the opposite, his downfall, as you might say. Why's that, do you think?'

Her last question was one I was to ponder over for many hours over the next days.

It was when Arabella (now looking deliciously brown and done to a turn from her day on the beach) and I were settling down later that evening to watch the new Dennis Potter series on television, that the day definitely lost every last glint of its shine. Even with the volume of Potter's heated dialogue, there was no mistaking the squeal, rattle and bang of Gus's Ford juddering to a stop outside. A moment later and I was answering his urgent banging on the back door, whilst Arabella switched on the video recorder so that we could view Potter at a later date.

At least on this occasion Gus did apologize for his bursting in on us without warning. Normally, he assumes the whole world gets wind of his intentions directly he forms any, and is thus always prepared both physically and spiritually (that means plenty of Heineken) for his visits.

'Sorry, old son, for coming round so late,' he muttered, as he stumbled through into the sitting-room. Then eyeing both myself and Arabella up and down, he added, 'Still, could have been worse, couldn't it? At least you weren't in bed.'

I proffered a seat and offered a beer. He accepted the first and to my amazement, declined the latter.

'No, old lad, thanks. Want to keep me head straight, don't I, till I've told you why I've come round?'

I saw Arabella's frown. It matched my own in depth, though not in tan.

'Well, Gus, fire away,' I smiled. 'It must be something pretty bloody important for you to turn down a drink.'

He sniffed and arranged himself symmetrically on his chair, as if order in his body might transfer itself to his mind.

'Yeah. Well, it is important in a way. Well, not to me, so much. But to Milly. Or rather, her friend.'

'Milly's friend?' My mind boggled.

He nodded. 'Never met her, mind. Woman called Ball.' Looking up at me, he added, 'Ring a bell?'

Again Arabella and I exchanged frowns.

'Ball ring a bell?' I asked, trying to hide a smile.

'Yea. Haven't you heard the wireless?'

By the blanket word 'wireless', Gus always means the local station, to which his set is super-glued.

'No, I haven't heard anything, Gus. You'd better tell us. What exactly has this Ball done to get on the radio?'

'Well, nothing. Or so his mother says.'

I tried to work it out. Not always easy the way Gus will insist on telling stories.

'Hang on. Are we to take it this Mrs Ball you've mentioned, friend of your Milly's, has a son, who has got on the radio?'

'Yes, that's right. Only he hasn't done anything to get on the wireless.'

'Then who's got him on it?' Arabella chipped in.

'That's the wholy ruddy trouble,' Gus muttered. 'You see, it's the police.'

I paused for a moment, then asked, 'You trying to say Mrs Ball's son has been arrested?'

'Not exactly. Well, nearly . . . well, it's like this 'ere. They came and took him away for questioning, like. And he hasn't done a blind thing, so Milly and his mother say.'

I hesitated before asking the next question. 'What do the police think he might have done?'

'What d'yer think?' Gus replied, somewhat irritably. 'Murder that toy collector man, that's what. Thought you'd have put that one together, Ercool Parrot.'

Ignoring the Agatha Christie Poirot allusion, one of Gus' regular gambits, I asked, 'So he's not exactly arrested. Just detained?'

'Well, I don't know quite. Mrs Ball's in a helluva state. He's been down at the station hours. That's why she rang Milly. Milly rang me.'

It didn't take a mind-reading genius to guess what Gus was going to say next. So I jumped in with, 'Gus, why did Milly ring you?'

He shifted uneasily in his chair. 'Well, you see, it's like this 'ere . . . I couldn't help it, really . . .'

I held up a calming hand. 'All right, Gus, I can guess. You have told Milly, haven't you, that I've done a bit of sleuthing in my time? And bingo, directly a friend of hers has any trouble from now on, she's going to leap to the old phone and ring you, so that you can come round and try to persuade yours truly to come to the aid of whatever party is up to his or her neck in the proverbial. Tonight it's her friend's son. Tomorrow. . . ?'

The rest of the sentence got swallowed whole by a sigh.

Arabella suddenly sat forward on the settee. 'Gus?'

'Yeah?'

'This son of Mrs Ball's . . .'

'Yeah?'

'He wouldn't happen to run an ice-cream van, would he?'

Gus's eyes lit up for the first time. 'Yeah. How d'yer guess?'

'And his pitch is down on the beach, the . . .'

'. . . stark, bollock naked end. Yeah, that's him.'

'I saw the police take him away this morning, Gus, that's how I know.'

'Oh.' He seemed quite disappointed Arabella hadn't been displaying second sight, after all.

'Gus.' He turned back to me. 'Gus, why have the police connected Mrs Ball's son with the Maitland murder? Do you know?'

'Toy collector, isn't he?'

'Is he?'

'Yeah. Mind you, Milly says it's only in a small way, 'cos, on his wages, he can't afford to be anything else.'

'But he loves old toys?' I persisted.

Gus held up a giant hand. 'Hold on, old lad. I know what you're getting at. He might love them so much, he'd go out and burgle to get some more.'

'Didn't say a thing, Gus.'

'But you thought it.'

I couldn't deny it. I tried another tack.

'Did your Milly say whether Mrs Ball's son has got an alibi?' I saw Gus's eyes flicker. 'Or is that the trouble? That he could have done it, Gus, because no one can prove he was anywhere else at the time of the murder.'

Gus shook his head wearily. 'No, seems there's no bloody mystery of where he was around that time.'

43

'And where was that?'

Gus blew out his cheeks and then exhaled like a mediaeval depiction of the Wind. 'Just round at the soddin' Maitlands' place, that's all.'

I missed a breath.

And Arabella stepped in with, 'What on earth would he be round at their place at that unholy time of night, if he wasn't. . . ?'

Gus cut her off with, 'I don't sorta like to say . . .'

I looked at him hard. 'Why not, Gus? Because your Milly has asked you not to?'

'No, no, nothing like that.'

'Then what's stopping you?'

I thought I detected a blush reddening his stubble fields, then I saw him shoot a fleeting glance at Arabella. She took the hint.

'Like that Heineken now, Gus? I'll pop into the kitchen and get one.'

Directly she had gone, I leaned forward and said, 'Out with it, Gus. Why was this Ball fellow round at the Maitlands?'

Gus cleared his throat. A major undertaking about which least said etc. 'Well, old son, you see, he's been had up for it before, so Milly says.'

'Had up for what?'

'Well, you know . . .'

'No, I don't.'

'Er . . . how can I put it, seems he's . . . er . . . well, a bit of a peeping Tom.'

He collapsed back in his chair, as if the strain of the admission had been too strong.

'Peeping Tom? You mean he creeps about people's gardens at dead of night, hoping to catch sight of . . .'

'. . . someone undressing,' Gus said quickly. 'And you see, his mum, Mrs Ball, knew he had a . . . well . . . "interest" in Mrs Maitland, ever since she started coming down to that end of the beach.'

'You mean. . . ?'

'Yeah. Seems this Mrs Maitland had taken up with that kind of thing earlier this year, directly it was warm enough to . . . well . . .'

'. . . take her clothes off.'

He nodded. 'Well, old son, now you know why I had to come round.'

'You didn't *have* to come, Gus,' I reminded him.

'But you'll try to help out, won't you, old lad? I told Milly you would, see, and she's told Mrs Ball.'

I hid my head in my hands and muttered through my fingers, 'Balls. Balls. Balls. Balls.'

'What's that, old son?'

'Nothing. Nothing at all,' I sighed, as I heard Arabella Heineking back into the room.

Four

After Gus had phutted and banged his way back down the lane to his cottage some two lagers later, Arabella and I were in no mood to enjoy Dennis Potter. So we rewound the tape and put it in our 'pending' pile by the TV.

'Here we go again,' Arabella grimaced.

I looked on the bright side or rather, at the only chink of light I could see in the whole shebang.

'Maybe, by the morning, this Ball fellow will be back with his mum. And I won't need to get involved at all.'

'With just a wag of dear Digby's finger warning him not to be a naughty peeping Tom again?'

She raised her beautiful brown eyes to the ceiling. 'But unlikely, isn't it?'

'Maybe not. Especially if he doesn't admit to his peeping pastime.'

'They could still get him for trespass in the Maitlands' garden, or whatever.'

'Maybe. But they would hardly detain him down at the station for just that. All they'd do is caution him not to leave town for a while, etcetera, etcetera.'

I went over and sat next to Arabella on the settee.

'It's a bugger, isn't it? If it was anybody asking but Gus.'

'But it *is* Gus. And he's asked. And I agree, damn it. You could hardly have said, "On your bike".'

I put my arm around her shoulder.

'Look at the other side of the coin for a second. It's dreadful to say, but maybe, this ice-cream vendor *did* kill Maitland. In which case, there's nothing for me to do anyway.'

'Because he found out about Maitland's toy collection?' she commented rather disbelievingly.

'Maybe.'

Arabella thought for a minute, then asked, 'You saw that photograph of Mr and Mrs Maitland in their home. How attractive did the wife look? I mean, the black and white photos I've seen printed in the papers and the ones we've got at the *Western Gazette* don't give much away. Other than she looks around thirty-five or so and is not exactly ugly.'

I shrugged. 'She looked quite tanned, which I guess is from all her altogether sunbathing that Gus has just told us about. But she didn't come across as someone peeping Toms would ogle, exactly.'

Arabella half-smiled. 'Maybe she looks better with her clothes off.'

'Maybe. Certainly her figure wasn't bad, at all. Quite well endowed, in fact, now I come to think of it.'

'Well, there you are. Maybe this peeping Ball got the hots for her when she came to buy an ice-cream from his van. Remember, I told you a lady on the beach this morning said she thought he was a bit of a dirty young man. Perhaps he finds out where all the ones he fancies live, then does the rounds of their houses in the small hours, when he reckons it's night-night time. Stranger things have happened.'

'But he's already seen them totally starkers. Why should he then want to see them getting into their nighties?'

'Nightie fetish?' she grinned. 'You men are always saying a half-clothed woman is much sexier than a totally nude one. Although I don't notice much evidence of that, when you actually get round to the job in hand.'

'Unfortunate phrasing that last, my darling, but I know what you mean. Anyway, for God's sake, let's now forget it all for tonight. For who knows, tomorrow we may find Gus rattling our door to tell us his Milly has phoned to say this fellow Ball is now totally in the clear?'

'Pull the other leg,' Arabella smiled.

'All right,' I said grinning. 'Done. But only after we have gone upstairs and you've got into your silk stockings and garter belt.'

'How about a nightie?'

'You don't own one.'

'Could look in Yellow Pages for an all night Marks & Spencers . . .' she laughed, but I'd risen from the settee by that time and was tugging at her arm.

*

The next day, Sunday, for once lived up to its name. The sun had donned his hat again and was out to play in no uncertain manner.

Over our breakfast muesli, Arabella commented between chews, 'I just hope this Gus thing doesn't ruin our whole day.'

I aligned my arm on the table against hers. The difference in tan was painful.

'I could do with a top-up on the beach. It hasn't been this fine since last summer.'

She looked up. 'Well, why don't we both just stroll on down, in the hope? I mean, we have to pass Gus's on the way, so we could pop in for a second and check on the latest . . .'

'. . . state of Ball play?' I grinned.

'Exactly.'

So that's exactly what we did.

We could see Gus through the murky window of his cottage. (But only because his newly installed phone is on a window-sill. By their opaque look, Gus last cleaned his windows after the putty had dried.)

As usual when he was in the front door was unbolted, so we just walked straight in, just in time to hear him say, 'Well, that's something, anyway.' Then a bit of muffled gobbledy-gook from the receiver, whereupon he said, 'So what time should we be down?' A pause, then, 'Eleven, eleven thirty. Right, I'll tell him.'

My heart sank and I made the thumbs down to Arabella out of Gus' eye-line.

More gobbledy-gook, then, 'No, don't be daft, Milly. Me mate's only too happy to oblige. All in a day's work to him.'

I raised my eyebrows at the liberty. Especially as I try never to work on Sundays, unless there's an important toy swapmeet I should attend.

'All right, Milly. I'll tell him. I'll ring you back later, when he's had a chance to talk to him.'

Gus glowered at us both, so we took the hint and retreated back into the postage-stamp hall. Even so, we couldn't help still hearing him.

'Bye, bye, Mill. Be over tonight, all being well . . . unless he needs some help, that is . . . Often calls on me, as I've told you, when he's investigating like . . . yeah, Sherlock 'Olmes and Watson, yeah . . . seen 'em, haven't I? Only I'm better looking than that berk who plays Watson . . .'

Then I'll swear I heard a blown kiss. Either that or Gus had burped down the phone, which I would hardly think he would do at such an early stage in his relationship with Milly. But you never knew . . .

'So what's the news?' I asked, when he at last surfaced in the hall.

'Goodish, old son.'

'Ball released?' Arabella smirked. Dear, oh dear, I wished the ice-cream man's father had answered to a different name.

'S'right. Two o'clock this morning, his mother told Milly.'

'So I'm not needed any more,' I tried on.

'Well . . . yes . . . and no.'

'Which is it, Gus?'

'Well, just for this morning, yes, I'm afraid, old son. You see, Mrs Ball told Milly her son's still terrified the police think he did it. They tried to get him to admit to it all night, from all accounts. Only released him, she says, because they haven't got any real evidence, see.'

'Evidence that he did the murder, you mean. Presumably, he has admitted he was there that night.'

'Only in the garden. He couldn't deny that because they've found his ruddy shoe prints in a flower bed.'

I sighed. 'So you've arranged that I have a chat with him, have you? Around eleven, eleven thirty. Heard you on the phone.'

I glanced at Arabella, whose crest, though well tanned, looked distinctly fallen at the prospect of a lonely beach vigil.

'Well, Gus, you'd better give me his address.'

His craggy face softened into a smile. 'Easy, old son. His address for this morning is where I can see you two are off to.'

'The beach?'

'Yeah. Milly says Sundays are by far his best day and he daren't not open up and lose all that business.'

'Good for him,' Arabella grinned, then added, looking at me, 'And good for us.'

'Oh good,' muttered Gus, looking quite relieved. He saw us to the door, then remarked nonchalantly, 'Might stroll up a bit later on.'

I hesitated, then said, 'Oh really? I thought you wouldn't be seen dead up that end of the beach.'

'Wouldn't normally. Don't hold with people wobbling all their bits about in public, I don't. But seeing as how this fellow Ball's van is parked back from the beach, like . . .'

I laughed. 'Gus, on a hot day like this, you won't be able to get near his van for wobbly bits.'

I don't know whether his eyes brightened or darkened at the thought, sod it, but they sure as hell narrowed.

We saw him arrive and open up his shutter. A queue of both the clothed and the unclothed formed within seconds and we relaxed back on the sand for a further twenty minutes, until the worst of it had evaporated. For I had no wish to cut him off from making a buck or frustrate the cravings of the volley-ball set for cooling drinks or spiralling ice-creams.

But at twenty-five to twelve, when there was only one child (in trunks) still proffering his cash, I (also in trunks) bade Arabella (in bikini) a fond farewell and strolled over to the dunes, where the van was parked.

The boy was just receiving his change when I arrived. So I had half a second to take in the vendor. He was about twenty-five and, if I say he looked a prime target to have sand kicked in his face, I'm only giving half the story. For though his body had struggled hard to keep up with his height – around six foot – the result was a droopy, gangly and almost tubercular physique. His face, though sallow and rather sad, had a certain sensitive strength to it, somewhat akin to those suffering saints you see depicted so often in mediaeval paintings or, come to think of it, like Ivan Lendl, the tennis ace.

When the child had gone, a thin voice asked, 'And what would you like?'

My answer rather took him aback. 'A chat.'

He frowned. 'A chat?'

'Yes. I'm Peter Marklin. I believe your mother has told you about me.'

He looked around furtively to check no one was in earshot.

'Yes . . . er . . . she has . . . er . . . Mr Marklin.'

He reached up for the latch of the shutter.

'Look, we can't talk here. Do you mind waiting while I just shut up the van? Then, perhaps, we can find a quiet place on the dunes . . . Won't be a minute.'

And he wasn't.

*

50

'So,' I said, re-arranging myself on the warm sand-hill, so that my buttocks did not boil. 'You took a shine to Mrs Maitland when she started buying ice-creams from you. You'd never met her before?'

He shook his head. 'No, never.'

I looked back towards the sea. 'And you'd never heard of her husband before?'

'No, no. I didn't even know she had a husband until I . . .'

He'd gone too far not to finish, so that's what he reluctantly did, '. . . followed her home one day.'

I looked at him and the red on his face wasn't sunburn.

'Do you make a practice of following your lady customers home?'

He rubbed his white and bony hands together in anguish.

'No, no, no. Never. Really. You must believe me.'

For the moment, I let him assume I believed him.

'Okay. So what was so different about Mrs Maitland that made you follow her?'

He hesitated, then said, 'I don't know . . . but she sort of . . .'

'Encouraged you?'

'Well, not exactly. But she always . . . well . . . was nice to me.'

'How nice?'

'She . . . er . . . you know, . . . asked questions, like. Always asked how I was. How business was doing. That kind of thing.'

'Hardly, though, an invitation to follow her home, I'd have thought.'

'It wasn't just what she said, really. More . . . well . . . she sort of . . .'

'Sort of what?'

'I don't know, exactly. It was just the way she . . . moved and . . . kind of wasn't shy about . . . showing herself off, I suppose.'

'Showing off her figure to you, do you mean?'

The blush reached the roots of his lank brown hair.

'Yes, I suppose so.'

'And you took her lack of shyness as an invitation?'

'No, no, not really. I guess I was just intrigued enough to want to know more about her.'

I flicked a basking ant off my foot. 'And how many times did you visit her house before that night?'

'Only the once. The first time.'

'Are you telling me the truth? I can't possibly help you if you lie to me or hold anything back, you know.'

His eyes brightened. 'So you're working to help me, Mr Marklin. I'm ever so . . .'

I held up a hand. 'Now I didn't say quite that. But I'm certainly willing to hear you out this morning. Let's leave it like that right now.'

'Thank you. I really do appreciate it. You ruining your Sunday morning just for me. And I am telling the truth about my visits to Mrs Maitland's house.'

'All right. Then let's move on to the night of the murder.'

I stopped, as two heads appeared over the next but one dune. When they'd passed on, I continued, 'I'm going to be quite blunt here, Mr Ball.'

'Please call me Ron. My name is Ronald.'

'All right, Ron. Now for the blunt bit. I gather you've been in trouble with the law before over, well, being something of what is known as a peeping Tom.'

He nodded and looked away.

'So am I right in assuming you were out that night, trying to catch sight of a few ladies getting ready for bed? Or were you out for quite a different purpose, as the police obviously think?'

He looked back at me, his head now shaking fit to fall off. 'I wasn't out to rob Mr Maitland, as they tried to get me to say. You must believe me. I like old toys, but I would never go so far, never, as to . . . steal any. Besides, how could I know that Mrs Maitland's husband had any toys?'

He got up from the sand and started to pace around. 'Why the hell doesn't anybody believe me?'

When I had at last managed to get him to calm down and resume his hot-seat, the sand being now at least regulo six, I said quietly, 'So you were just out in the hope of catching sight of Mrs Maitland, that it? Wasn't it a bit late for that?'

'I'd been for a walk. I have trouble sleeping, see. Always have done. Even when I do manage a bit of sleep, I get these funny dreams.'

'So you went for a walk?'

'Oh yes . . . well, I went for a walk and it wasn't until I was on my way back that I decided to drop by Mrs Maitland's house.'

He put his face in his hands. 'Oh God, I wish I'd never gone out that night.'

52

'So you didn't really go specifically to catch a glimpse of Mrs Maitland, say, going to bed or. . . ?'

He shook his head. 'No, no, no. I just went, well, because . . . I like her, I suppose. She's the first lady who's ever really been nice to me, you see.'

I saw. Only too well.

'So you dropped by her place, just for . . . sentimental reasons?' I was not sure 'sentimental' was quite the right word, starting with 's' that is, but there you are.

'Yes, I guess you can call it that.'

I thought for a moment, then said, 'So you're saying you must have been in the garden some time before the murder took place, are you?'

'Must have been, I suppose.'

I eyed the digital on his thin wrist.

'You didn't look at your watch?'

'No. And it wouldn't really have helped, as the police admit they can't pinpoint the time of the murder to an exact minute.'

'But it would have been around twelve thirty or so, I gather.'

'Probably.'

I moved my weight on to the uncooked buttock. 'Now tell me, whilst you were in the garden or around the house, did you see anything unusual or suspicious? Like a car parked where it shouldn't be. Or someone loitering in the area. Or . . . anything that might just give us a clue as to what actually did happen.'

He took a deep breath. His chest didn't seem to expand one iota.

'No, I can't say I did. I wish I had. For I bloody well know that unless I do think of something or other, the police are going to try to nail Mr Maitland's murder on *me*.'

'Not necessarily. After all, they've released you, haven't they?'

'I bet only so that they can have more time to get up a *real* case against me. That's why I need your help so badly, Mr Marklin. Mum says you've been ever such a godsend with other people wrongly accused . . .'

I cut him off with, 'What kind of toys do you collect, Ron?'

It took him a second to recover, then he replied, 'Wind-ups mainly. You know. I guess you'd call them clockwork toys. But I've called them wind-ups since I was a kid.'

'Just wind-ups? They're pretty expensive these days.'

'I know. It's terrible, isn't it?' He smiled wanly. 'Well, maybe

53

not for you, being a dealer in them and all, but for instance, the last Minic I could afford – a streamline tourer – set me back forty-five pounds. *And* it was scratched and without a box.'

'But you have *other* toys?'

'A few. Yes.'

'Die-casts? Dinkys, Corgis and so on?'

'Yes.' He turned round to face me. 'I know what you're getting at, Mr Marklin. The police showed me the list of what was stolen. Mainly die-casts, they were.'

I held up a hopefully calming hand. 'Now, come on, Ron, I'm not hinting at anything. Just trying to get a few facts straight, that's all.'

I saw Ron Ball look back towards his vehicle. We could only see its top half from where we were sitting, but it was sufficient to see a few heads gathered round it, in hope.

I went on, 'Now don't get all het up with my next question, either.'

'Try not to,' he blinked.

'All right. So, have the police searched your house?'

'Not *my* house. It's my mum's. Can't afford a place of my own. Not on what that van brings in.'

'Okay. But I take it they've searched it?'

He nodded. 'And how. Even dug up some of the flower beds. Mum's ever so upset.'

'And found nothing?'

He bridled. 'Of course, they've found nothing. Well, none of what was stolen, anyway.'

I frowned. 'What are you saying, Ron? That they've found something else?'

Again the red invaded his hair-roots.

'I suppose you'd better know everything, if you're going to be kind enough to get involved.'

'Yes. It would help.'

He looked away. 'All right. Well, they found some . . . magazines in my bedroom. Took them away, they did. But not before . . .' A bony finger went to a now watering eye, '. . . they showed them to my mum.'

I hardly needed to ask what kind of magazines.

'That's all they found?'

'Yes.'

'It's not a crime to have magazines, you know. Otherwise people like W. H. Smiths would be in real trouble.'

After a sigh, he said quietly, 'I didn't buy all of them from Smiths.'

'Oh. Under the counter stuff?'

'No. Direct mail. From Holland.'

I saw now why the police had taken them away. Girlie magazines were one thing. Hard-core from Holland was another. I could also see why Ron had taken Digby's fancy. But what I still did not know was how he had latched on to the ice-cream vendor in the first place. So I asked.

'Oh, that was simple enough,' was his resigned reply. 'The police said they'd received an anonymous phone call.'

'Saying what?'

'Oh, you know, that I collect toys and am always moaning about how I would like more but can't afford them. That kind of thing. And . . .'

He stopped suddenly, so I helped him. '. . . that you are a bit of a peeping Tom?'

'Something like that.'

'Do you know who could have made a call like that? After all, it must be someone who knows you.'

'Yeah. I reckon so.' He wiped both his eyes with his hand. 'There's a nosy parker who lives just up the road from us. Hates me parking the van outside my mum's. Says it lowers the tone of the street. He knows about my, well, previous brush with the law, as you might say. Wants Mum and me to move. Throw enough dirt around . . . you know . . .'

'And he knows you collect toys?'

'Right. Saw my collection one day when he barged in to complain about my van again.'

'So you reckon it was him?'

He nodded. 'Who else could it be?'

I shrugged. 'You know better than I do.' I changed tack. 'Tell me, Ron, do you think you might ever have actually met Mr Maitland? I mean, without your really knowing it.'

'What do you mean?'

'I mean, was Mrs Maitland always alone when she came to your van? Or for that matter, have you ever seen her with a man on the beach? If you have, it could well have been her husband.'

He combed a lock of hair back from his forehead with his hand.

'I never spotted a man with her. Though I can't see much of the beach from where I park. And certainly she was never with a man, when she came for an ice-cream or rather, a drink. She's not big on ice-creams, is Mrs Maitland.'

'Did she come with anybody else at all? I mean on a regular basis?'

'Yes. Just a few times she's been with another woman.'

'Another nudist?'

'No. Always dressed prim and proper, she was. Bit older than Mrs Maitland, too.'

'But a friend?'

'Yes. I suppose so.'

'You didn't catch a name, by any chance?'

He pondered for a second, then offered, 'Chrissy, I think it was. Yeah, that's right. It was Chrissy. I remember because it reminded me of a girl at my school – she was called Chrissy, Christine, really.'

'No surname?'

'No. Never heard one. Sorry.'

'All right. I don't suppose it's important.'

I was now starting to run out of meaningful questions, so turned to him and said, 'Mind if I pop and see your mother some time, before I decide on whether I can be of any help?'

He looked a bit doubtful at first, but then agreed. 'If it helps you help me, I can hardly say no, can I? Can I say when you'll be likely to come round?'

'I'll leave it until tomorrow, if you don't mind. Say, just before lunch. It'll give me time to sort out my own mind and who knows, hopefully, you may not need my help by then.'

'I will, I know I will. That lot is not going to leave me alone . . .'

'By the way,' I interrupted, 'does "that lot" include an individual called Digby Whetstone? Inspector Digby Whetstone? Big flab of a man. Carroty hair. Moustache. And more freckles than you can shake a truncheon at.'

'Yea. He was there, all right,' he sighed. 'Worst of the bunch, he was.'

'Oh,' I smiled, 'he's not so bad – once you've got to loathe him.'

Then I upped from the griddle of the sand and after he had given me his address, made my way back to the briny.

By the time I had finished recounting my conversation with the

Lad of the Dunes, Arabella had also finished anointing my back with oil. I lay down on my towel, resting my head sideways on my folded arms.

Arabella laughed.

'Why the merriment?' I enquired. 'I don't see anything to laugh at in the poor man's tale. Quite the reverse.'

'I wasn't laughing at Ron Ball. I was laughing at you.'

'For getting involved even this far?'

'No, for the direction in which you've got your head pointing.'

I suddenly got her, well, point. 'Oh, you mean. . .?'

'Yes.' She lowered her voice. 'Right towards the wobbly bit lot.'

I looked back towards her. 'Pure concidence, my beloved.'

'Impure ogling, if you ask me,' she grinned.

I took immediate umbridge. 'Please. I'm no peeping Tom.'

'No, you're a peeping Peter.' Then her expression suddenly changed and not because of her joke. 'By the way, what do you think of this Ball fellow? Reckon he's telling the truth?'

I held my hand up to my eyes against the sun. 'I don't know. That's why I decided to see his mother first, before I agreed to help any further.'

'Like mums know their sons better than anybody?'

I nodded. 'Only she obviously did not know about his pornography.'

'So she might have missed a few other peccadilloes of his, you mean? Like a tendency to steal and hit people with their own ornaments.'

'Well . . . it's the least I can do, really. See his mother. Otherwise I'll be disappointing old Gus.'

A thought suddenly hit me. 'Good Lord, where is he, by the way? Would have thought he'd have come rolling across the sand by now.'

Arabella ferreted in her bag for her watch. 'Gone yardarm time,' she announced. 'Possibly preferred a wobbly brown ale to wobbly brown bodies.'

I laughed. 'Don't be fooled. He's not against wobbly bits as much as he . . .' at the last second I changed the phrase from 'would like to make out' to '. . . would like to be. I just reckon he doesn't like ogling in public, that's all.'

'Could be. Anyway, I'll lay bets the public for him right now means only one thing. Public bar . . .' She stopped suddenly as a giant shadow cut us both off from the sun. We both whipped our heads round and looked up into the eyes of a man definitely not in a public anything.

'Wotcher,' was his yuppy-style greeting.

'Howdy,' we both drawled, praying Gus hadn't overheard our speculation. I noticed he continued to look down on us, rather than spread his gaze across the acres of flesh all around.

'Seen him, then?' He pointed a thick digit towards the ice-cream van.

'Yes. Yes, I have.'

'Well?'

'Well, what?' I needlessly asked.

'You know well what. Are you going to help, that's well what?'

'I am going to see his mother. Tomorrow lunch-time,' I sidestepped.

Gus took the weight off his feet and applied it with his bottom to the sand. 'Oh well, thanks, old son. Milly'll be pleased. That there mother of his seems to be her best friend.'

'Met her?' I asked. 'I mean at art class?'

'Think I did and she says I did. But she introduced me to so many that day, their old faces all merge into one.'

So I wasn't exactly going to get any guides from Gus before I met her. Then I changed the subject before he could probe me more deeply about my reaction to her son. 'Where have you been all this time, then, Gus? We expected you earlier.'

He sniffed and ran his finger round the top of his sweater. How Gus can wear winter clobber all the year round (except for the new art class days, of course), I'll never know. Must be a relic from his seafaring years. For fishing in deep water can often be chill, even when the sun has got his hat well and truly on. All depends on the wind, so I'm told.

'Yes, well, I did a bit of snooping of my own, now didn't I?'

I looked down at Arabella. She, wisely, had closed her eyes, so her expression wouldn't show.

'Oh yes? And where did it take you, Gus?'

'Here and there.'

I raised my eyes to the skies. 'Oh, great. Two of the nicest places in England.'

He leaned towards me. 'Want to know where?'

'No.'

'No?'

'No.' I heard Arabella trying hard to stifle a giggle.

58

'All right, I'll tell you,' he said. 'Been to Wareham, haven't I?'

I pinned back my ears. Wareham rang a bell. The bell, in fact, of a certain fancy-dress shop. But I hadn't yet updated Gus on the tittle-tattle from Arabella's office secretary.

'Have you? Why Wareham?'

'Milly phoned me again soon after you two had come down here.'

'Oh, yes. What did she say?'

Gus leaned over towards me, confidentially. 'Heard a rumour, hasn't she, that old Maitland had a bit of stuff on the side.'

He waited with bated breath for my 'Good Lord's and 'Whew's and 'Can't believe it's. But he waited in vain.

'Don't seem surprised, old son.'

So I told him why I wasn't. He seemed quite put out that I had not put out with that juicy piece of information before.

'Might have told me,' he grumbled. 'Then I could have gone and seen her before.'

'Who?' I asked, knowing the answer.

'The Fairchild woman, who do you think?'

I thought for a second. 'Her shop open on a Sunday?'

'Open? I'll say it was bloody open and bloody full of people returning the stupid fancy dress they had worn the night before. 'Ere, there was one daft 'aporth who'd gone as 'itler, swastika armbands, Charlie Chaplin moustache and all. And his missus must have gone as ruddy Mussolini by the size of the costume he was returning.'

I held up a sand-covered hand. 'Okay, Gus, spare us what everyone round Wareham was wearing last night and get to the point. You went to see this Fairchild woman, right? Presumably because your Milly thinks she might be able to shed some light on the murder.'

'Yeah, yeah, that's right.' He puffed himself up. 'Well, old son, I think you'd have been proud of me.'

My heart sank.

He went on, 'I pretended I was just another customer, see. Looking for something to wear. So she wouldn't suspect a ruddy thing.'

'Okay. So you had to speak to her at some point. So what did you say?'

'I left it until the shop was almost empty, so that I'd have a little time to watch her, like, see what I might be dealing with.'

'And. . . ?'

'She's a cool customer, old lad. Well, not a customer 'xactly, but you know what I mean.'

'How old?' Arabella asked, from her supine position.

'Oooh. Round thirty, thirty-two. But I could be wrong. Not good on ages.'

'Did you fancy her?' Arabella grinned across at him.

Gus patted the front of his pullover. 'Me? Naaah. Not me. Too snooty a bit, she was. Too thin, too, by half. But I can see some daft idiot might go for her.'

'So she's not bad looking?' I half-asked.

'S'pose not, if you like that sort of thing.'

'Come on, Gus, get to the point. What in the end did you say to her?'

'Asked if she'd got a costume that might suit me.'

'Pretty definitive brief,' I muttered under my breath, but I'd been premature.

For Gus then shattered us both by saying, 'Said I wanted to go as a murderer, I did. Get it, old son?' Beaming, he awaited my reaction.

'Very subtle,' I commented.

'Yeah. Wasn't it?' Gus agreed, then went on, 'Watched her face, I did, when I said "murderer". Her poncey eyelashes flickered a bit, I'll tell you. Then she asked if something like Dr flipping Crippen would be up my street. I said, "no," so then she asked what kind of murderer did I want to be.'

This time it was Arabella and I who waited with bated breath.

'And I said – still looking at her tarted-up eyes – that I wasn't yet sure whether I wanted to go as a man or a woman murderer. Get what I was after, old son?'

'Trying to keep up,' I sighed.

'Well, then, that seemed to really worry her.'

'Not surprised,' came from Arabella.

'So, while I'd got her on the run, so to speak, I followed up with, had she got a blunt instrument or something that I could use as a murder weapon at my party? Well, that did it.'

It wasn't too hard to imagine that it must have done. But by this time I was becoming less and less amused by Gus's sleuthing initiative, as I could see how it could well now have put the fancy-dress lady on her guard for life, whatever her innocence or guilt of any damn thing.

'All right, Gus. Let me guess what she did. She threw you out, right?'

'Not exactly. But she went all severe like and looked daggers at me. Then, because some army officer type had come into the shop, she made an excuse to leave me and go and serve him.'

'So you left?'

'Not right then. I hung around a little longer, to see if I could button-hole her again, when she'd finished with the army chap. But he didn't seem to know what he ruddy wanted and she kept showing him stuff and he'd turn it down, showing him more and he'd turn it down. Dear, oh dear, if the bloody British Army is run by blokes like him, who can't even make up their mind about flipping fancy dress, Lord help us if the perishing Russians turn nasty once more.'

'So he kept you from speaking to her again?'

'No, not exactly. See, when he'd gone – and still without choosing anything – she came up to me and said it was closing time and if I really wanted any fancy-dress stuff, I'd have to come back. And with that she turned the sign on the door to "Closed" and bingo . . .'

'Yes, bingo,' I concurred.

Gus rested an elbow back on the sand. 'So I got the measure of her,' he said with satisfaction.

'And what does your measure read, Gus?'

He took a deep breath. 'She's not to be sneezed at, that woman.'

'Leaving sneezing out of it for a moment, what do you mean?'

'Well, I reckon, if what Milly heard is right, and she was Maitland's bit of stuff, then I reckon I know who wore the trousers.'

Oh Lord, if only Gus would stick to good old plain English once in a while.

'I take it you mean Maitland would have to have been a pretty strong character to stand up to her.'

He nodded. 'That's how she struck me,' then he grinned and added, 'Come to think of it, that's how she may have struck him, too.'

Good old Gus. Just because this Fairchild lady had taken umbridge at his totally unveiled innuendoes and more or less thrown him out of her premises (understandably), he was all

61

ready to lob a label round her neck reading 'Murderess'. Still, I didn't throw any stones. After all, for all I knew, he could be right. What's more, I didn't want to stifle his enthusiasm for helping out. Who knew, if I was to get further involved in the Maitland case, I might well need him. For you can always say this about Gus. In a crisis, he can either be your salvation or a further pain in your arse. Curiously, though, in either case, you're rather glad he's there, if you know what I mean.

The rest of Sunday was, really, just that. A rest. After Gus had gone, Arabella and I grabbed a sandwich from the beach café, then lazed in the sun until early evening. But I'm afraid my tan never caught up with hers, or those of any of the wobbly bit brigade just up from us.

Five

'I'm ever so grateful, Mr Marklin, I really am.'

I waved my hand. I did not want Mrs Ball to be too grateful at this point, before I had finally made up my mind about her son.

She came up to my chair and I caught a whiff of Pears' transparent soap, a real trigger for memories of my childhood. My mother had sworn by Pears', believing the soap company's claim implicitly, that transparency proved its purity.

'Are you sure I can't tempt you to a little drink, Mr Marklin? After all, it is nearly lunch-time.'

'No, really. Want to keep a clear head.'

She nodded and her double chins did a dance. For Mrs Ball was as plump as her son was puny and positively glowed with ruddy health, whilst her offspring just looked ruddy poorly.

'My son went off this morning feeling much better after your little chat yesterday,' she smiled. 'And knowing you were coming round today, of course, as well.'

'Oh good,' I said. 'I take it the police haven't been round again.'

The smile instantly left her voice. 'Don't talk of them, Mr Marklin. Poor Ron. They really put him through the wringer and all because he's keen on old toys.'

'*All* because . . .' I began and Mrs Ball, I'm glad to say, took my point.

'Perhaps not *all* because. But mainly because, I reckon. Not fair. Now you'll agree with that, I know you will. Seeing as how you like old toys too. Seen your shop, haven't I? My Ron has always said that one day he'd like to give up the ice-cream business and open up a place like yours. Buying and selling toys, I mean.'

I tried to get her back to my point. 'Mrs Ball, let's talk for a second about the other interest your son seems to have.'

She put a plump hand to her perm and a blush doubled her

ruddiness. 'Oh, that's nothing, Mr Marklin, really. It's just that my Ron, you see, doesn't get to meet many girls. Far too shy. I keep telling him he should get out and go to a dance or two. Give himself a chance to meet someone nice. Know what I mean? But he won't. Prefers to stay at home up in his room, playing with his . . .' She caught my eye and proceeded smartly on with, '. . . toys and that.'

I cleared my throat. 'Look, Mrs Ball, I'd better tell you Ron has told me all about the magazines the police found.'

She turned away and her fingers toyed with a cheap china figure of a crinoline lady standing on an even cheaper chipboard sideboard. Indeed, practically everything in the cramped sitting-room (or should it be termed parlour in a Victorian terraced cottage such as the Balls'?) seemed to be made of chipboard, except the black cat as big as a gorilla, and of course, Mrs Ball and her son.

'Oh those . . . yes, well . . . he's a young man, isn't he?' she said quietly. 'Young men like . . . that kind of thing some-times . . . don't they?'

I refrained from commenting 'And not only the young', and instead asked, 'Mrs Ball, why do you think your son went to the Maitlands' house that night?'

Slowly, she turned back to me. 'Why are you asking? Don't you believe what my son has told you?'

I looked her in the now watery eye. 'Do you?'

She nodded, then took a handkerchief from her apron and dabbed at her eyes.

' 'Course I do. It's like he said. He only went round there, 'cos he liked her, like.'

'Why do you think he likes Mrs Maitland so much?'

She finished drying her eyes and pocketed her hankie.

'Well, I don't think it was . . . you know . . .'

'Sex?'

She nodded. 'Despite her always coming to his van without covering herself up and that. Don't hold with it myself. Nudity may be all right in its place, but . . .'

'. . . an ice-cream van isn't that place?'

She sniffed. ' 'Course it isn't. But I know some women. Like nothing better than parading themselves in front of young men . . . and then they wonder when something happens.' She looked at me. 'Anyway, what was I saying?'

'If it wasn't sex, it was. . . ?'

'She's always been kind to him, from what he says. Asking after him and all that. Flattered him, I think. So he took a shine to her. Wanted to know more about her, I suppose. Young men sometimes fall under the spell of older women, you must have heard that.'

I had, of course, but not nearly as often as the other way round. But be that as it may . . .

'So you think there's nothing more to it than that? Your son was out for one of his midnight walks and decided to come back via the Maitlands', because he's rather taken with the owner's wife.'

She frowned. 'What are you hinting at, Mr Marklin? Really, I thought, when Milly recommended you, . . .'

I got up from my Ercol chair and went over to her. 'Now calm down, Mrs Ball. You must realize I have to ask all sorts of questions, explore all sorts of theories, when I'm trying to get at the truth.'

The hankie was out again. Once it had performed its function, she said, 'All right. Sorry. Didn't mean to get huffy. Really.'

'Fine.'

'Now tell me what's in the back of your mind, then.'

'Why Mr Maitland was killed, Mrs Ball.'

'For the toys,' she offered instantly.

'Maybe. Maybe not.'

'What are you suggesting?'

I just had to say it. If I hadn't, dear Digby might well have beaten me to it. 'Could be Mr Maitland was killed for more intimate reasons. Like someone . . .' I cleared my throat, '. . . had fallen for his wife and wanted him out the way.'

Her red-rimmed eyes flared out at me and she snapped, 'There you go again, Mr Marklin. I know what you're thinking. My Ron killed him, because he admits he likes the wife.' She hid her face in her hands. 'Oh God, can't everyone see, Ron couldn't even kill a fly? And, anyway, he would never then attack someone he likes so much as Mrs Maitland.'

I made to put an arm on her shoulder but she instantly pulled away.

'No, don't go soft-soaping me, Mr Marklin. That's what you think, isn't it?' She prodded an accusing finger towards me. 'If you think the poor man was killed for love, then why the hell don't you go after his fancy mistress over in Wareham, then? From what Milly's heard, she's no better than she should be and as hard as nails, from all accounts.'

I gave her a breathing space, then said quietly, 'What exactly has your friend Milly heard?'

She took a deep breath, then said slowly, 'Friend of her nephew's is a police constable. He told him the police have found out Mr Maitland had a woman friend. Seems she runs one of those fancy-dress hire places over in Wareham. They went to see her yesterday . . . or the day before . . . I get muddled . . .'

'The police went?'

'Yes. That's right. So you see what I mean? She might have a far greater motive for killing Mr Maitland than my poor son. Like, perhaps, he'd told her he was giving her up or wouldn't divorce his wife to marry her. I don't know. And perhaps she stole a few toys just to throw the police off the scent.'

I shrugged. The theory, after all, wasn't that wild. And no doubt, by now, was buzzing around in my favourite Inspector's freckled head too. Gus was going to be a mite disappointed to hear that he'd been beaten to the post by a nag like Digby. I'd have to be careful how I told him.

'Any other thoughts, Mrs Ball, before I get out of your hair?'

She brooded on the question for quite a time, then shook her head. A curl escaped from the prison of her perm.

'Not that I can think of right now, Mr Marklin. Sorry, I don't seem to have been of much help.'

This time I did succeed in putting a hand on her shoulder. 'Well, if you think of anything, ring me at the shop. "Toy Emporium". It's in the book.'

Her eyes lit up. 'Does this mean. . . ?'

I smiled in lieu of a direct reply. 'If the police don't bother your son again over Mr Maitland's death, then you won't be needing me, really, will you?'

I don't think the thought had occurred to her. Presumably because she and her son were both pretty sure the police had not yet finished with him over the murder. I wondered whether they were both holding something back that made them think that way. Or whether they felt that once you've been in trouble with the law, as Ron had been over his Tom-peeping, you were always then prime suspect for any other shenanigan in the neighbourhood. Which gave me a thought.

'But if the police do come round again, Mrs Ball, then do inform me. But for goodness' sake, don't inform them that I am having anything to do with the case. I've had enough tickings off from the Bournemouth division for interfering in their affairs, to last me a lifetime.'

She forced a weak smile. 'Already forgotten your name, haven't I, Mr . . . er . . . er. . . ?'

Gus shambled into the shop later that afternoon to be brought up to date. And to my great relief, proved not to have performed any more subtle sleuthing on his ownio.

Just before he left – to wash and wring out his 'smalls', he claimed – an assertion I could hardly credit, as one, Gus hardly washes anything himself but gets his latest lady to bung it in her washer. And two, the word 'small' could never be applied to anything this hunk of a hunk might force himself into, anyway – Gus asked, all bushy-tailed, 'Well, what next, old son?'

I hated to disappoint him. 'Nothing next, yet. The fellow's back home and unless the police come back, we've no cause to do anything.'

He sniffed an 'Oh,' then added, 'What shall I tell Milly, then?'

Ah, so he's over to his lady friend's to get his misnomers washed and wrung out.

'What I've told you. The police have no real evidence against him, as far as we can see. Except that he'd been in the Maitlands' garden that night. So . . .'

He bit a lip. 'But . . . er . . . I mean, could I tell Milly, now you've met Mrs Ball and her son, that you think this Ron is, well, innocent?'

Oh, Lord. I could see Gus wanted so badly to impress his Milly with something more than dirty washing when he went over.

'Gus, I would love to be able to say that. But I can't. Really. All I can say is . . .' I chose my words carefully. '. . . that I don't think Ron Ball is quite the type to murder anyone for a few toys.'

He thought for a minute and though Gus may be slow sometimes and, most times, leaden footed, he's no fool.

'Yeah . . . well . . . yeah. I'll tell her that, then,' he muttered and with a half-hearted wave of the hand, went back out to his dreaded Ford Popular.

The main event of that afternoon, curiously, proved not to be the sale of a Günthermann tinplate Golden Arrow record car, in good, though not mint, condition, for a most welcome one hundred and seventy-five pounds (twenty pounds down on my asking price, but it had been gathering dust in my shop rather long), but a phone call from Arabella.

Ostensibly, she was ringing me from the *Western Gazette* offices to tell me she thought she'd discovered the full name and, indeed, the address, of the lady called Chrissie, that Ron Ball had told me about on Sunday – the prim and proper one who sometimes seemed to be with Mrs Maitland on the beach.

'The reporter who covered the murder while I was away said Mrs Maitland was looked after by a woman called Christine Cartwright, after she had come back from the police that day. Christine . . . Chrissie . . . probably the same person, don't you think? She lives quite near the Maitlands. At a house called Blindwell, Windy Lane. Thought you might be interested.'

'Thanks,' I said. 'But its only relevance might be if the police come bothering Ron Ball again. Then, I suppose, this Chrissie might be able to give me a clue as to how Mrs Maitland and dear Ron seemed to react together. I mean things like, did she lead him on at all or did he always ogle her wobbly bits or. . . ?'

'. . . or anything else,' she chuckled.

'Exactly,' I agreed. 'Poor old Ron, I think, is very naive and might develop great expectations out of the merest of gestures or remarks, who knows?'

'Who, indeed?' Then the real purpose of her call came tumbling out. 'By the way, darling, talking of great expectations . . .'

My heart instantly skipped a beat and then pounded into double time, sounding as near the pitter-patter of tiny feet as damn it. Hell, it couldn't be . . .'

I only just managed to gargle a 'Yeees?'

'What's the trouble?' she asked instantly.

'Nothing,' I falsettoed.

She broke into roars of laughter. 'No, no, no, you idiot. I don't mean *those* expectations. Don't have a heart attack. I'm not pregnant. Yet!'

I swallowed. 'So what expectations are you talking about?'

'Maybe I shouldn't get too excited at this stage. But I've had a call from a guy I met when I was covering the break-in at the television studios, last month. Remember?'

I dimly recalled a burglary.

'Well, anyway,' she went on, 'the purpose of his ringing was to ask me if I would be interested in switching from newspapers to television. You know, try my hand as a television reporter. That is, as he warns, if I'm any good at a few screen tests.'

'What did you say?' I asked, as if I didn't know.

'I said I might be. After all, I've been at the *Western Gazette* quite some time and there's precious little scope for expanding my career here. What do you think, darling?'

'I think it's great,' I said genuinely. 'Now I can watch you at work as well as at home.'

'Aw, shut up,' she chided. 'Be serious.'

'I was being serious. I'd jump at the chance if I were you.'

There was a pause and then she said, 'Got a worry, though.'

'Oh? What's that?'

'I don't want to be away too often. Or too long. You know, filming, and all that. And I would have to work pretty late some evenings.'

'Don't worry about me.'

'I'm not. Well, I am. But I'm mainly worried about me. I like our life just the way it is. I like us, just the way we are. Come to think of it, working on a local paper is just about right, isn't it? Not too demanding.'

'Local TV may not be too bad, either. After all, you won't be asked to work all hours that God made, like you might in London, working on national programmes.'

'Hope not. I'll check all that out, if I go for the interview.'

'You'll go for the interview,' I said firmly. 'You know you want to.'

'We'll talk about it tonight,' she said quietly.

'Right. We'll do that.'

And we did. Long into the night. But Arabella was not willing to come to any hard and fast conclusion – except that only a complete nincompoop would turn down the chance of at least going and sussing out the pros and cons of it all. And as Arabella remarked, 'My nincompooping is, as yet, by no stretch of anyone's imagination, *complete*.'

You can see why I go for her, can't you?

I was extremely relieved when the next day, Tuesday, went by without calls for help from Ball, Milly or Gus. Not only because I was loath to get involved further with the Maitland murder, but also because the silence and a fairly slack time in the shop gave me time to think further about Arabella's TV opportunity.

For the previous evening had, quite rightly, been spent mainly on exploration of my enamorata's attitude towards the likely ramifications of the job change and latterly, on whether she really was the kind of personality, who would be happy exposing her face on countless thousands of screens across the South and West.

'I may not be extrovert enough,' she had complained. 'Somehow, I think once I see that red light blink on the camera, I'll lose all confidence and just dry up. You've got to be a bit in love with yourself, I'm sure, to succeed on screen.'

'Well, won't my great passion do?' I'd joked, but I knew what she meant. For appearing on the screen is, to me, a bit like . . . well, the wobbly bit brigade on Studland beach. Worse, in a way. For you are exposing not just the physical, but every chink, flaw, wrinkle and wart on your psyche as well. There's nowhere to hide when those cameras start turning. A million eyes are dissecting you, piece by piece, gene by gene, particle by particle. Stripping you down, way past your bones to the nitty gritty of your soul. And worse, I guess, if you are a woman. For the mental stripping, no doubt, then lingers awhile over your flesh, on its way through. There must be thousands of men making love to attractive newsreaders every night of the week.

'I have a feeling that you're either born a TV reporter, or you're not,' Arabella had concluded.

'Don't tell me you didn't conduct interviews with other kids from your pram?' was my completely unhelpful comment. 'I'm sure people like Robin Day and Barbara Walters did.'

'Nope. Never had the hankering. I'm not sure I've got it now, really.'

'The hanker?'

She nodded. 'I think I'm more flattered by the guy's invitation than turned on by the thought of appearing live on the box. At least with a newspaper, only the person being interviewed sees the interviewer. And I don't mind that.'

'Whatever you say,' I had said, before switching off the light on the night. 'I bet you'll be a smash hit on the screen test.'

'If it ever gets that far,' she'd muttered, then added, 'which I very much doubt.'

Well, I didn't doubt it. On her looks alone, she'd probably get that far, let alone her journalistic experience, brain, talent, creativity and the uncanny discrimination she often displays as to what in this life is phoney and what is worth half a damn. In my view, any TV manager worth his salt would jump at the chance of having her. (On screen, I mean, of course.)

The only thing I personally had doubts about was my attitude towards the whole thing. Selfish questions like, did I really want Arabella to become public property? Could I live with the idea, one day, of perhaps being known as an appendage to a local screen personality, rather than someone in my own right (or wrong)? Would I like evenings spent with a 2D girl-friend made up of 625 separate lines? Can you cuddle a TV set without getting a nasty shock? Or even worse, what's a TV like in bed?

The intellectual ramifications of my ponderings become a trifle too much for me that Tuesday. So I was quite glad, in a way, that Arabella, when she came home, made scant mention of her possible new career, save to say they'd fixed an interview for her on the coming Friday.

Wednesday, however, proved quite a different kettle of fish to Tuesday. For I had only been open about an hour and a half, when a kettle of fish called Gus spilled into the shop, waving his arms like a dervish.

In typical fashion, he opened obliquely. 'Have you 'eard, old son?'

' 'Eard what, Gus?' I said, a little irritably, cupping my ear.

He came up to the counter, but was obviously too agitated even to plonk himself down on the stool.

' 'Bout Ball, of course.'

I closed my eyes and held my breath. In measured tones, I said, 'No, Gus, I have not heard about Ball. Now calm down, sit down and explain yourself.'

He dithered, flapping his great hands about.

'SIT,' I commanded, like some dog trainer.

He sat down. A tip for the future.

'Can't stay, though, old son. Nor can you.'

'Nor can I? Why, what on earth's happened?'

'They've bloody arrested him, that's what's happened.'

'Ron Ball?'

'Who do yer think? Man in the moon?'

I didn't rise to it. 'Why? What have they found out now?'

'Came and dug again, didn't they? Found these ruddy toys behind a tool shed.'

'Found the toys?' I frowned.

Gus raised his hedgerow eyebrows to the ceiling. 'Cor, luv a duck, do I have to say everything twice? The police found . . . the ruddy toys . . . in the garden . . . early this morning. Right? Got it?'

'Got it first time, Gus. I just wanted you to explain it a bit more, that's all.'

'Nothing to explain. They came and dug, found the loot, arrested Ron Ball and carted him off to the police station. 'Nough for you?'

I thought for a moment . . . 'Hear it from Milly? Or direct from Mrs Ball?'

'Milly. She got the call immediately after they'd taken him away.'

'I'm surprised Mrs Ball didn't ring me too.'

'She would have done, probably, only Milly said she'd look after telling you.'

'Via you?'

'Why not?' He fidgeted around on the stool. 'Anyway, old love, we shouldn't be just sitting round 'ere, gassing. Milly says Mrs Ball is beside herself with worry, all cryin' and that on the phone.'

'I can well imagine.'

Gus got up off the stool. 'Well, old lad, are you coming or not?'

Good question. Crunch time had come round with a vengeance. I felt like a hesitant juror at a trial, called upon to pronounce sentence by an impatient foreman, before he'd really had time to weigh the evidence. Was Ron Ball guilty or not guilty? Come on, man, hurry. We can't wait all day. Right, if we can't, I guess I'd better give him the benefit of the doubt, hadn't I? Not guilty, me lud. Unless, perchance, I find out later that I'm dead wrong, of course.

I fiddled with the keys in my pocket. 'Better lock up,' I said.

Gus winked at me. 'Knew you would, old son.' Then he added, 'My car or yours?'

'Look, Gus,' I began, 'since when, given a choice, have I ever. . . ?' I stopped abruptly, as I saw him wink again. Lord, when will I ever learn?

*

As I parked my old Beetle convertible outside the Victorian terrace cottage, I glimpsed Mrs Ball's face peering out through the net curtains. The next moment, she was at the door.

'Oh, Mr Marklin,' she tearfully exclaimed, 'And you, Mr Tribble . . . I don't know how to thank you for bothering about . . .'

'Gus,' Gus cut her off. 'Name's Gus. Not Mr Tribble.'

He smiled broadly and Mrs Ball blinked, then swallowed, then looked a deal less suicidal. This was a new side of Gus I was seeing. The charmer of mature ladies. And semi-tactful with it. Still, I suppose I should have guessed Gus had to have another side. After all, he never seemed to have a shortage of Phyllosan-fortified ladies queuing at his un-blancoed doorstep.

She ushered us into her parlour, where Gus dominated the tiny room, like a giant grandfather clock. (It's not his height, so much as his . . . well . . . overall Rock of Gibraltar-ness.)

After rather hasty pleasantries, I asked, 'So tell us what happened this morning, Mrs Ball. I gather the police came round to do some more digging. Do you know why?'

She shook her head. This time no curls escaped from her perm, because they were already out. I guess when your son is carted off by the police, you don't fuss too much about how you look while they're doing it.

'No. They just turned up. Minutes after seven it must have been. I'd just heard the weather forecast on the radio and a bit of the news, when I saw their two cars pull up outside. Then a constable came to the door and said they would be doing a bit more digging in the garden.'

'How long were they digging before they found anything?' I asked.

'Not very long really. Under the hour, certainly.'

I looked at Gus. He nodded.

'Did they dig all in one place or in different places?'

'Well,' she sighed, 'they hadn't got many places they hadn't searched last time they came. So all they'd got left was behind the tool shed and down the end by the hedge. They dug over both.'

'And where did they find the toys?'

'Behind the tool shed, they said.'

'Did you see the toys yerself?' Gus grunted.

'I saw the big plastic bag they were in. It was transparent see, so I could see a few of the boxes inside, like.'

'And then what happened?' I asked.

She looked a trifle amazed at my question. 'Well, nothing really, 'cept what I told Milly and I expect she told you. They said that Ron must come down to the police station with them, right away . . .' She wiped an eye with the edge of her apron. 'And off he went in one of the cars. I had to stay because they left a constable and a plain clothes man behind, see. They searched the house and garden all over again. They haven't been gone long. It was awful, Mr Marklin, Mr . . . er. . . , Gus, just terrible. What on earth do you think they imagined they would find?'

'I don't know, Mrs Ball,' I lied, so as not to worry her further. But it didn't take an 'Ercool Parrot' to see that the boys in blue might well now be suspecting her son of rather more burglaries or, indeed, crimes, than just the one.

So I went on hastily, 'I take it the police didn't actually arrest your son. I mean, like read him his rights and all that, before they took him away.'

'Well, not exactly, but they took him off all the same, didn't they? Probably by now they'll have done all that, have him behind bars and . . .' Her voice disintegrated into sobs and Gus had an arm round her shoulder and was helping her to a chair, before you could say 'social worker'.

After a discreet pause, I said quietly, 'Look, Mrs Ball, if you like, I'll go down to the station now, myself, and see if I can find out anything.'

She blinked her tears up at me. 'Oh, that would be kind . . . are you sure. . . ?'

I wasn't sure, but I nodded.

'Would you like Gus to stay until I'm back?'

She shook her head. 'No, you both go together . . . please. Milly tells me you're like Sherlock Holmes and Dr Watson, you two. What one doesn't think of, the other does.'

I looked at Gus. He looked away. Dead right. I dread to think what tales old Gus spins to impress his lady friends. For I'll swear, however adept any of them may be at embroidery, Augustus 'Did I ever tell you about the time?' Tribble has them all needled into a cocked hat.

Our mission to Bournemouth, however, added next to nothing to our knowledge, but did produce a crumb of comfort for Mrs Ball. For the station sergeant on duty assured Gus that no formal arrest had yet been made, but that her son was still being detained so as to help the police with their enquiries.

I myself stayed outside in my Beetle, at the urging of Gus, who maintained that if Digby Whetstone saw me hanging around the station, he'd put two and two together and make the correct number four. Not that Gus's face is much less familiar to the Inspector, but I swallowed his argument that, should he be recognized, he could always claim to be a friend of Mrs Ball, whereas such a story would hardly wash from me.

On the drive back, Gus asked what I thought our next step should be.

'Well, I know what yours is,' I replied. 'That is to stay and comfort Mrs Ball for a while.'

He looked miffed. 'Why, where you going? Don't forget I've got no car to get home in.'

'I won't be long. Thought I'd just pop round and see that Chrissy friend of Mrs Maitland's. The one Ron Ball told me about. That is, if she's in. Then I'll come straight back and pick you up.'

'What you want to see 'er for? She's not likely to have ruddy done the murder.'

'No, Gus, she isn't. But how else am I going to find out all about the Maitlands' friends? And, more to the point, enemies? I can't ask Whetstone and I don't know anybody else. I'm hoping she can fill in some of the background, anyway. Like Digby mentioned that Maitland had a business partner, who has a fancy house. She's likely to know a bit about him, I would think. Or at least, know his name and where I could contact him.'

'Yeah,' Gus admitted with his usual grace. 'Might be him who did it, I suppose you're thinking. After all,' he grinned, 'business partners usually hate each other anyway, don't they?'

I ignored his obvious reference to the stories I'd told him about my days in advertising. A profession which I'm surprised has not yet given birth to human beings with the mutation of back to front heads, so that the daggers can at least be glimpsed before they strike. (Mind you, I've known a few clients who think people in advertising *do* see life back to front.) And it was this rat-race mentality that had, as much as anything, prompted me to swap the profession some years ago for the rather more innocent world of old toys.

'Now don't jump to conclusions, Gus,' I cautioned. 'Anyway,

last time I heard, you reckoned that fancy-dress-shop lady might have had something to do with it.'

'Well,' he sniffed. 'Got to be somebody, hasn't it?'

'Certainly has,' I smiled, then added, 'Unless, of course, Maitland beat up his wife first, then struck his own head with his own trophy.'

After I had dropped Gus at Mrs Ball's, I looked up in my diary the address of this Chrissie Cartwright that Arabella had telephoned through to me on the Monday.

'Blindwell', Windy Lane, proved to be what estate agents would call a comfortable, mature home set well back from the road in a third of an acre of beautifully landscaped gardens. In other words, a fairly ordinary four-bedroomed house, built circa 1928–30, but in this case the lack of architectural originality was partly disguised by the ivy that was now devouring everything save the windows and roof. The garden, mainly lawns and rockery, was as prim and proper as Ron Ball's description of the lady occupier.

I parked the car in the short gravelled drive and rapped the somewhat heavy brass knocker which was in the shape of a discreetly breastless mermaid. The door was opened fairly promptly by a tallish woman of around forty, with thick greying hair that reminded me of a squirrel's coat.

'Yes?' she enquired in a no-nonsense manner.

'I'm sorry to call on you like this with no notice, Mrs Cartwright,' I explained, 'but I would like to talk to you about Mr Maitland's death.'

She frowned at me. 'Are you from the police?'

'No,' I assured her. 'I'm just trying to help an acquaintance of mine, that's all. Her son, you see, is under suspicion for the murder and . . . er . . .'

'. . . you don't think he did it. That it, Mr. . . ?'

I held out my hand. She shook it with a fair old grip. 'Marklin. Peter Marklin.'

'Christine Cartwright. But then you must know that already otherwise you wouldn't have called on me, would you?'

She looked me up and down, from my casual, open-neck shirt to navy blue corduroys and striped trainers. I had the feeling I should have changed before I came calling on Mrs Cartwright. Like into a vicar. Or, at least, an accountant.

However, she did then let me in. But with the caution that she had already told everything she knew to the police and that she did not wish to get further involved, except to continue comforting the widow as and when necessary.

The sitting-room into which I was ushered seemed almost as grey as Christine Cartwright's hair. Only discreet pink flowers, about the size of a very primrose, relieved the grey loose covers on the over-heavy three-piece suite and the grey stroke lavender, but not stroked very much, wallpaper's only lighter touch was the green of a climbing ivy motif that was repeated every two foot or so. The rest of the furniture was straight out of the pages of 'The Plain Woman's Guide to being equally boring about Home-Making'.

Once she had installed me in one of the armchairs, she said quite bluntly, 'To be honest, Mr Marklin, you don't look or sound the kind of person who would know people like . . . well . . . that ice-cream man's family.'

'Oh, don't I?' I smiled between my teeth. But by then, my hostess's thoughts had obviously moved on.

'Marklin, Marklin. Now where have I heard that name before?'

'There was a famous German toy manufacturer of that name,' I tried, but it was a try I was instantly to regret. For she suddenly flashed a long finger at me with a, 'That's it! Toys. Old toys. You must be the man poor Mary told me about.'

'If you're talking about Mrs Maitland, I'm afraid I've never met her. That's really the reason I have come to see you today.'

'No, I know you two haven't met. But the Inspector on the case said he'd had a man in to give a value to the toys that were stolen. And it was he who told Mary your name – Marklin. The name stuck in her mind, she told me, because she knew her husband had one or two toys made by a firm of the same name.'

She bent forward towards me. 'You *are* the same man, aren't you?'

I nodded. ' 'Fraid so. Inspector Whetstone knows I run a vintage toy shop in Studland, so . . .'

But she did not let me finish. 'That's not all he knows, though, is it, Mr Marklin?' she said, with a fiercely knowing look. I could guess what was coming, but there was, damn it, nothing I could do about it.

'You see, he warned Mary about you as well. Said you fancied yourself as a bit of an amateur sleuth, or words to that effect and if you were to come round bothering her at any time, she was to give him a ring.'

I held up my hand. 'Look, Mrs Cartwright, I'm making no secret of why I'm here. I want to find out more about Mr and Mrs Maitland, their friends and colleagues, enemies even, if they had any, in case I can be of any slight help in tracking down the murderer.'

She pursed her thin lips. 'Does this Inspector Whetstone know what you are doing?'

'No.'

She looked at me, almost as if her dark eyes were having trouble finding focus. (Later, I was to learn, she normally wore contact lenses, but my calling without notice had caught her on the lens-less hop.)

'Going to tell him?'

I shrugged. 'I suspect he will find out soon enough.'

She closed her eyes, then suddenly, to my amazement, burst into a peal of laughter.

'Not from me, he won't, Mr Marklin. Not from me.' She immediately sat down and pulled up her chair towards mine. 'Oh, if my dear husband were still alive, wouldn't he just have loved this?'

'Loved *what*?' I asked, hesitantly.

'All this private eye stuff. He and I are martyrs to detective fiction.' She pointed towards the sitting-room door. 'The walls of his little study are still lined floor to ceiling with detective fiction. Everything from Raymond Chandler to Dashiel Hammett, from Agatha Christie to people like Creasey, Durbridge and A. E. W. Mason.'

I breathed a little easier. 'Does this mean, Mrs Cartwright, you might be willing to help me?'

'Willing?' she laughed. 'You just try and stop me. And by the way, before we get any further down the trail, my name is Chrissie, not Cartwright. Prissie Chrissie I was called at school. Been trying to live it down ever since.'

Would you believe it that in the end I stayed for a quick lunch. That's the last time I judge a woman by her decor. For Chrissie Cartwright proved to be what my mother would have termed a 'live wire', and plugged herself into my activities with high voltage enthusiasm. But I run ahead of myself, so I'll rewind a little.

I began by further elaborating on my connection with Mrs Ball and her son – via Gus – whereupon she naturally asked, 'So you must think this Ronald of hers didn't kill Maurice Maitland?'

I shrugged. 'I really don't know. My instinct sort of says it's a bit unlikely. That's why I've been willing to get involved – but then, I could so easily be wrong. His extreme naivety, that I'm interpreting as a not guilty sign, might be the very thing that could drive him to kill. Who knows?'

I explained what both mother and son had told me about the nature of Ron Ball's feelings for Mrs Maitland.

'So you see, he might have been so infatuated with her that he became intensely jealous of her husband. Jealous enough to want to get rid of him, in the mistaken belief that then Mrs Maitland might turn to himself for love and comfort.'

Chrissie shook her head. 'Oh Lord, Peter (yes, by then she'd shed the Marklin), if only Mary had listened to me.'

I looked up. 'Listened to you? About what?'

'About . . . well . . . not . . . er . . . showing herself off so much.'

'You mean on the beach?'

'Being starkers *on* the beach these days is not such a big deal.' She smiled sheepishly. 'Not that I myself indulge, you understand. Ever since Mary got bitten by the nudist bug earlier this year, she has been trying to persuade me to throw off my inhibitions with my clothes as well, but, somehow . . . I don't know, with all my feminist talk, I'm still not quite as unshackled as people tend to think I am.'

'So you advised her to pop on the odd garment when she went off the beach to get ice-creams and so on?'

She nodded. 'Yes. Ice-creams. The public conveniences. I tell her, "You never know, Mary. There may be funny people about who will quite misinterpret your parading naked once you're off the beach." And now, you say, you think one might have done just that?'

'Could be.'

'I must say, I was always a teeny bit embarrassed when I was with her, getting drinks at that van. Much as I love poor Mary, recently she has become . . . well . . . I suppose you could call it, a bit of a tease. I think she suddenly realized, probably for the first time in her life, that she really is quite attractive to men. And it's undoubtedly her new-found enthusiasm for nudism that has exposed it, as you might say.'

I thought for a moment, then asked, 'What was Mrs Maitland like before, then? I mean before she, well, shed her clothes?'

Chrissie smiled. 'Would you believe, rather timid and shy? For years I was always telling her she should come out of her shell and live a little. She used almost never to go anywhere. Except into Bournemouth or Dorchester to shop. That kind of thing. And then she'd always rush back in time to cook her husband's dinner.'

'So she had no enemies really, as far as you know?'

She looked amused at the thought. 'Mary? Enemies? I doubt it. Until just recently, she has always been a bit too compliant, in my view, too eager not to offend anybody.'

'You say, until recently?'

She waved her hand dismissively. 'Oh, I don't mean anything bad by that. It's just that, obviously, you're more likely to make enemies if you're outgoing than if you are quiet and introspective. Now her poor dead husband was quite a different kettle of fish. Don't get me wrong. He wasn't a show-off or anything like that. But he did know his own mind and was not afraid of letting people know it.'

'Did he dominate his wife?'

'Dominate is not quite the right word. It suggests brow beating to me and bullying and all that. Maurice wasn't a bully. He was too taciturn for that. Undemonstrative, I suppose. But what few words he did use, were always to the point. Bit . . . well, secretive, I always found him. About his emotions, I mean. Other things too, I suppose. Take that toy collection of his. You've seen it. But I don't think, before his death, that anybody had ever seen it, except Mary, that is. And precious few even knew it existed.'

She smiled to herself. 'Funny, isn't it? There he was sitting on a fortune. Or rather, under it, I suppose, seeing it was kept in the attic.'

I readjusted myself in my chair for my next question.

'Would you say Mr and Mrs Maitland were a happy couple?'

She hesitated for a second and then replied, 'Well, happy isn't quite the right word, really. Maurice was always too undemonstrative to be called a happy anything. Not that I've ever seen them quarrel or anything like that. You see, I don't think Mary has ever expected too much of life. And with all his faults,

Maurice Maitland was undoubtedly a better husband than a lot you hear about. He worked hard at his business, didn't get drunk or knock her around or anything. Even helped out occasionally in the house and kept the garden immaculate. That's why it's come as such a shock to discover . . .'

She stopped suddenly, then rose from her chair and went over to the window. I waited, not being willing to complete her sentence until I was sure of my facts.

Eventually, she turned back to me and asked, 'Have the police told you anything about Maurice Maitland?'

I shook my head. 'Not really, no.'

'Then perhaps, I shouldn't tell you either.'

'Tell me what, Chrissie?' As if I didn't know.

'Well,' she swallowed. 'Maybe Mary wouldn't want me spreading it around, either.'

I tried a sucker punch. 'But Mary must surely want to help track down her husband's murderer? And any information . . .'

It worked. She resumed her seat and leaning forward towards me, said confidentially, 'You mustn't ever say I told you, then.'

I promised.

'Right, well,' she took a deep breath, 'the Inspector has told Mary that Maurice had a woman friend over in Wareham.'

'Oh?' I feigned surprise.

'Yes. Seems she runs that fancy-dress hire shop in the High Street. Name of Fairchild, I believe.'

'H'mmm,' I digested. 'Maurice Maitland certainly was a bit secretive, as you say. How long had the relationship been going on, do you know?'

'Only since early this year, apparently. Mary can pinpoint almost the exact date. You see, it was probably through her that Maurice met this Fairchild woman in the first place.'

'Go on.'

'As I've told you, Mary has really come out of her shell this year, at long last. The first signs of it appeared just after Christmas. You see, Mary had seen an advertisement for a Fancy Dress party in the local paper. Over in Bournemouth, it was. Being staged on behalf of the Tunisian Earthquake Appeal. Well, she suddenly took it into her head that she would like to go. Not like the old Mary at all. And after days and days of badgering, she got Maurice to agree to take her. Well, you can guess the rest. They both went to choose their costumes in this woman's shop and bingo . . .'

I frowned. 'Bingo on one meeting?'

'Not quite,' she smiled. 'You see, Maurice offered to take the costumes back on the Monday, as he was going through Wareham that day, on business. And that's when poor Mary reckons it might have all started. Ironic, isn't it? I mean, that Mary coming out of her shell seems to have caused her husband to stick his . . .' she hesitated, then smiled, '. . . well, head out of his.'

'And Mary never guessed that anything was going on?'

'No, not a thing. Seems that whatever they were up to, must have been "up-to-ed" during the day. Mary says that Maurice was not often late home.'

'She must have been shocked when the police told her.'

'Yes. I think it hit her almost as badly as his murder, poor love.'

'By the way, how did the police find out about this Fairchild woman?'

'Someone rang them, I believe, saying he or she had seen someone who looked like Maurice in the shop often.'

It wasn't hard to guess who that must have been. I laid odds it was the 'she' Arabella had told me about – the newspaper typist's mother.

'I must say, I was a bit shocked too,' Chrissie went on, 'after Mary had told me. Had to have a stiff drink.' She suddenly got up from her chair. 'Talking of stiff drinks,' she grinned, 'I should have invited you to have one ages ago. I don't know about you, but I've talked myself dry.'

Thereafter, a light lunch seemed the most natural follow-up to drinks that anyone could wish for. Especially when that anyone only had a sausage or two left back in his own fridge.

Six

What was left of that Wednesday afternoon, I spent in my shop. And not just so that I could try to earn enough to keep the wolf from the door. (In fact, on that particular afternoon, I might just as well have invited the wolf pack in, to start with. For not even a G & T deigned to cross the threshold.) But I also wanted a little time on my own to digest what my new partner against crime, Chrissie Cartwright, had told me. For whilst I'd been recounting my time with her to Gus, after I had picked him up from Mrs Ball's, I realized there were still quite a few questions about the Maitlands left unanswered.

Like, what had her husband thought of the newly hatched Mary? Of her naturism and her baring all to the world on Studland beach? And, for that matter, what had triggered her emergence from the shell in the first place? After all, women by their mid-thirties, even more so than men of the same age, have usually found their permanent life-styles. Maybe they shouldn't have, but that's quite another story.

Then, whilst keeping lonely vigil in my shop, I remembered Chrissie's comment about her constant efforts over the years to get her friend to live life a little more adventurously, get out and around a bit more. I guessed, if you keep a tap dripping long enough, it must wear a hole in almost anything. And I reckoned Chrissie could be quite a forceful faucet when she got going. For there was certainly one thing you couldn't do with that dear lady and that was ignore her.

So by the end of the afternoon, I'd worked out the odd answer or two for my lurking question marks about Mrs Maitland. But her husband still remained somewhat of a mystery. For here was a man who seemingly had lived a very straight and narrow life and been a dutiful, if not over-caring or communicative, husband, suddenly taking a shine to the Morgan-driving owner of a fancy-dress shop. The only explanation I could come up with was that, perhaps, the boot was on the other foot. She had taken a shine to him, for some reason or other. Yet, from Chrissie's description of him – and certainly from photographs I'd seen of Maitland – he hardly seemed the type to sweep ladies off their feet or, rather, out of their dresses, fancy or otherwise. Yet, I said to myself, appearances are not everything. After all, hadn't I just made the terrible error myself with Chrissie Cartwright, of confusing outward manifestations with inner character? And for that matter, as Arabella had often pointed out to me, it's hard for anyone to judge the real attraction of members of their own sex to the opposite one. And she's right. If I'd been a movie producer, for instance, I'd have booted Robin Williams out of my first casting session, without as much as a 'How d'yer do?' But even so . . . I made a note to drop by Wareham some time on the morrow, as I suddenly felt an urgent need to attend a fancy-dress party coming on.

Of the dead man's public life, I knew a little more. Over lunch, Chrissie had told me something of his business affairs and had described the character of his partner, a man called Malcolm Savage.

It seemed that Maitland had been in printing all his life. First as a compositor on a local paper and then, after he had moved to Corfe, he had joined a small printing firm in Poole, where he worked for some years, eventually becoming its manager. Then, some fifteen years ago, when he was thirty, he had met this Malcolm Savage, who was the manager of a competing printing house. Their aims seemed to be in common, so they decided to go into partnership and set up their own printing business with money borrowed from the bank. This was, essentially, the same business they, until Maitland's murder, had still been running in Poole. Bank loans long repaid and profits fair, if not fabulous.

But it seemed that recently, Savage, the extrovert salesman side of the team, had been trying to persuade Maitland, his conservative, technically minded partner, to expand by buying a largish printing house that was up for grabs the other side of Bournemouth. And Chrissie gathered, from what little Mary had told her, which was all apparently her husband was willing to divulge to her, that they had reached an impasse on the issue. Maitland had maintained that he had no desire for their firm to grow to a larger size than it was at present and, anyway, where were they to get the finance for expansion? Savage had retorted, quite understandably, that no firm, if it wants to survive, can stand still, and finance should really be no problem. He personally was willing to go so far as to take out a second mortgage on his house, whilst he pointed out that all Maitland had to do was sell some of his beloved toys to raise his contribution.

This last piece of information was the first I'd heard that the partner had even heard of the attic hoard and I'd pointed the fact out to my hostess.

'Oh, don't go jumping to conclusions,' she'd smiled. 'From what little I've seen of that Savage man, he's as likely to steal old toys as fly in the sky. And if you're thinking he might just have been after what they'd fetch, forget it. Savage comes across to me as far too impatient a type to go that roundabout route to raise money.'

'Impatient is he?' I'd asked with a wry smile.

She wry-smiled back. 'I see what you mean. Savage might have lost patience with Maurice for stalling on the expansion plans? H'mmm.' She'd brooded on the thought, then remarked, 'But losing patience is still quite a stone's throw from murder, isn't it?'

I had to concur. But all the same, neither I, nor Chrissie, nor Mary Maitland, it would seem, actually knew all that much about her Maurice's business affairs. I could see that a little trip to a certain printing house was also on the cards for me next day, if I was to learn more.

So by the time I had shut up shop that Wednesday evening, I could see the Toy Emporium would be unlikely to open again until the Friday. Unless, of course, I could persuade Gus to hold the fort next day. I always hesitate to ask him, at the best of times. For he has a tendency to completely ignore the prices marked on my stock and ask what he's guestimated each punter's good for. Overall, I have to admit, I tend to gain by his mental arithmetic rather than lose, but the stories he weaves as to why the price asked varies from the price marked often live on to haunt me for many a day, as customers retell them to me when they return for another purchase.

However, as times were somewhat hard, I decided I had no alternative, so I put Bing on a lead and we both strolled down to Gus's cottage. A misty drizzle was by then drifting in from the sea and there was not a soul on the road. And there was not a soul at

Gus's either, more's the pity. I didn't need to knock to know. For if Gus is in, his Ford Popular is bound to be treading weeds outside.

So I looked at Bing. He looked at me. And I'll swear he shrugged before pulling at the lead in the direction of the beach. So I had no alternative but to follow. After all, there was no point in the two of us being frustrated.

But by the time we returned up the lane some fifteen minutes later, our hair and fur damp and our eyebrows jewelled with mist drops, Gus's upright old banger was standing guard outside his cottage. As Bing and I went up to the front door, I was rather disappointed to see through the window that Gus was not alone.

'Gor,' he grunted at me. 'I've just been trying to ruddy ring you. Where've you been?'

I pointed down at Bing. 'We've been to London to seek our fortune. But the streets weren't paved with gold and . . . Gus, where do you *think* we've been?'

He took the last bit literally.

'Beach, most likely.'

'Right in one, Gus. But we were actually coming to see you as well, because I've got a favour to ask. But if you've got a guest . . .'

'So've I,' he muttered. 'Got a favour to ask, I mean, old lad.' He pointed a thick digit towards his living-room. 'Milly's in there. Better come in and meet her.'

I frowned, as I whispered, 'That the favour? Meeting Milly?'

'No, you berk. Use your brain. Why do you think she's here?'

'I dread to think.'

He waved his great hand irritably and Bing took refuge from the draught created and crouched behind my legs.

'No, no, no, none of that. It's just that, well, Milly wanted to come over and thank you, like, personal, for what you're doing for her friend.'

'I haven't done anything yet, Gus.'

'But you will be, old lad. Yes, you will be.'

My heart sank to Bing's level, as I saw the look in his rheumy eyes.

'You mean. . . ?' I began, but his nod cut me off.

'Yea. They've gone and done it now.'

'Arrested Ron Ball?'

'Yea.'

86

'For murder?'

'Not yet. But next worst thing. For nicking Maitland's old toys.'

'They've detained him?'

' 'Course. See their little scheme a mile off, I can. Charge him with something small, so that they can hold him until they've got enough evidence to nail him with something big.'

Gus was probably right. I could almost hear Digby Whetstone urging on his troops to dig up the damning evidence pronto, if not before.

'Anyway,' Gus concluded, 'now you know, you'd better come in and meet Milly, hadn't you?'

I looked down at Bing. He blinked a weary blue eye.

'Welcome to the club,' I thought, as I trundled on through behind Gus.

Milly proved to be as small as Gus is big, as soft and cuddly as Gus is craggy and as sweet and charming as Gus is gruff. And there the dissimilarity ends. For she certainly shared his down-to-earth quality (although with considerably less fertilizer mixed into her conversation) and also, I guess, his sharp suspicion of anything that smacks of pretension.

I put her age at around sixty-two or three, which would make her around mumble, mumble years younger than Gus. (Sorry about the uncertainty, but on the few occasions I have asked Gus his age, I've always got a mumble as a reply.)

The first few minutes in her company were spent, as Gus had prophesied, on effusive thanks for anything and everything I might have done or might be doing on behalf of her friend and her son.

'He didn't do it, you see, Mr Marklin. I know he didn't. Not our Ron. You believe that, now don't you? I can see you do.'

She obviously had better eyesight than I have but there you are. I countered by saying I'd do all I could to try to track down the real murderer, in the hope her penetrating peepers did not spot the side-stepping. Luckily, they didn't seem to. Then I asked a question of my own.

'Have you got any theories, Mrs Millicent?' (Yes, that was her name, Milly Millicent. The imagination of her parents must have been mind-boggling.) 'I mean, as to who might have killed Mr Maitland?'

Her marble-round eyes lit up. 'Me?'

I nodded and saw her flash a glance at Gus. Whereupon he nodded. So I guessed I had asked the right thing.

'Yes,' she said, her round face flushing somewhat. 'I have thought quite a bit about it, since it all happened. And talked about it with my friend, Mrs Ball, of course . . . and Gus, here. . . .'

'And. . . ?' I prompted.

'And . . . er . . . well, I reckon it isn't nothing to do with those toys they're now accusing Ron of stealing, any old road.'

'So what do you think it is to do with, then?' I asked.

Again she shot a glance at Gus. Again he nodded.

She filled her chest with air, then went on, 'I reckon you'll find, when truth is known, that Maitland man had it coming to him. Those who get theirselves murdered very often do. Only got to read the papers to see that.' She wagged a careworn finger. 'Go a little bit too far for their own good, they do. And then . . .' she sliced the air with her whole hand, '. . . down comes the chopper and off go their heads.'

'Wasn't a chopper, Milly,' Gus observed. 'Bronze ornament.'

She looked up at him from under her eyelashes, then saw his earnest expression change to a broad grin. Instantly, she prodded him in the stomach. 'Oh, go on with you, Gus. There you go again, kidding me on.'

There he went indeed. But I was somewhat relieved to note that I obviously wasn't the only person in the world who fell for Gus's wind-ups.

'Any ideas as to where and how you think Maitland might have gone too far?' I asked.

'Not really. Gus here thinks it may have something to do with that fancy lady he'd got over in Wareham. But neither of us really know enough about any of it to make a proper guess.' She put her chubby hand to her mouth and grinned like a small – correction – large-ish, child. 'But I suppose you should call Gus's guess about the fancy lady a bit improper, really.'

'Gus? Improper? Never,' I asserted with a smile.

And she laughed. 'I can tell you know him backwards, Mr Marklin.'

'Less frightening than from the front,' I said.

' 'Ere,' Gus suddenly interjected, 'that's enough about me, thank you very much. What I want to know right now, is what we're going to do next, seeing as how this Ron Ball's now ruddy well been arrested?'

I blanched at the thought of 'we', but let it pass.

'Right now there's nothing much we can do. It's too late. The fancy-dress shop will be closed. So will the printing works that Maitland owned with his partner. And I don't have their home addresses. Besides, even if I did, I don't want to beard them in their dens at this early stage. Rather get a feel of them first. And prepare my thoughts a bit.'

'Can't we go round and see Mrs Maitland?' Gus suggested. 'After all, she's the only one who's actually seen the ruddy murderer.'

I shook my head. 'Her friend, Chrissie Cartwright . . .' I turned to Milly, '. . . a woman Gus has probably told you about. I saw her earlier today . . . well, she says Mrs Maitland is still pretty unwell after her beating up.'

'Not surprised, poor dear,' Milly sympathized. 'Might have got killed herself too, she might.'

'Apparently, she spends quite a bit of the day in bed still,' I continued. 'So I hesitate to call on her until she's a little bit better. Certainly I can leave her until I've at least seen the other two.'

Gus rubbed his hands together. 'So what time are we off in the morning, old lad?'

I hesitated, then played the joker. 'Milly,' I began.

'Yes, Mr Marklin?'

'If I'm to be off to Wareham and Poole and so on, tomorrow, I've got a bit of a problem with my shop.'

'Oh . . . Yes . . .' she pondered. 'That's true. I keep forgetting you've got a shop to run. Isn't that awful of me?'

'Not at all,' I beamed. 'But I was just wondering if you . . . er . . . might be able to hold the fort, perhaps, whilst I'm . . .'

I got no further, as, suddenly, I felt a vice gripping my forearm.

'No, that's all right, old son. Don't you fret yourself. Nor you, Milly. I'll look after the shop. Done it before. Know the ropes. Nothing to it. Only too 'appy.'

The joker had turned the trick, much to my relief. For I've often sensed that Gus displays an almost proprietorial feeling towards my shop. Oh, I know he's always making disparaging remarks about old toys and the silly grown-ups who won't grow out of them, but even so, I had a suspicion that if I ever dared to introduce an outside party into the mix, he might well feel a mite miffed. Jealous even. Serving in the shop have only ever been myself, Arabella and Gus. Arabella he adores, quite rightly, and regards, even more rightly, as family, and not by any measure a third party.

'Sure, Gus?' Milly checked. 'I mean it's no trouble for me to do it, if I could be just picked up.'

Then her eyes checked with mine and she gave a subliminal wink. Yes, I liked Milly.

I arranged for Gus to come round not before ten thirty on the next day, as I had got a little behind on my mail-order business and the sending out of my latest listings. I wanted to catch up before the day caught up with me.

As there was no point in keeping the shop closed from nine thirty and thus lose an hour of potential business, I opened up at the usual time and continued addressing envelopes and sticking on stamps (second-class), whilst seated behind my counter.

Needless to say, the only customer I had for the first forty minutes or so was Sweet Fanny Adams, which was not a great surprise. But at least, the last quarter of an hour or so of my lonely vigil was not wasted, as just after I had brewed a quick if not instant cup of Nescafé, I caught sight of a punter peering in at my recent great advance in salesmanship – the military Diorama in the window. And lo and behold, he not only peered, but popped in with a buying look in his eye.

'Good morning,' I said breezily. 'Seen something you fancy in the window?'

'Yeees,' he drawled in an 'anyone for tennis?' style delivery that spoke of the Home Counties and away from home education. 'The old tank on the slope.'

I came out from behind the counter. 'Which one would that be? I have two crawling up slopes, as I remember.'

He smiled. 'Think it must be a Vickers Medium. Certainly looks like it.'

'Ah, the Dinky toy.'

I went over to the window and by dint of a contorted lean-cum-gorilla arm extension, managed to extricate said tank without knocking over the skyscrapers of boxed toys that surrounded and backed the Diorama.

I proffered the little die-cast item and hoped he wouldn't notice its wireless aerial was missing.

'Ah. That's the one. Thank you.' He cradled the tank in one hand and rotated its turret with strong well-kept fingers.

'Interested in military stuff?' I asked.

He looked up. 'Yeees. Yeees. A little. Let's say the bug has just begun to bite.'

He smiled and his close-cropped moustache seemed almost to disappear into the fold between his slightly over-long nose and broad, fleshy lip. Not that he was bad looking. He wasn't. It was just that, like his accent, his features were a trifle exaggerated.

'Just starting a collection?'

He nodded.

'Well, you couldn't really have a better start than a Vickers Medium. And then you could go on to the rest of the Dinky pre-war military range. The light tank, the reconnaissance car, the 18-pounder Field Unit, the various lorries . . .'

'Hold on, Mr . . . er . . .' he cut me off.

'Marklin. Peter Marklin.'

'Mr Marklin, I'm sure you're right and the Dinky range is where I should concentrate first, but . . .' He turned the tank upside down and read the price, '. . . at sixty-five pounds a time, I'm afraid I will have to build gradually.'

'They won't all be that price,' I persevered. 'You can still get a good light tank, for instance, for around fifty. I haven't got one in stock at present, but I'm sure I could get you one fairly quickly.'

He handed the Vickers Medium back to me and for a second, I thought all my salesmanship had been in vain.

But then he asked, 'Take sixty, Mr Marklin?'

I pretended to think about it. 'Well . . . considering you might become a good customer of mine, sixty it is.'

He reached into his well-cut hacking jacket, produced a lizard-skin wallet and shelled out three twenty-pound notes.

I accepted them with a, 'Well, if you'd like me to look out a Light tank for you, I could give you a ring when it's in.'

'Yes, why don't you do that, Marklin. But no immediate obligation to buy, I hope.' He patted his breast pocket. 'Funds, you know. Got to see where they stand, when the time comes.'

As he made for the door, he appraised the rest of my stock, then remarked, 'People like you must be very relieved the police have at last traced the fellow who stole those old toys last week. Remember? From the house where that man was murdered. Or haven't you heard? It was on the local radio this morning.'

'Ah, yes,' I nodded, '*that* man. Yes, I had heard. And yes, of course, we're all relieved. We just hope old toys haven't now joined family silver, paintings, Sheraton and Chippendale as the burglar's best buys. Correction, non-buys.'

He chuckled. 'Yes, indeed. I dare say that fellow they've arrested will turn out to be rather more than just a common burglar. What do you think?'

'Could be. But it depends a bit, I suppose, as to whether he actually *was* the burglar.'

My tank-buying customer seemed almost to drop his purchase at the idea that the great British police could ever be wrong. Though I guessed his age at only around thirty-five, his manner was almost that of a previous generation, when questioning the Establishment wasn't really cricket, old boy. Drum you out of the regiment. Turf you out of your club.

'Mark my words, Mr Marklin, the police have got the right man, all right. That's the thing about living in Britain, whatever the loony left in the big towns says. You can trust the Law. Especially in quiet country backwaters like this. Nice feeling, isn't it?'

I smiled, then changed the subject. 'Well, if you'd like me to ring you about the Light tank, I'll need your number.'

He held up a finger. 'Ah, tell you what's easier. I pass this way every once in a while, anyway, so I'll just pop my head in. Save you bothering and save the cost of the call.'

With that, he left. I didn't see a car, so assumed he must have parked it round the corner, as many did. If I'd had to guess its make right then, I'd have said a five-year-old but well-kept BMW. He seemed that kind of customer. Know what I mean?

Gus turned up almost as soon as he'd left. And I proudly recounted the success of my dioramic window dressing that he had so recently poo-pooed.

'Wasn't your dio-whatsisname, old love, that sold that tank. Don't kid yourself. Bet he'd have bought it, even if it had been perched on some old shoe boxes or a stack of lavatory seats, for that matter.'

I love Gus. He's so encouraging to have around.

So with a certain trepidation, I left him minding the store – having read him the riot act about changing prices and embroidering stories – and left for the Sandbanks ferry and the address in Poole that Chrissie Cartwright had given me.

Once there, I had difficulty parking my Beetle, as the ugly

concrete building that housed Purbeck Print, as Maitland's business was called, was hemmed in behind other newer office blocks that reduced the street width to anorexic proportions. I could see immediately one reason why his Savage partner would want to expand and take over the company the other side of Bournemouth. Forget seeing a better future, how about seeing a better view from your window. For contrary to popular belief, brick walls *do* a prison make.

A diminutive girl telephonist cum receptionist and cum dogsbody, I suspected, seated at a chipped formica desk, asked me, in a voice well overdue for oiling, whether I had an appointment with Mr Savage. I replied, 'No', but if he could spare a few moments, I wished to speak to him about some personal matters connected with his deceased partner.

She fiddled with her tangled assortment of plugs and wires and transmitted my message. A garbled crackle later and she turned to me and asked, 'You're not from an insurance company, are you? Mr Savage makes a practice of never seeing anyone connected with insurance.'

I smiled and shook my head. I had great sympathy for his feelings. 'No, I'm not. Tell him I'm just here as a private individual. Nothing to sell. Promise.'

More crackling, then she squeaked, 'Mr Savage says he hopes it won't take long, as he has to go out shortly.'

'No, it shouldn't take long,' I assured her, then she pointed to some stairs behind her.

'Third floor. His office is second on the left. Name on the door. Just knock and go in.'

As I passed her on my way to the cold and uncarpeted stairs, she sniffed and said, 'Sorry about walking up. Lift's broken, see.' Then she smiled. 'Just as well, really, with all the rude messages people keep scratching on its walls. That's the trouble about being in printing, I suppose. Get all sorts coming and going in here, we do. Not casting no aspersions, mind.'

I tipped the brim of my non-existent hat. ' 'Course not,' I smiled. 'I forgot to bring my penknife today, anyway.'

If the look on her face could have been bottled, she would have made a fortune.

'Well, Mr Marklin, what's your problem, this so far unrewarding morning?' Malcolm Savage asked, without taking his eyes off

93

what looked like a printer's proof of a handbill that he held in his hairy hands. 'I gather from my receptionist that it's something to do with my late, lamented partner. That right?' But before waiting for an answer, he grumbled on, 'God, I wish I didn't know what my problem is. Bloody incompetent staff, that's what it is. This'll be the fourth time I've had to send this simple poster back to be reproofed. Look at it.'

For the first time he glanced up at me as he proffered the offending article. And for the first time, I could take stock of him. But first I did as I was bid. Though to my untutored eye, the poster – for a disco called Drango, opening up in Dorchester – looked fine.

'See the bloody "S" on Saturday? Smudged, Mr Marklin. And the whole damn word is still set too near the border. Let this thing out as it is and the whole world will think we're a bunch of bloody amateurs.'

I wasn't too sure about the whole world bit, but didn't argue. I was too busy, anyway, trying to sum up the speaker. For in the few minutes I had been allotted, I did not want to miss a trick.

It did not take a genius to see the accuracy of Chrissie Cartwright's comment about his impatience. To this I now added irascibility and after a quick glance at his clothes, the words 'show off' and 'colourblindness' sprang to mind. Physically, he was short, at the most, five five, which went some way to explain his obvious need to be noticed, but stocky with the kind of shirt-bulging chest that is normally the preserve of night-club bouncers and the muscled beach brigade. Age? Forty or thereabouts. It was difficult to be too precise, as his hair was black enough to have been boot polished or, at least, dyed, and he had not left any snow-white bits at his temples to give the game away. (Carlos Menem, please note.) What's more, his face was the kind that's round as a schoolboy's football, but with none of its lines. The kind that stays more or less inflated that way to the grave, unlike us more angular mortals whose features lose pressure and sag into deep kinks and furrows.

To my relief, Savage put the poster down, without expecting me to betray my printing ignorance. Then in turn, his over-active eyes started to appraise me.

'So, Mr Marklin, what is your connection with poor Maurice Maitland? I don't ever remember his mentioning your name and I have certainly never seen you around, either here or at his home.

If I had, I'd have remembered.' He smiled coldly. 'You see, I have a photographic memory. Never forget a face. Never.'

'I'm just . . .' I began, but narrowing his eyes, he cut me off.

'You're not one of Mary's friends, are you? That Matilda's husband maybe, or someone like that?'

'No. I've never met Mrs Maitland.'

'Oh,' he nodded. 'Well, who are you then and what do you want with me?'

I took a deep breath. 'I am a vintage-toy dealer. Have a shop in Studland. The police called me in after your partner's death to value his toy collection and also the items stolen.'

He leant back in his chair. 'Oh, so you're the fellow. I have only seen Mary once since that terrible night. She was so badly knocked around she hasn't been up to visitors. But she did tell me then that some toy dealer had been round. Well, well, well. So what do you think of my late partner's little hoard, then? Impressive, eh?' Then he quickly added, 'Mind you, I've never seen it myself, but Maurice used to refer to it once in a while. Go into reveries about some blasted car or ship or something. Must say, I didn't pay much attention.' He raised his eyebrows in knowing fashion. 'I'm into more adult pastimes myself.'

After his nudge-nudge, I asked, 'Do you know who else knew about the collection?'

He scratched his blue but still razor-smooth chin.

'Mary, of course. But even she didn't know its real value until you came round. Staggered her, it did, she told me. Said she had no inkling her husband could well be a millionaire. If she had, I reckon she'd have been at him more to take her on decent holidays once in a while or buy a better house or car, or how's your father. Poor Mary. Old Maurice did rather keep her on a tight rein over money. But then he was like that about everything. The number of arguments we've had over the years about expenses in this modest little business, you wouldn't credit. Looked at every penny, he did. I had a tremendous fight to get him to agree to the two of us having half-decent cars off the company. Even then, all we've got are ruddy Vauxhalls. People owning a company half our size run Rovers and Jags. Mercs, some of them, too.'

'So, Mrs Maitland, you think, was none too happy about . . .'

'Rubbish, old man,' Savage cut in. 'You don't know Mary. She was happy enough with her lot. I think she'd come to terms with the boredom of it all over the years. My wife wouldn't have, no

95

way. But it takes all sorts . . . Besides, recently, Mary has branched out a bit. Taken up nudism, would you believe? And I must say, she certainly looks a hundred times better now she's got that tan. Trying to make up for her husband never taking her abroad, I suppose.'

He smiled. 'I remarked to poor old Maurice a few days before he died that Mary was looking a treat these days, all brown and so on. And d'you know? I think he'd hardly noticed any change in her.' He shook his head. 'Cor, what a man. I hate to speak ill of the dead, but Maurice was hardly a charmer, you know.'

He suddenly stopped, then leaned forward over his desk. 'Hang on a minute. Here am I rattling on about the Maitlands and you still haven't told me, really, what you're here for.'

I had been praying he would not notice the omission.

His eyes now changed their sparklers for ice-picks. 'God, I'm slow sometimes, aren't I? Thousand to one, Mr Marklin, you thought by coming to me, I might be able to persuade Mrs Maitland to sell her husband's toy collection to you, rather than to anyone else.'

He rubbed a forefinger and thumb together. 'Money. Money. Money. Money makes the world go round, eh, Mr Marklin? Thought you'd probe me about Mary's weak spots, did you, so that you can come up with a sucker punch offer? Well, it ain't on. I've never accepted a bribe in my life . . .'

I almost completed his invitation for him. '. . . and I'm not stopping now.' Instead, I held up a hand. 'No, you've got it all wrong, Mr Savage. I am not here to enlist your help in buying the toy collection. It's entirely up to Mrs Maitland and no one else, what she does with it and whom she might one day sell to.'

He punched a finger at me. 'So, if you don't need my help, why are you here, Mr Marklin, asking all these bloody questions?'

'I didn't say I don't need your help. But not over buying toys. Over finding who *really* killed your partner, Mr Savage.'

I watched him carefully. But his ice-pick eyes now became blank screens, blast it. A trick I had observed many times in my old advertising days, when my colleagues were confronted by questions that rather fazed them.

'Sure you won't have one?' Savage asked, as he poured himself at least three fat fingers of Famous Grouse into a glass a goldfish would have been proud of.

I shook my head. He shrugged and came back over from a gilt-ridden cocktail cabinet that bore more relation to a sixties juke box than a piece of furniture. If Savage's home was any reflection of his office, he might one day get a good offer for its contents from someone short-sighted like Elton John.

'So you don't think this ice-cream bloke did it, then?'

'I don't know. That's what I'm trying to find out.'

He resumed his seat behind the desk. 'So why come to me? I hope you don't think *I* might have killed poor old Maurice.'

Luckily he gave me no time to react before adding, 'And for that matter, why come at all? Why not leave it to the police? They seem to have got things well in hand. At least they've found the toys and the burglar. And who knows, he may turn out to be the murderer as well?'

I looked at him. 'Do you think he is?'

'Why not? He bloody admits he was prowling round their garden that night, according to the radio. And he's a toy nut. And he'd met Mrs Maitland several times at the beach, as well.'

'How do you know?'

'Mary told me.'

I frowned. 'When? When you visited her the other day?'

'No. This morning. On the phone. I rang her to see how she's getting on.'

'And how *is* she getting on?'

'Not very well, she says. Feels giddy. And the headache has come back. Must say she sounded rather groggy. Advised her to see her quack and get an X-ray or something. Who knows but that bloody fellow may have done her more damage than we thought.'

'I'm very sorry to hear that.' Doubly sorry, in fact, because I could see that it might further postpone my visit to her. 'Tell me, Mr Savage, did your partner have any enemies that you know of?'

He smirked. 'Enemies? Oh dear, Mr Marklin, I suppose you people in the old-toy trade are a bit different, but outside in the big business world, you can't do a single deal without treading on somebody's toes.'

'So he had enemies?'

'No more than I do. Probably less, because I do all the outside selling and fighting for business. That's where you tread on toes. Maurice mainly restricted himself to keeping the actual printing

97

side going. Good at it too, he was.' He tapped the side of his forehead. 'Had it up here, he did, for machines. Anything technical. Not my forte, that, more's the pity. Still you can't have everything.'

'What about the other printing firm I believe you yourself are keen to take over? Anyone there who might have resented Mr Maitland's negative attitude towards them.'

He smiled. 'Where did you get all that from, then?'

'Mrs Cartwright told me.'

'Oh, *her*.'

This one I felt I had to proble.

'What do you mean, "Oh, *her*"?'

He shrugged. 'You want to watch what she says a bit. Troublemaker she can be, like a lot of these ruddy feminists.'

'Has she caused any trouble with you?'

'No. Not really. Not with me. But old Maurice wasn't too keen on her.'

'Any reason?'

'Oh, I suppose he felt she was a bad influence on Mary.'

'In what way?'

'Well, feeding her with all sorts of women's lib-type chat. You know the kind of stuff. All us men are chauvinist pigs and women should get out from under their husband's thumbs et-bloody-cetera. Maurice blamed the Cartwright woman for Mary joining the health and efficiency nutters. Didn't like it at all, he didn't. People seeing his wife without any clothes on. Don't blame him. Wouldn't like my wife parading around naked, either.'

'Do you think they ever quarrelled over it?' I tried.

'Doubt it. Mary's not the quarrelling kind. If she'd wanted to quarrel, she'd have started it years ago, not wait until she's thirty-five.'

'Ever see the Maitlands argue over anything?'

He thought for a moment. 'Not really. Can't say I have. But then that doesn't mean to say they didn't have the odd bicker in private. But I wouldn't reckon that happened often, if at all. Mary, in a way, was a perfect wife, you know. Not one to grumble much, really.'

I didn't comment.

'And your late partner didn't grumble about her either?'

'Not really. Mind you, Maurice wasn't exactly the talkative type. Especially about his private life. That's why I never guessed for a minute that he'd got a . . .' He stopped suddenly and looked away.

'Mistress?' I helped him out.

He looked back. 'So you've heard? Mrs Chrissie-cursed-Cartwright, no doubt.'

I sidestepped once more with a question, 'So you've never met Fiona Fairchild?'

'Never.' A tiny sparkle replaced one of the ice picks. 'Maybe I should. I've done a few checks since Mary told me about her. With one or two of my customers. Seems she's quite a number. Flashes around in a camouflaged Morgan, they say. Crafty sod, Maurice, having a piece like that on the side. The mystery is what she saw in him. As I've said, he couldn't be called a charmer in the wildest stretch of anyone's imagination. Shaken Mary bloody rigid, I can tell you, finding out about her from the police. I should think that's probably putting the stoppers on her recovery more than anything.'

'Any friends she can turn to? Besides Mrs Cartwright, that is?'

He shrugged. 'I don't know really. Because I haven't met any of her other friends. Though Maurice had mentioned one or two occasionally, when she's been off visiting them for the day. Especially recently, now that she's been going out a bit more.' He sniffed. 'Libbers. Got in with a few of them, apparently, according to Maurice. Friends of that Cartwright woman, no doubt.'

Savage looked at his watch, then back at me.

'Well, that it, Mr Marklin? Because I've got to get over to Dorchester before lunch.'

'For the moment, yes,' I conceded, as he got up and went over to a coat-stand to get his jacket from a hanger. As he came back towards me, the checks on his coat flashing like lurex noughts and crosses, he observed with a salacious smile, 'I'd advise that your next move should be to pop over to Wareham and get a shufty at this fancy piece of Maurice's. Who knows? From what I hear, the visit might well be quite rewarding – whether she knows anything about his ruddy murder or not . . .'

Then, slapping me on the back, he saw me to the door. His dirty chuckle followed me almost the length of the corridor.

Seven

It was as I started to walk back to my Beetle, parked a street and a half away, that I saw the white Ford Escort. Oh dear, the Dorset constabulary still have something to learn about covert surveillance. First, it was parked on double yellows. Second, the dimwit driving it had stopped at a T-junction. Third, said driver, although in plain clothes, looked as much like an ordinary man in the street as the Archbishop of Canterbury looks like Arnie Schwarzenegger. Fourth, taking into consideration the three above, white Ford escorts are only second to white Rovers as cautionary tails. The T-junction stop was only understandable in the sense that from there, one could see who and what might be going in or coming out of the printing works. But an ounce of common sense might have suggested leaving the car just back from the junction and watching the entrance on size twelve feet.

But right then, it was certainly more my problem than dimwit's. For the last thing I wanted was to be spotted around the print works and thus, by implication, trespassing in Digby Whetstone's parish. So as I approached the T-junction to turn left towards where I had left my yellow advertisement for myself, I hunched my shoulders and kept looking away to the left, as if the graffiti on the concrete wall I was passing had been sprayed by a Tolstoy, or at least an Auberon Waugh.

It was only once I'd turned left at the junction that I felt it safe to shoot my first glance at the driver. To my intense relief, he was not swivelled round in his seat staring at me, nor looking in his mirror. His gaze was still firmly set towards the printing works. I smiled to myself. So Digby was still interested in people other than Ronald Ball. Which could well explain why he had not yet charged him with Maitland's murder.

It was not until I was back seated in my Beetle that another possible explanation for having the printing works under surveillance occurred to me. That the Inspector was not so much keeping tabs on Malcolm Savage, as keeping guard on him. For after all, it was his partner who had been murdered. And who knew, if the motive was connected with the business, then Malcolm Savage could well be the next juicy item on the murderer's menu.

Such ponderings kept me from pulling out of my parking space for quite a few minutes, so that by the time I reached the main road, I was not too surprised to see that the Escort had gone. For by then, no doubt, it would have been haring after Savage's Vauxhall, as he made his way to his pre-lunch appointment in Dorchester.

To my disappointment, but not real surprise, 'Make Believe', as the fancy-dress shop in Wareham turned out to be called, was closed for lunch. So I took me to a hostelry – nauseatingly called 'The Compleat Tippler' – just down the High Street on the opposite side. Clutching a lager and ploughman's, I seated myself at a window-seat and kept a beady eye out for the first sign of life returning to the shop. Which, yawn, yawn, was not until an hour and forty minutes later.

And what then returned to 'Make Believe' was a Morgan in World War II desert camouflage of sand and dark earth. Out of the Morgan's diminutive door stepped a not so diminutive but coolly elegant lady dressed over all in white, from leather flying helmet to silk blouse and limb-hugging trousers.

I gave her five minutes to open up and sort herself out, then went across the road to play customer.

Upon going through her door, I was rather fazed by the smell of what seemed to be joss-sticks and moth-balls in a sixty to forty ratio. Of 'Morgan' Fairchild there was no sign, but over the many racks of wild and exotic clothes, I could see a door to what was obviously an office, so I assumed she was still de-helmeting or whatever in there.

To attract some attention, I ferreted rather roughly through the rack nearest the office, making the metal hangers clack and click against each other and the rail. The clothes here, rather unfortunately, seemed to be all for the opposite sex, varying from black cat costumes and mermaid outfits to historical costumes fit for a Queen Elizabeth or Victoria and adult schoolgirl outfits seemingly by the score. (Complete with canes too. I must say, I hadn't realized dear old Dorset was quite that sophisticated. Maybe Arabella and I just don't get invited to the wrong parties.)

But even all this click-clacking failed to elicit a response and I was about to shout the fancy-dress equivalent of 'Shop', when I heard a click from inside the office. Followed a moment later by the emergence of quite a different creature from the White Queen I had seen de-Morganing. Oh, the elegance was still there all right, but now it had obviously fallen head over heels in love with the colour chart as used by professional rainbows. For Fiona Fairchild was now sporting a ravishing shot-silk blouse with blue, red and yellow curlicues on a dark-green background with matching green leather skirt, slashed to the well-tanned thighs at the side. All in all, quite an eyeful to digest at that hour, especially after a ploughman's lunch.

'Can I help you?' she asked in a voice that hit the low registers as much as her ensemble hit the high.

'Yes, perhaps you can,' I recovered. 'Thanks.'

Her dark eyes drank me in from head to toe. Then slightly pursing her purple painted lips, she asked, 'Private party, is it, or public do?'

She tinged the former with a hint of excitement, the latter with a note of disparagement.

'You have different . . . ranges . . . I mean for whether it's public or private?'

She laughed. 'Really, Mr . . . er . . . er. . . ?'

I hooked a fish on her line. 'Marklin. Peter Marklin.'

'Really, Mr Marklin, you don't look the kind of man who doesn't know the difference.'

I took it as a compliment. Whether it was meant as one was another matter.

She went on, 'Private parties are a chance to be . . . well . . . a little more outrageous, aren't they? You can let your hair down in your choice of gear far more than you can if the "do" (there was that dismissive word again) is in the town hall, church hall or, for that matter, the Bournemouth Conference Centre.'

I swallowed and decided it was time to unpin my locks. 'It's a private party, actually.'

She moved comfortably close to me; so close I began to wade knee deep in her Chanel.

'How private?'

I Woody-Allened, 'Oh . . . you know . . . private . . . er . . . private.'

'Going alone?'

'No, no, no. With a friend.'

'Girl or . . . boy?'

'G . . . g . . . girl.'

'Right then.' She moved past me, her hip just saying hello to my hand, then asked, 'How naughty do you want to be?'

Before I could think up an adequate answer, she had come back holding what was clearly a black, academic gown, complete with mortar board, which she handed to me.

'Or rather,' she smiled, 'perhaps I should have asked how naughty do you want your girlfriend to be?' She leaned across to the rack I had been inspecting and took down a cane. First swishing it in the air, she then hooked its handle over my arm. 'This is a very popular little double act right now for young couples. The headmaster and his pupil.' She pointed at the gymslips and blouses on the rack. 'We have the outfits in various sizes, as some couples like going vice versa. The man dressed as a schoolgirl, the girl going as the master. Swish, swish, naughty boy and all that.'

She touched my arm with a purple ended finger. 'See what I mean? Might not go down too well in a church hall.'

'No, I . . . don't suppose . . .' but I got no farther, as she went on, 'But you don't look like the sort of man to me who'd let someone else have the whip hand. Am I right?' Her hip nudged the dangling cane.

I decided it was high time to move on from Frolics at St Freda's and put the gown, mortar board and cane down across the nearest chair.

'Look, I think . . . er . . .'

'Name is Fiona,' she cut in, 'but most of my friends call me Morgan.' She pointed outside to her car. 'Because of that little beast I drive.'

'All right, Fiona, I'd better come clean and tell you . . .'

Again, she cut in. '. . . you haven't come for fancy dress at all.' She fluttered her mascara. 'You've come to see me.' Suddenly, all flutter and flatter ceased and she glared at me. 'You shouldn't have used your real name, Mr Marklin. Then you might have fooled me for a while. But not a long while, I assure you. I'd have cottoned on to your line of questioning pretty fast. I'm nobody's fool.'

I was sure she wasn't. But what I wasn't sure of was how she knew about me.

'Inspector Whetstone?' I tried.

'He'll do,' she smiled coldly. 'He must be a clever man. He warned me there might be a possibility that you would turn up on the doorstep, sniffing around. Said you had a habit of interfering in affairs that are nothing to do with you. A bad reputation to have, Mr Marklin.'

'I'm only here to try to discover the truth about Mr Maitland's death. If that is reprehensible, then I plead guilty on all counts.'

'Are you *really* after the truth or do you just like being around to snort the sick smell of other people's tragedies?'

I looked at her hard. 'Do I really look like a car-accident groupie?'

She held my stare for quite some time, before replying, 'All right. Well, you'd better go into my office, while I shut up shop again. But I warn you, I can't afford to be closed for long.'

She sat down in a tubular chrome chair opposite me and crossed her legs, no doubt so that the split skirt would do its seductive best to distract. (It performed this function remarkably well, damn it.)

'I'm waiting, Mr Marklin. What do you want to know? And for that matter, why?'

I quickly explained how I came to get involved in the case, but deliberately did not refer to Gus by name, in case he might prove useful on what would be his second trip as a fancy-dress shop spy.

Then I went on, 'As to what I want to know, I have to admit I'm not as yet quite sure. I guess a good starting point would be the Maitlands themselves. How . . .'

'. . .well did I know Maurice Maitland is what you really mean, isn't it?'

I didn't disagree.

'Well, I think that's my affair, don't you?'

I liked her use of the word 'affair'. I cleared my throat, then persisted, 'So you're not willing to tell me anything about your friendship with Mr Maitland?'

'Except to confirm a friendship existed, no.'

'And is that all you've told the police? You and Mr Maitland were just good friends?'

The edge of her wide mouth curled – luckily in the right direction – at my *Time*-magazine-style phrase.

'What else should I say? Anyway, it's not yet a crime to have friends, you know, Mr Marklin.'

I tried another tack. 'This . . . er . . . relationship was quite recent, wasn't it?'

She pursed her lips. 'Ooh, we didn't know each other since childhood, certainly.'

I was starting to get a little tired of Miss Oblique, but patience is a virtue, so my impatient mother used to claim.

'You knew he was married?'

She laughed at what she no doubt considered my naivety.

'Of course I knew he was married. Dear, oh dear . . .'

'What else did you know about him?'

She frowned at my question, then raised an elegant purple-tipped hand and started to fold down the fingers one by one as she answered, 'First, that he was forty-four last birthday. Second, that he ran a printing business in Poole with a partner called, as I remember, Savage. Third, that until he met me, he claimed the only way he got his kicks was through dreaming about those old toys of his. Fourth, that his wife had bored him for years. And fifth, that said wife had become even more boring of late, now that, as poor Maurice termed it, she'd "gone all Women's Libby" and got those "dragon lady" friends of hers.' She unfolded her fingers, then shrugged her silken shoulders. 'That's about it, really. Oh, yes, and Maurice hated her new "naked is natural" notions, too.'

'Do you actually mean "hated", or just disliked?'

She fluttered her mascara, as she gave my question some thought. 'Oh, I think I see what you're after, Mr Marklin,' she said eventually. 'Your computer has punched up on the screen a sequence showing Maurice having a violent argument with Mary over her Libbing and flashing it all around. Then when she won't agree to go back to being a nice quiet mouse of a wife, laying into her with his fists. Whereupon, she says, "Excuse me for a moment," rushes to wherever poor Maurice kept that heavy trophy, then returns and asking him to hold his head really still, thumps him with it. Then she lies down to think up a nice covering story of a burglar, for when the police turn up.'

She moved a hand up over her brown thigh. 'Is that it, Mr Marklin? Well, if it is, then I would recommend that you take your computer back to the electrical shop toute suite and ask for your money back.'

'Why do you say that?'

She screwed up her eyes. 'You don't know too much about old Maurice's murder, do you?'

'Do *you*?' I asked, trying to probe through the slits her eyes had now become.

She laughed. 'Think I might have killed him, Mr Marklin? Is that your next gambit?'

I shrugged. 'I have no idea who was the murderer, Miss . . . er . . . Fairchild, I promise you. But let's go back a bit. You implied that the scenario described by my mythical computer could not be accurate. Would you mind telling me what makes you so sure?'

'Not at all.' She recrossed her long legs and at that angle, the slit in the skirt was far less blatant. My temperature dropped back to only just above ninety-eight six. 'And it's not what makes me so sure. But who. You see – I'm a bit ashamed of it now – I suggested a scenario, more or less as I described just now, to that Inspector fellow who knows you.'

'Whetstone?'

'That's right.'

'And *he* said?'

'Couldn't be, that's what he said. Mainly on physical grounds. The blow was of such force that it was highly unlikely to have been a woman of his wife's size or strength who struck it. Anyway, the angle of the blow suggested someone much taller than her.'

She caught my eyes appraising her. 'There you go again, Mr Marklin. Yes, I'm a good deal taller than Maurice's Mary. I'm as tall as he was, actually. One of the things he liked about me, he said. Yes, and I guess I'm probably stronger too. Should be. While she's been lying back on beaches tanning her all, I pump iron, as they say, in the gym. Three times a week. And quite a few evenings, I work out with Jane Fonda. Maurice used to want to watch . . .'

She stopped suddenly, then smiled coldly. 'So I suppose I might be physically qualified to be the murderer, or is it murderess? But the fact remains, I wasn't. I liked Maurice. We never, ever, had a quarrel. And besides, what possible motive could I have?'

106

I assumed she did not want me to answer her question literally, so I asked, 'Any other reasons Digby give you for the scenario being impossible?'

'Oh, that Mary Maitland had been quite severely beaten up and so was extremely unlikely to have been able to fight back. Besides, the Inspector said there were no other marks on Maurice's body or clothing to suggest that any kind of fight took place. Those were, as I remember, the physical objections to my neat little theory.'

'There were others?'

'Yes. Temperamental ones, I suppose you could call them. He said that he reckoned, from all he'd learnt of the . . . loving couple . . . that neither of them was in the least way violent or even impetuous. So he doubted very much that Maurice would have had a savage up-and-downer with his wife, whatever she'd done, or that his dear wife would have upped with a blunt instrument – and to boot, stood on a chair to do so – and banged it down on his head. Those were more or less his actual words. As you probably know, the Inspector is not exactly a magical weaver of words.'

I said nothing for a moment. For my mind was still trying to digest the matter-of-fact way Morgan Fairchild had described the death of the man who had been her lover. In fact, come to think of it, her whole demeanour throughout our meeting had been rather more that of a detached outsider and a brittle one, at that.

'Dumbfounded, Mr Marklin?'

'No . . . not really. Sorry for going silent on you.'

Her legs suddenly reversed back into the tropical zone, blast it. And I could have done with another cooling Heineken.

'No, don't apologize. I rather like . . . silent men.'

Well, that might be one reason she'd gone for Maitland. I must say I could not, right then, see many others. Mind you, I had a feeling this Fairchild liked men out of any barrel, silent or otherwise. As long, that is, as they had . . . what? I wondered. Beyond the obvious, as it were.

'So, since the Inspector poo-pooed that particular theory of yours, have you come up with any others? After all, someone killed Maurice Maitland. And that someone must have had a good reason, unless, of course, it eventually turns out to have been some nutter who kills just for kicks.'

She inspected an immaculate nail. 'Can't say I have. I don't remember Maurice ever mentioning that he had any enemies particularly.' She shrugged and leant back, and her nipples prodded at their silk prison. All I needed.

'So,' she went on, 'I guess someone must have been after his blasted toys, like the Inspector says. Caught in the act, panicked and picked up the nearest heavy object he could find . . . Probably that ice-cream seller fellow they've already arrested. Why not? Sorry and all that.'

Why not, indeed, blast it?

'Did Maurice Maitland talk much about his collection?'

I could see by her eyes that she instantly saw the inference of my question.

'Well, he told me about it, yes. But not in great detail. Why should he? I'm not interested in toys. He knew that and anyway, we had better things to do when he came around.'

'Did you realize how valuable they might be?'

She swivelled round irritably in her chair. At least the slit closed up a bit.

'There you go again. Really, I've had just about enough . . .'

I held up a hand. 'I promise I'm not insinuating anything. I'm just trying to discover whether Mr Maitland was in the habit of disclosing the financial worth of his collection,'

Her blink rate went down to just above par. 'Oh . . . well, in that case, . . . yes, he did once mention he thought they were worth quite a bit.'

'Mention a figure?'

She hesitated, then replied, 'Not exactly.'

'So what did he say?'

'That . . . er . . . they might well raise enough to buy a couple of houses, small ones, that is, if he cashed them in.'

I thought for a second, then asked, 'Houses? Houses for whom?'

But I had overstepped the mark and, as it turned out, overstayed my welcome. For suddenly, Morgan Fairchild rose from her chair and strode across to the door.

'That's it. That's enough, Mr Marklin. I should have listened to the Inspector's advice and thrown you out the moment I knew who you were. But better late than never.'

I had no option but to get up and leave. But at the shop door, I decided that as I'd already blotted my copybook with the dear lady, I might as well tip over the whole ink-well and see what pattern it made – if any.

'Just one last question,' I said. 'You don't, by any chance, know the contents of Mr Maitland's will, do you?'

If I hadn't moved with the speed of light, I'll swear I'd have been picking splinters of door glass out of my nose for ever and a day.

Eight

I got back home a couple of pips before four o'clock. To my considerable surprise, the Toy Emporium was closed and there was no sign of Gus or his old car.

I let myself in and the only one to greet me was Bing; I repaid his fidelity by opening a new can of Whiskas, then went into the shop. And there, on the counter, I saw a scrap of paper, torn from that morning's copy of the *Independent*. I picked it up with somewhat bated breath and there, scrawled across the corner of an advertisement for Singapore Airlines, majoring on the sex appeal of a dusky stewardess (I wonder how many letters they get from irate feminists), was the following wonderfully explanatory message:

'No one about much, so gone off for a bit. Won't be long.'

Typical Gus. Probably not had a customer all day, so, bored out of what he likes to call a brain, he had upped and . . . That's what worried me. He had upped and . . . whatted?

Determined not to lose what little was now left of the afternoon, I opened up shop and sat behind the counter, a mug of tea and Bing my only companions. But for over three-quarters of an hour, there was not a soul through my portals. Still, it did give me time to mill over my day's activities and come to some assessments of the two wildly different characters in the Maitland drama that I'd now met.

I started with the lady. One, because she was freshest (if that's the right word) in my mind and second, because she had undoubtedly made the greatest impression on me. And maybe, there was a third reason. She intrigued me. Don't get me wrong. I had not fallen under her sexual spell or anything – I prefer ladies to be wrapped up in a little warmth and consideration and not in ice-cold cellophane, through which you can see every chip and wire of their calculators. Maybe I should have said her motivations intrigued me. Why, for instance, had this sharper than sharp, elegant creature gone for the kind of man Maurice Maitland was reputed to be? What had she seen in him that others obviously could not? It was much easier to see why he had taken a shine to her. And I suspected it had gone deeper than mere superficial sexual allure. Her whole personality must have been next door to electrifying to a man whose wife – until very recently anyway – appeared to have acquiesced to the role he wrote for her. That, apparently, of a door-mat: a mat upon which he could rub off the detritus of each day, without a thought for the wear and tear on the fabric.

So . . . where did that leave me? I had to admit, not only still in the dark, but bulbless to boot. For I realized I really didn't as yet know enough about this Morgan Fairchild to come to any conclusions about her motivation – and particularly, why she should have singled out Maitland from all her customers, as a lover. Unless, of course, he had told her about the value of his toy collection. But even then, she would have no motive to kill him, unless he had just made a will in her favour. And I had a feeling I would have heard by now, if he had. Surely Mary Maitland would have informed a close friend like Chrissie Cartwright, if such a bombshell of a will had been discovered. And Chrissie would hardly have refrained from telling me, as it would quite plainly land dear Morgan up to her neck in the proverbial.

So, with a sigh, I moved my mind on to the pugnacious printer, Malcolm Savage. Here, at least, was someone with a possible motive. At one stroke (in this case, of a blunt instrument) he would gain control of the company from an obstructive partner, who was far less enterprising than himself. Once in control, he could carry out any plans for expansion he desired, his only constraints then being financial.

I made a mental note to check with Chrissie what happened to Maurice Maitland's shares in Purbeck Print. Had they passed to his widow? Or was there some provision in the company that decreed that, upon the demise of one partner, the shares were automatically offered to the other. Either way, Savage had to come up with a tidy sum to get one hundred per cent control; which might well delay his proposed take-over bid for his competitor the other side of Bournemouth.

So if Savage were his partner's murderer, then, maybe, the stealing of some valuable toys could have been part of the plan from the start. After all, it did not take a genius to see that vintage toys, unless they happened to be unique survivors of their kind, are hard to trace, especially if they are sold, say, a hundred miles or more from the scene of the burglary. The flaw in this theory was, unfortunately, obvious – the value of the number actually stolen was not nearly sufficient to fund Savage's acquisition of shares, let alone of new companies. But then, I argued to myself, the burglar/murderer seemed to have been interrupted and, in all probability, therefore, had intended to take many more.

Then I remembered how short and stocky Savage was. And the ice-cream vendor, right then languishing in police custody, was long and lanky. And Mrs Maitland had, I assumed, seen her husband's killer and her own assailant long enough to get a rough idea of his size and height. Therefore, she would have given his description to dear Digby Whetstone and he, with all his faults and short-sightedness, was unlikely to arrest a James Stewart in mistake for a James Cagney.

So that seemed to eliminate Savage. Unless, of course, everything happened so quickly that Mrs Maitland, still only half-awake from her interrupted slumbers, could not really give the police an accurate description of the intruder or she was deliberately misleading them for some reason. What reason? Protection? Self or another? If the latter, then, wild one, perhaps it was Savage. Motive? I was really clutching at straws here. Well, maybe Savage had some hold over her. God knows what, though. Or perhaps she was too terrified of him to come out with the truth. Or, wilder still, could Savage have pointed out to her that she could become quite a rich woman, if her husband was dead. One, through what he could achieve with Purbeck Print, given freedom to expand; and two, through the sale of the old toy collection. After all, if Mary Maitland was bequeathed her husband's shares, then under this conspiracy scenario, Savage would not have to drum up the money to buy them. At least, at first. For his dead colleague's wife, knowing next to nothing about the business, was unlikely to be much more than a sleeping partner and thus, Savage would reckon he would enjoy effective control of the company.

Then this condom-thin thought balloon burst with a bang, as I remembered Mary Maitland's injuries. Don't get me wrong. I was pretty certain someone like Savage could inflict them, but I could not see any sane woman agreeing to being beaten up so badly that she was still very groggy days later. Besides, I could

112

see no need for her to be attacked at all, under the conspiracy theory. All she had to do to protect Savage would be to give a false description of the intruder. That would be quite sufficient a role for her to play.

It was at about this point in time, when I was sitting despondently at my counter, surrounded by the tattered and torn rubber of punctured thought balloons and assorted debris from kites I had attempted to fly, that I heard the squeal, rattle and bang of Gus's Ford Popular shuddering to a halt outside. And for once, I didn't raise my eyebrows at the racket. For by that hour that afternoon, any interruption of my tangled and tortuous thoughts was a welcome relief.

I blanched, however, at Gus's apparel, when he shuffled through the door. For he was back in his 'artist' set of choker, clean shirt and dark-blue corduroys.

'Didn't know you had art classes in the evenings,' I remarked.

'Not surprised,' he dead-panned. 'They don't hold classes in the evenings.'

I pointed at his gear. 'So. . . ?'

'So what?' he retorted. 'Took the afternoon off to paint, didn't I?'

I frowned. I couldn't quite see the artistic muse suddenly alighting on Gus's shoulder whilst he was minding the store.

However, he went on, 'Got me stuff still in the car. Easel and all.'

Solely on the basis of 'wonders would never cease', I asked, 'What have you been painting then, Gus?'

'Nothing,' he replied.

'Nothing?'

He nodded. It was clearly one of his more enigmatic days.

'You got dressed up, packed all your gear in the car and went off to paint *nothing*? Or do you mean, you've found your true metier in abstraction?'

Now it was his turn to frown.

'What?'

I waved my hand dismissively.

He sniffed and recommenced. 'Didn't go out to paint nothing, now did I? Well, yes, I did, but then I didn't. Least wouldn't have, if I hadn't been interrupted, like.'

Now if you can make any sense of that, you should ring MENSA. Or at least join an ESP society.

'Gus, what on earth are you blathering about?'

'Not blathering, old son. That's what happened. Just after I'd got all me stuff out of the car and all.'

I cleared my throat. 'Begin again, Gus. Like, begin with why you suddenly decided to shut up shop and satisfy your artistic soul by whipping your brushes out.'

He subsided on to the counter stool, which creaked an early warning to his buttocks.

'Was nothing to do with arty-crafty stuff, old lad. Had a thought, didn't I, when I was sat here doing nothing, waiting for customers who didn't ruddy call.'

'What was the thought?' I asked with trepidation.

'Well, you were out sleuthing, so I thought I'd do my little bit, like, seeing as how trade was slack.'

'Oh, yes. . . ?' Well, what else could I have said?

'Yes, so I thought I'd pop over and . . . er . . . give the old Maitland place the once-over.'

I swallowed hard. 'You don't mean . . . paint it?'

He smiled a smile broad enough to give a dentist a heart attack. 'Naah. Pretend to paint it, see. Little cottage scene and all that. Had to have some excuse for hanging about there, now didn't I? Didn't want to arouse no suspicion, nor nothing.'

I smiled at the last thought. Gus, in any garb, looks as much like a sensitive artist as Dan Quayle looks like a credible Vice-president.

'So you wanted to keep watch on the house, or what?'

'Both,' he answered. Do hope your MENSA membership's come through.

'Both?'

'Yeah. Thought at least one of us should see the scene of the crime now, didn't I? You know, in case there were any clues old Digby and his lot didn't pick up. And while I was painting, like, I could keep a watch on what was going on, at the same ruddy time.'

'What on earth did you think might be going on, Gus?'

I shouldn't have asked.

'If I knew that, old son, I wouldn't have needed to go, now would I?'

'Yes' and 'No' and 'Both' is what I suppose I should have answered to that. But instead, I said, 'Let's skip a bit now, Gus, and tell me how you got interrupted.'

He held up a hand. I moved out of its shadow.

'Now, hold on. Wasn't interrupted right away. Had time to have a shufty at the garden.'

'And what did you see?'

'French windows.'

'In the garden?'

'No, don't be bloody daft. On the house. Look out, don't they, on the garden. Reckon that's how the murderer got in, don't you?'

I shrugged. 'Might have. Haven't heard exactly how he or she got in.'

He grinned. 'Noticed the "she" bit, didn't I? Come round to my way of thinking, have you, now you've seen that fancy-dress woman?'

'No, I haven't, Gus. Not yet, anyway. But before I go into my story, let's finish with yours.'

He looked disappointed. 'All right, then. Well . . . where was I . . . oh yes . . . the garden. Easy to get into, it was. No fences, see. And the hedge is very thin in places. Walk straight in, you can. Can sort of see why a bloke like Ron Ball would think it was worth going round. Most of the upstairs windows are at the back. Get a good view from the garden, if the lights were on and the curtains not drawn.' He sniffed again. 'That's how I saw them clearly.'

'Saw them? Saw who?'

'Ambulance men.'

'Ambulance men?'

'Yeah. That's how I was interrupted, see.'

'What, you mean they came out and asked you to move on?'

He laughed. 'No, no, no, old son. No, it was all the dee-dahhing when the ruddy ambulance arrived that did it. Didn't see it, 'cos I was round the back, wasn't I? But next minute, I saw the figures of two of them at an upstairs window.'

I held my breath and he went on, 'Put down all me stuff then, didn't I? Nipped round the front. Just in time to see them popping a stretcher into the back of the ambulance.'

'Could you see who was on it?' I queried, in not much above a whisper.

'Not clearly, no. But from where I was standing, it looked like a woman, it did. Too many bumps under the covers for a man.' He looked across at me. 'Mrs Maitland, I wouldn't wonder. But by the time I'd run up to the bloody thing, it was blaring its way down the street.'

Gus rattled off to see his Milly, after I had brought him up to date with my Savage/Fairchild encounters.

'She'll be glad to hear we're at least doing something, old lad,' Gus had grunted, as he left. I chuckled to myself as I watched him mount his ancient chariot outside. 'Doing something' is only a comfort if you know what that something you are doing is . . . or am I starting to sound about as lucid as Gus?

Directly he had gone, I lifted the receiver and dialled Chrissie Cartwright. Luckily, she was in.

'Must be psychic, Peter,' were her first rather breathless words. 'I was just going to ring you.'

'About Mary Maitland?'

She hesitated. 'Why, yes. How on earth did you guess?'

'Psychic,' I by-passed.

'Oh, well, yes, er . . . anyway, what I was going to ring to say is that she's been carted off to hospital. I only just heard. She got the hospital to ring me.'

'What's happened, then? Has she been attacked again or what?'

'No, thank God. It just seems she's not really recovering from the first attack. I knew she was getting terrible headaches still and odd giddy turns, but this afternoon, apparently, she blacked right out in the bedroom. When she came round, she was still so woozy it was all she could do to crawl to the telephone and ring her doctor. He phoned the hospital to send an ambulance round right away. Isn't it awful? I thought you should know, in case you were thinking, sometime, of going round to see her.'

'Thanks. Yes, I was contemplating a visit, but I would have checked with you first, naturally.'

'Obviously, now, that will have to be postponed until poor Mary is a good deal better,' she sighed. 'Now I've told you my news, let's get round to why you were ringing me.'

I decided to lie a little, to save telling her about Gus's artistic escapade.

'Oh, just the odd query or two.'

'Fire away.'

'First, you don't happen to know the provisions of Mr Maitland's will, do you?'

'No, not in detail. But Mary has mentioned that she is the sole beneficiary. Why do you ask?'

'Well, I saw Malcolm Savage this morning and I was wondering who now inherits Mr Maitland's shares in Purbeck Print. I mean, is Mary now his new partner or do the shares get offered to him first, with Mary just getting the proceeds of the sale?'

'Oh, I hadn't thought about things like that. Though I guess it would make little difference either way. I know Mary well enough to know she wouldn't really want to get involved with running her husband's business – let alone with a partner like Malcolm Savage.'

'So, you mean, if she had inherited half the company, she would sell out to him anyway?'

'Yes, I'm pretty sure of it. Business life is not what Mary has ever been about, otherwise she could have got herself involved before.'

I thought for a moment.

'Any other questions, Peter?'

'Er . . . yes. After I'd seen Savage, I went out to Wareham . . .'

'. . . and saw the fancy lady?' Her voice pulsed with animated curiosity. 'Tell me, what did you think?'

'Some lady, is Morgan Fairchild.'

'Morgan?'

'Yes, after her car. Most people seem to call her that, rather than Fiona.'

'I don't blame them,' Chrissie chuckled. 'Anyway, what's the question?'

'She said Maurice hated his wife's new passion for nudism and also the women's lib-type friends she seemed to be making. I was just wondering if you knew any of them, that's all.'

She laughed. 'Oh, Peter, so now I see the whole thing. You're ringing me because you think, like Maurice did, that I'm behind Mary's recent emergence from a mousehole. And that it was me who introduced her to all her new friends. Well, you're wrong, Peter. I have certainly encouraged Mary over the years to stand up for herself once in a while, I admit. And I myself am certainly more Libby than most of my contemporaries. But I assure you I'm not and never have been a militant, crusading feminist. I have met quite a few who are and, frankly, we just don't get on. They seem to be throwing away all the advantages women have always had over men, in return for posing as the men they can never actually be. So, fact is, I don't really have any Libby friends of my own. Those Mary has mentioned to me are all of her own making and nothing to do with yours truly. In fact, I've never even met any of them.'

'Chrissie, I didn't mean to . . .'

'I know you didn't, Peter. It just annoys me that if a woman speaks out occasionally and stands up for herself, she is automatically branded a "Libber" or a "feminist" or whatever. We're not, most of us. We're just women, who want to be reckoned as people, not as pretty pieces of furniture men like to have around to decorate their lives.' She took a deep breath. 'Anyway, so all I know about Mary's new set are a few of their names. That any good?'

I reached for a pen and the nearest piece of paper – a receipt pad.

'Okay. I'm ready.'

'Right. Well, there's a Matilda. Matilda what, I have no idea. Mary's never said.'

The name rang a bell, but right then I couldn't quite remember where I had heard it.

'Then there's a Mrs Valentine. She's mentioned her a couple of times. Oh, and a Miss or Mrs Churchill . . . that's about all I can recall at the moment. I'm sorry, but I don't know any of their addresses. Mary's never offered them and I've never bothered to pursue it, frankly. No, I tell a lie. The first name, Matilda Somebodyorother, she lives in the Bristol area somewhere, I believe. I only remember because Mary told me once that she was going up to Bristol by train to meet her. Sorry, but that's the lot. But may I ask why you want to know?' Then she added, 'As if I can't guess.'

I decided it might be interesting to call her guess. After all, I wasn't quite sure exactly why I was bothering about Mary Maitland's new set of friends.

'Go on, Chrissie. What's in your mind?'

'I reckon you reckon it just could be that poor Maurice was killed for his chauvinistic views. You know, just punishment for keeping Mary under his thumb all those years. Wild one, Peter, wild one.'

'It's your guess, not mine,' I pointed out. 'Anyway, from what I gather from Morgan Fairchild, the police say the fatal blow was delivered with considerable brute force and therefore, at present, they seem to be excluding women as likely suspects.'

Chrissie laughed. 'Poor frail little souls we all are, no doubt, in their macho-ridden imaginations. But they may be making a big mistake, Peter. Women do even pump iron these days and I'm told that a month of Jane Fonda taken religiously can make an Amazon of the weakest of us.'

I laughed, especially when she added, 'And I'd back a good butch feminist, like some of those Greenham Common protesters, against your average constable on the beat any day.'

'You may be right, Chrissie, who knows? But still, I can't quite see your friend so inflaming her new acquaintances with horrifying stories of her subjugation that one of them comes round and bumps off her oppressor. Anyway, surely Mary would have recognized the intruder if it had been one of her friends? Or at least, known it was a woman.'

'Why?' was Chrissie's immediate retort. 'Men and women often wear the same kind of clothes these days. And lots of women have short hairstyles. Don't forget he or she was wearing a stocking over his or her head and as far as I know, Mary did not hear the murderer actually speak.'

Notch up a few more points, Chrissie.

'A minute ago,' I pointed out, 'you said the theory was a really wild one. Now you sound as if you're warming to it.'

She sighed. 'No, I guess I'm just warming to my own rhetoric and devil's advocacy, if you like. So don't get me wrong. I'm no further forward now than I was at the beginning in really having any worthwhile theories about Maurice's murder. Are you?'

I had to admit I wasn't.

'So the police may be on the right track after all,' Chrissie observed. 'I heard on the radio earlier this afternoon that they've now charged the ice-cream seller with stealing the toys. And I'm sorry to say it, knowing your interest in the case, but whoever stole the toys is most likely to have been the murderer, surely?'

'The toys and the murder seem to be connected, certainly.'

There was silence for a moment, then she said, 'Tell you what, Peter. The hospital people said I could go in and see Mary for a minute or two later this evening, when they've finished their tests and X-rays. So I'll go and maybe pop by your place to report on the latest on the way back from the ferry. Would that be all right, or are you going out?'

'No, that's fine. Arabella and I have no plans for this evening.'

'Looking forward to meeting her. Sorry I can't give you both an exact time, but you know what hospitals are.'

'Yes,' I signed off. 'A carbolical smell and acres of highly polished floor to break a leg on. So watch your step.'

Arabella lowered her glass and looked at me.

'Chrissie may not be our only visitor tonight, you realize.'

I blinked. 'Oh? Surprise me.'

She laughed. 'No surprise about it. You know who I mean. Begins with a "D" and ends with trouble with a capital "T".'

I looked at my watch. It was almost nine. 'If dear Digby was going to call tonight, I think he'd have done so by now. After all, even policemen like to put their feet up in front of the telly of an evening.'

Arabella smiled knowingly. 'Ever actually seen one?' she enquired.

I had to admit defeat.

'Still, you're right. I'm a bit surprised he hasn't been in touch. I'd have thought I'd done enough poaching on his territory by now for him to get some inkling of what I'm up to.'

'Especially after what you've told me of your meeting with that fancy-dress woman. She sounds just the type to run to the old blower and ring the police the second she'd thrown you out of the shop.'

I thought for a moment, then commented, 'You'd think so, wouldn't you? But maybe, she needs more contact with the police like a hole in the head.'

'Like she's got something to hide?'

I shrugged. 'Maybe.'

'Like what?'

'Don't know.'

Arabella looked at me, her big brown eyes Liza Minelli-ing my own. 'Did she seem strong enough?'

'Physically? To brain old Maitland, you mean? Difficult to say. After all, women can actually be much stronger than they look, these days. Stronger than their flabby husbands, I guess, if they spend a lot of time at the gym or working out in front of their videos. And for all I know, Morgan Fairchild's elegant frame may be all one giant muscle.'

Arabella held up a cautionary finger. 'Well, if you have to see her again, don't pinch her to find out, will you?'

I boy-scouted a promise, then reached for my own glass of wine and held it aloft. 'Anyway, my darling, enough of murder and mayhem for today. Let's drink to the success of your interview tomorrow.'

Even grimacing, as she was now, Arabella looked delectable in the dying light of the day. I just knew the TV cameras would love her – but not as much as I did.

'I'm terrified,' she said quietly.

I leaned forward in my chair. 'What of? You've met the guy before. The only thing you haven't met is the camera and . . .'

She stopped me. 'No, you don't understand. I'm not terrified of the actual interview or any camera test they may or may not carry out. It's just that . . . well, what we've discussed before. Where tomorrow might then lead.'

'To a much more productive career than local newspapers can ever give you.'

She took a deep breath. 'M'mmm. Yeah . . .'

I let the silence play out. Then, after a while, she said, 'You see, one side of me loves the idea of being a television reporter. I've sometimes had childish and stupid dreams of one day becoming a Kate Adie, a Barbara Walters or an Anna Ford. Or even a Selina Scott. That is, as long as I wasn't asked to do some ridiculously shallow programme like The Clothes Show. But the other side of me sort of recoils at the whole prospect. I guess it's the parading in front of the camera, as much as anything.' She gave a self-conscious smile. 'No, I'm not nervous of its "penetrating eye" and all that guff. Least, I don't think I am. It's just that . . . well, I'm not sure I've got the right kind of ego for it all. I don't crave for self-publicity. I wouldn't really relish the power over camera crews and so on, that people like Kate Adie must exercise. And to a certain extent enjoy. And I suppose, most important of all, I'm not certain that I want to be devoured by a million eyes every night or however many might be watching. I'm not that type. Never have been.'

'But you're not shy,' I pointed out. 'It's one of the things that attracted me to you.'

'No. But there's a difference between lack of shyness and a desire to become public property. And also . . . well, you men don't really understand. It's different for male presenters on television. They don't get . . .'

She hesitated, so I helped her. '. . . get mentally undressed by every frustrated Tom, Dick and Harry.'

'Especially "Dick",' she grinned. 'And male reporters don't get their vital statistics bandied about in pubs, either. Or their likely worth in bed evaluated at great length at shove-ha'penny tables or around dart boards. After all,' she added, laughing, 'have you ever heard a woman claim she'd like to be given one by Martin Lewis or Michael Buerk. Or, heaven forbid, Robin Day?'

But before I could answer, we heard the sound of a car pulling up outside.

'Digby?' sighed Arabella.

'Doubt it,' I replied. 'Not a Rover. No V8 rumble. That's a four cylinder. But it's a million times too smooth for Gus. So it's probably Chrissie.'

When I went to answer the doorbell, my guess was proved correct.

'So how is she?' I asked, after I had welcomed her in and introduced her to Arabella.

Chrissie Cartwright took the proffered glass of Muscadet from Arabella and settled back in her chair.

'Oh, much better than I was expecting. Amazingly perky, in fact, considering everything. They have really gone to town on her since she's been in. She says countless doctors have seen her, prodded her, probed her and then they've dragged her off to X-ray and taken more shots of the inside of her than she says she's ever had taken of her outside.' She smiled. 'Those were more or less her exact words, so you can tell how surprisingly bouncy she was while I was there.'

'That sounds promising,' Arabella remarked. 'Do they say what they think caused her to black out?'

'Not yet. It's too early. But it doesn't take a genius to see it must have something to do with the beating up she received, does it? My guess would be – though obviously I did not say so to Mary – that she may have suffered slight haemorrhaging from the blows to the head. She made a great mistake refusing to have X-rays when it first happened, in my opinion. It might have saved her all the headaches, giddiness and what-have-you she's suffered since, if my haemorrhaging guess turns out to be right. So her fainting today may be a blessing in disguise. Who knows? At least, if they discover anything like that, they can start proper treatment right away now.'

'Might mean an operation,' I sighed; my sigh being not only for

Mary Maitland's condition, but for any delay such an operation might cause to my, at last, seeing the lady.

'It might. Let's hope not.' Chrissie raised her glass. 'Here's to Mary's quick return to health.'

We all drank to that, then she looked across at me and said, 'By the way, Peter, I told Mary all about you. Thought it might take her mind off her own worries a bit, if she knew that more than just the plodding police were on her side and trying to find the real truth about it all.'

I glanced at Arabella. Her eyes indicated she'd crossed her fingers too.

'Oh, and what did she say? I hope she doesn't mind an outsider getting involved with . . .'

Chrissie held up her hand. 'Quite the contrary, my sleuthing friend. She really warmed to the whole thought right away. Wants to see you, in fact. Soon as possible, she said. Tomorrow, if the quacks will let her. Though you'll have to see her in the hospital, as they've already said they'll be keeping her in for observation for at least the next two or three days.'

'Sure it still isn't too soon?'

'Well, short of a bombshell like she's got to have an immediate operation or something, I don't think so. If I judge Mary's present mood rightly, she's as anxious to get this whole ugly thing solved and out of the way as soon as possible. As she says, if you can help in any way, why, let's get right on with it. Though she did add, she's not quite sure what help she herself can be. Beyond what she has already told the police, that is.'

'Well, it sometimes helps to hear things first hand,' I remarked. 'Though she may be right and we'll end up learning nothing new.'

'Tell me, Mrs Cartwright,' Arabella began.

'Chrissie,' our visitor interrupted.

'All right, Chrissie,' Arabella continued, 'I was just wondering whether Mary voiced anything new tonight about who she thinks her assailant was.'

'No, not really. As she's told me before, it was all so sudden. Coming downstairs and then being attacked, I mean. And it was over in no time at all. Poor Mary was in such a state of shock and then pain, as you can imagine, that the assailant's identity was not really uppermost in her order of priorities – mere survival, I guess, being everything.' She ran a strong finger round the rim of her glass, which prompted it to give out a tiny squeal. 'Sorry,' she smiled.

I asked, 'Did you talk about Ron Ball, the ice-cream fellow, at all?'

'Only for a second. When I asked her again whether she thought he could have been the murderer.'

'And she said?'

'What she said before. Yes, she thought he was the most likely suspect. Especially as he has admitted to being in the garden around that time and now the police know he stole the toys.'

'Correction,' Arabella pointed out. 'The police *think* Ron Ball stole the toys. Finding them buried at his place does not constitute proof that he put them there. They could have been a plant to incriminate him.'

I nodded my agreement, then added, 'And don't forget too, that the stolen toys were all die-casts.'

Chrissie frowned. 'Er . . enlighten me, Peter . . .'

I leaned forward in my chair. 'Well, old toy buffs often fall into categories. That is, they concentrate on one type of toy. There are very few catholic collectors who range over every blessed thing made in the toy world.'

'And this Ron Ball does not collect die-casts? Is that what you're saying?'

'Not quite. He has a few, apparently, but his main interest is in wind-up models. Clockwork, you know. Minics, Schucos . . . the cheaper end of the tinplate market.'

Chrissie thought for a moment. 'Maybe he stole just what he could lay his hands on before he was interrupted by Maurice Maitland. Or for that matter, his intention may have been to sell the stolen die-casts to raise money to buy the wind-ups he really wanted.'

I shrugged. 'Who knows?'

'The murderer,' Arabella grimaced, then remarked, 'Or maybe I'm wrong. Maybe Ron Ball did steal the toys that night but wasn't actually the murderer. Could be there were two people involved, not just one.'

'Bit unlikely, isn't it?' Chrissie commented, then blushed slightly. 'Sorry, Arabella. Didn't mean to squash your theory as bluntly. My late husband used to tick me off sometimes for my bluntness. "Chrissie," he used to say, "your bull-at-a-gate tactics will get you into big trouble one day." ' She shrugged. 'Still, that's the way I'm made, I guess. Can't fight your genes all the way, now can you?'

None of us reacted for a moment or two, though Arabella did shoot a quick glance at me. And it was fairly easy to guess what it was saying. Or rather, asking. Something along the lines of, 'Do my Arabella Trench genes say Kate Adie, or not? Hell, I've got to know by tomorrow's interview.'

My molecule musings gave me a thought.

'You're right, Chrissie, we should all act the way we're made. And not pretend to be something or somebody we're not.'

'Thanks, kind sir,' Chrissie smiled generously, then turned to Arabella. 'You've got a gem here in Peter, you know.'

My beloved ran her hand through the close-cropped lawn of her hair and laughed.

'Really? What would I get for him in Ratners?'

'A big raspberry,' I offered, then tried to bring the conversation back to what I hoped was some form of sanity.

'Tell me, Chrissie, talking of genes. Mary Maitland's recent life – her conversion to naturism and feminism and what-have-you – do you think this is her real genes talking for the first time in her life, or is it all just a temporary reaction against being ignored for all those years? And one day soon, now that her husband is gone, she'll go back to being a . . .'

'. . . mouse?' Chrissie held her hands wide. 'Peter, it may not be that Mary has really changed as a woman. But that the whole of woman's role in society has now changed, so all that Mary is now doing is to react to that. Catch up, if you like, rather belatedly I admit and rather quickly, with all that women are starting to make happen, after years of struggle and strife. I think the realization that women aren't, after all, just the side-kicks of men, has hit dear Mary like a ton of bricks. Knocked her, if you like, into a new world, where she, perhaps, feels a little lost, but nevertheless, is determined to try everything, like a kid let loose in a sweet shop.'

She stopped to sip her wine, then ended, 'So, in answer to your question, I don't think for a moment that Mary will go back again to being a fully paid-up member of the church-mouse muster. No woman in her right mind need ever join those furry friends these days. Praise the Lord, or whoever pulls the strings from on high.'

She suddenly looked at her watch, then downed the last of her drink in a gulp. 'My God, is that the time? I must get out of your hair.'

She rose from her chair and we followed her example.

'Thanks for the drink, Peter,' then she turned to Arabella. 'And I'm delighted to have met you, Arabella. Maybe next time, you and I can have a proper chat. I'd love to know more about you. What you do and all that.'

'By then it may be something different from what I do now,' Arabella smiled.

Chrissie's eyebrows ascended. 'Oh? Thinking of changing jobs, then?'

'Just thinking. I've got an interview tomorrow.'

'May I ask who with?'

Arabella hesitated before answering, 'Local television.'

Chrissie took one step back, hands now on hips.

'Oh, my. On screen or off? Silly question. With your stunning looks, there can only be one answer, can't there? How marvellous. You must be very excited.'

Not hearing any 'hurrahs' or 'youbetchas', Chrissie frowned. 'Oh, come on, Arabella, don't kid me. At your age I'd have killed to get on television. Every time I watch those women reporters and newsreaders, doing jobs that used to be the sole preserve of men, I get a sense of pride in what we've achieved. But also a considerable feeling of envy.' She patted her hair. 'Still, I was born too late and, no doubt, too ugly, blast it. But you, on the other hand, have everything going for you.'

She took Arabella's hand. 'So grab it, lucky one. Grab it and hold on to it. It is still offered to too few, unfortunately, but we're getting there.'

A moment later, she was gone. The room seemed empty without her.

'Wow!' Arabella grinned at me, as we resettled ourselves after the whirlwind exit. 'I wonder what her husband was like.'

'Leading light of the church-mouse muster, wouldn't wonder,' I smiled back.

Nine

Next morning I managed to make an appointment at the hospital for eleven o'clock.

'Not really visiting hours, Mr Marklin, but seeing as how Mrs Maitland now has a private room and has some further tests this afternoon . . .'

So, after I had seen Arabella off on her Big Day, I had a little time to kill before I need make for the Sandbanks Ferry and Bournemouth General. My time-murder consisted of despatching two more mail orders that had come through that morning's letterbox (nothing world shattering – a Spot-On Daimler Dart, mint boxed, and a pre-war Tootsie airship, 'Los Angeles', somewhat playworn) and a slight reorganization of my stock on display so that regular punters would not imagine I had sold nothing since their last visits. Not that they really care one way or the other, I suppose. More a case of my own pride not wishing to be hurt.

Thereafter, I opened up shop for the last half an hour or so and waited. Not so much for customers, really, but for the dring-dring of the telephone or the sight of a whiter than white Rover pulling up outside. For, in my judgement, a vermilion-faced Digby Whetstone had to be on the boil by now at my activities. After all, I'd obviously been seen going into and coming out of Malcolm Savage's Purbeck Print and I could not really see my fancy-dress friend not informing the law about my little visit to her shop. Who knows, I might have been observed at Chrissie Cartwright's house or Gus, in his arty gear, at the Maitlands' place.

By the end of the half hour, I was a little surprised to admit to myself that an eerie silence from the dear Inspector was becoming almost as disturbing as his usual bombastic and booming broadsides. For at least with them, you knew where you stood in his book. Like nowhere you can describe in polite circles.

My unease was hardly helped by Gus shuddering round in his Popular, just as I was flipping my 'Open' sign round to 'Closed'. But at least, he was dressed normally this time. Correction. Dressed in his only too habitual gear.

'What yer doin' shutting at this ruddy hour?' was his kindly and considerate greeting.

'Going to the hospital,' I replied.

His rheumy but knowing eyes gave me the once-over.

'Look all right to me,' he muttered. 'No wonder the bloody Health Service never has enough bleedin' money. People go to the hospital these days with next to ruddy nothing wrong with 'em. In my day, everyone was carried to the hospital. If you could walk, you didn't need to go. Better off in bed back home with a bottle of whisky. And if you couldn't afford any Scotch, a good woman wouldn't come amiss.' He chuckled. 'Or even a Mrs. Or even a bad woman . . .'

'Thank you, Gus, and goodnight,' I muttered back. 'It's not me that's ill, you idiot, it's your Mrs Maitland. Remember? You saw her carted off to hospital, when you were Toulouse Lautrec-ing in her garden.'

His eyes lit up, or as near as they could get to it, with all the water surrounding them.

'Oh. So you've at last got a chance to see her, have you? Well, good luck, old son. Milly was on to me again this morning to see how we were doing. Tells me Ron Ball's mum is now half-way round the ruddy bend with worry. No bloody wonder, either.'

No wonder, indeed. But I was by no means sure that anything I, or even Gus, could achieve was actually going to make the clouds that were lowering upon her house, glorious summer.

'Must go now, Gus. Got to be there by eleven,' I hustled.

He let me pass to lock up.

'Want me to come with you?'

'Expect the hospital would rather only one visitor at a time, Gus,' I weaseled. 'She's still pretty poorly.'

'Yeah.' He took a deep breath, which he then expelled with the balloon cheeks of a superannuated, stubble-ridden cherub.

'Well, then, you go to the hospital, and I'll . . .' He suddenly stopped. I held the shop key poised in the lock.

'You'll *what*, Gus?'

He looked away. 'I'll . . er . . .'

'On the side of caution,' I grimaced.

128

'What?'

'Nothing, Gus, nothing. And that's just what I want you to do. Absolutely nothing. No more gallivanting in gardens or getting up to your neck in anything to do with the Maitland affair.'

'Why not? I want to help, don't I? After all, it's my friend what . . .'

'I know you do, Gus. But I'm terrified old Digby's going to get our scent any minute and send the Dobermanns round. Surprised he hasn't already. So I don't want to give him any chance to . . .'

But I could see from Gus's expression, I'd lost him.

'Where did you go, Gus?'

He beckoned with a massive forefinger. I finished locking the door and followed him meekly along the pavement to the corner. His digit now unfolded to point down the lane towards his cottage. I held my hand up to my eyes to keep off the glare of the spring sun. Instantly I saw a shaft of said sun glinting off something white and shiny, half-hidden behind a clump of rhododendrons.

I looked at Gus. He nodded sagely.

'Perhaps he's just taking a break,' I tried. 'You know, patrol cars can't be on the go all the time. Britain would never be able to afford the petrol.'

'Got binoculars,' he grunted. 'Saw him put 'em down when I passed him on the way up to you.'

'Bird watcher?' I sighed.

'Oh yeah,' Gus chortled. 'Must be the tits in me thatch.'

'Or that rara avis – a greater spotted Tribble.'

'In a minute, I reckon, it will be an easily spotted Marklin, if you're not bloody careful.'

I smiled an inscrutable smile. 'We'll see,' I said softly. 'We'll see.'

But I did not actually spot him again until aboard the ferry and then only as the crew was about to chain off the car deck before departure for Sandbanks. He had, at least, been cute enough to leave it to the last minute to board.

In the short time it took to clank across the entrance to Poole harbour, I was half-tempted to go up to him in his patrol car and ask him to give my regards to Digby. But discretion this time prevailed. After all, one, I could not be a thousand per cent certain that he was actually tailing either me or Gus, and two, I knew my good wishes would be interpreted in exactly the same spirit as they were delivered. And a Digby Whetstone deliberately provoked might be a thousand times worse than one accidentally jolted.

Being one of the first on to the ferry, I was one of the first off. I used every horse-power my old Volks could muster to put distance between myself and the law, before it was his turn to disembark. As a result, I reached Bournemouth General via a circuitous route without anything white appearing in my mirror, except my own eyeballs.

Upon enquiry, I discovered Mary Maitland's room was on the third floor. I shared the lift with an old lady in a wheelchair who kept calling me her son, despite the corrections supplied by her nurse; so that by the time I emerged, I was hardly in my most composed frame of mind. So much so, I mistook a St John's ambulance man striding towards me up the third floor corridor for a police constable about to 'Hello, hello, hello and goodbye' me.

When my heartbeat had stopped imitating a spaced-out, heavy metal drummer, I knocked on the door whose number I had been given. But there was no reply from within. Three raps later and still no response, I tentatively turned the handle and popped one eye and half a face around the door.

'Come in, Mr Marklin,' a rather breathy voice invited from the bed.

Clearing my throat and attempting to do ditto with my brain, I did as I was bid.

A tanned hand patted the blankets next to a cane-seated upright chair.

'Sit down by me. Sorry the chair will hardly win any comfort awards, but there you are.'

There I was. Now sitting down and looking across at someone a deal younger looking than I had been expecting. In fact, she was a deal more attractive too than any photograph I'd seen had depicted her, despite the traces of bruising and abrasions still apparent.

She smiled at me, her generous mouth carefully outlined with recently applied lipstick (terracotta shade, not scarlet).

'I know what you're thinking. Doesn't she look a fraud? Why is she taking up a valuable bed in hospital?' She chuckled. 'I see it in some of the nurses' faces. That's the trouble with having a good tan. It often hides what the body is feeling. You know, a bit like paint applied on a rotting window-sill.'

'Some window-sill,' I replied.

She looked away and sighed.

'Yes. Some window-sill.' Suddenly turning back to me, she said, 'I didn't answer when you knocked. Know why? I wanted to see how pushy you were. Whether you'd hesitate or go away and check with a nurse or doctor before entering or . . .' She shrugged. 'But you went ahead and came in.'

'That good?' I frowned.

'Might be. Good in a . . . what do you call yourself? . . . a private eye, I suppose.'

'I'm not a private detective, Mrs Maitland. I'm just an old toy dealer, who has a friend who has a friend . . .'

'. . . with a son in big trouble?'

'More or less.'

She looked at me, her large brown eyes now displaying the pain that lay behind them for the first time.

'Are you like those defence lawyers who take on a case even though they know full well that the accused is guilty?'

I shook my head. 'No, I'm not. I'm only interested in finding out the truth, that's all. If the truth is that Ron Ball is guilty of attacking you and your husband, then so be it.'

'But you obviously don't think he is?'

'No, that's not quite true, either. I just don't know, that's all.'

I tried to change the subject. 'By the way, I meant to ask the moment I came in, how are you this morning?'

She held up her hands. Though tanned, they were obviously those of a capable housewife rather than of some lady of leisure. 'How am I?' After taking a deep breath, she went on, 'I'm not dead yet, so they tell me. And the pills they're dishing out have cut back on the headaches, so I suppose I shouldn't complain.'

'On the mend?'

'Round the bend, I wouldn't wonder.' She forced a smile. 'Anyway, Mr Marklin, enough of my health. Let's get back to you. And what you, no doubt, want to ask me about that dreadful night. I warn you, it all happened so quickly, I'm not sure I will be of much help. You probably know already that the murderer wore a stocking over his head.'

I nodded, then said quietly, 'You said, "his head". Does that mean you're sure it was a man?'

'Pretty certain.' She played with the edging of the bed sheet. 'You know, if you're a woman, you can almost sense the sex of someone, say, if they've come into a room and you can't see them. Men and women seem to give off different . . .' She shrugged, '. . . I don't know, the old cliché "vibrations" is as near as I can get.'

'And the assailant's vibrations were male?'

'It felt that way.' She looked at me. 'Anyway, it's hardly likely to have been a woman, anyway, is it? I mean, from what I gather, women don't collect toy cars. Dolls, yes, automata, maybe, but vehicles?'

'True,' I admitted, 'but that's assuming the burglary and the murder are directly connected. It's just possible they may not be.'

She raised her rather over-thick eyebrows. 'Really, Mr Marklin? We know for a fact that the toys were taken. And what's more, found again. In the garden of the man you're befriending.'

I could see I would get nowhere much by pursuing that avenue – except thrown out of the hospital for raising the temperature of one of its patients. But Mary Maitland did not seem to want to let the matter drop.

'Besides, why should *any* woman want to attack me or my husband? It doesn't make any sense. What on earth would be her motive?' She stopped and looked at me.

'Have you been to see that Fiona Fairchild woman?'

I nodded.

'Is it her you're thinking of?'

'Not particularly.'

She propped herself higher up in the bed and her nightdress did little to disguise her well-developed attractions.

'Why not, come to think of it? If it's a woman you're after, surely she must come highest on your list? At least it's just possible with her to imagine some kind of motive. A dotty one, but then, maybe, she is dotty. Probably have to be dotty to think of running a fancy-dress shop. And certainly anyone would have to be round the twist to have an affair with old Maurice . . .'

'What motive are you thinking of?'

'Why, maybe Maurice wouldn't go as far as she wanted. Like leave me or marry her or something. I don't know. Or could be he'd just given her the brush off and she didn't like it. She strikes me as a woman you don't cross in a hurry.'

'You've met her, have you?'

'Of course. When we went round to hire fancy dress for that party I had at last persuaded Maurice to take me to. I went as a cat and guess what he chose to be? Napoleon, no less. I should have guessed what he'd choose and just gone by myself to pick the costume up. Then he'd have never met that awful woman at all.'

'And you never had an inkling that he and she. . . ?'

'Never. Not for one moment. I never ever doubted Maurice the whole of our marriage. Never had the slightest suspicion that he would ever be unfaithful.' She smiled ruefully. 'It wasn't because I trusted him as a man. Dreadful, isn't it? I just trusted other women's good sense and taste. Assumed they would always totally ignore him and certainly reject any advances, if he ever made any. I still can't quite see someone even as weird as that fancy-dress woman going for Maurice.'

'Do you know if she knew about his toy collection?'

She shrugged. 'Who knows? Maurice never really talked about it. But, perhaps, he had to with her. I mean, brag about how much it might all be worth, so that she'd be impressed enough to . . . well, do what he wanted.' She looked away, towards the window. 'Whatever that may have been.'

That was an avenue I was not about to pursue. After a moment's silence, I said, 'Know of any person who might have had some motive?'

'A woman, you mean?'

'If you like.'

She felt a fading abrasion on her cheek. 'You've got a thing about women, haven't you? Don't tell me you're a chauvinist pig, like Maurice used to be. You certainly don't look it.'

I waved my hand by way of reply.

'No, I just want to probe every possible area, that's all.'

Mary Maitland thought for a while, then answered, 'No, I can't think of any other woman in the whole wide world who would want to cause either of us any harm.'

I decided to take a flier.

'Not even amongst your new friends? I gather you've made quite a few over recent months. And you may not know all of them very well.'

She closed her eyes. 'Who's been telling you all this? Chrissie, I'll be bound.'

'Not just Chrissie.'

She whipped her eyes open and aimed them at me.

133

'Who else?'

When she elicited no reply, she softened into a knowing smile.

'I bet it was dear Malcolm. Malcolm Savage. You must have seen him too.'

'Yes, I have.'

She exhaled dejectedly. 'Oh dear, what have they been telling you?'

'Only that you've . . .' I hunted for the right words, which she now readily supplied.

'Blossomed out a bit. Begun doing my own thing. Become a naturist. Flaunted my body about, no doubt. Made new friends, all no doubt described to you as militant feminists. That right?'

'Not quite.'

She shook her head and a lock of hair tumbled across one eye. She ignored it.

'All right. I'm sorry, Mr Marklin. To be so tetchy, I mean. Blame it on my condition.' She smoothed the sheet out in front of her. 'Okay. So what do you want to know about my "new" friends? But I assure you, they've as much to do with that night as the man – sorry, or woman – in the moon.'

'I was given a few names, that's all.' I delved into my memory. 'There's a Mrs Valentine, I gather. And a Mrs Churchill.'

'Miss Churchill,' I was corrected. 'Go on. Who else?'

'A Matilda somebody. Lives Bristol way, I believe.'

'You believe correctly.'

Nothing more was volunteered, so I soldiered on. 'Mrs Valentine and this Miss Churchill. Are they local?'

'Were.'

'Were?'

'Well, they still are, I suppose. But they are both in America right now. Molly Valentine left some days before that terrible night. And Christine flew out on the very day. So you can see why I say they have as much to do with it all, as whoever's on the moon. They are both attending a big feminist convention in Chicago, then going on to meet some distant relations of theirs. They wanted me to attend too, originally, but I said I couldn't really leave Maurice.' She smiled at me. 'See what a dutiful wife I made? Looking back now, I should have gone. At least then, I wouldn't have been there to be knocked about that night.'

'And Matilda . . . er . . . er. . . ?' I tried.

She laughed and turned towards me in the bed. I wondered if

134

she was conscious of how much of her brown self her nightgown was now exposing.

'It's not Matilda Ererer. It's Matilda Vickers. She's married and lives near Bristol, as you seem to know. Apart from a complete lack of any possible motive, she's hardly likely to have travelled all the way from Bristol in the dead of night to kill my husband or rob him of old toys, now is she?'

I had to admit there was a deal of sense in her statement.

'So there you are. That accounts for all my so-called new friends. There aren't any more. Besides Chrissie, that is. And she doesn't count. She's an old friend and quite different.' She nodded to herself. 'I owe her a lot. Should have listened to her years ago, then I would have come out of my shell a lot sooner.' She looked at me. 'When I was younger and had more time ahead of me to enjoy life.'

'You've still lots of time, Mrs Maitland,' I smiled encouragingly.

She shrugged. 'Who knows? I mean, how long any of us have got really? That's what I told Chrissie last night when she sort of hinted I might be going a bit far, a bit fast. You know, she's never approved of my naturism. And I do believe she might be just a teeny bit jealous of my new liberated friends, who take their feminism a little more seriously than she does. So I'm afraid I told her she was being a bit old fashioned.'

She looked at me. 'But that's by-the-by. You don't want to hear all this liberation stuff, I'm sure.'

'No, please . . .'

'You mean, please no.' She grinned. 'So let's get back to Maurice's death. What else do you want to know? How about some male suspects? Other than Ron Ball, that is.'

I was on the point of replying, when she went on, 'If you've met Malcolm Savage, he must be on your suspect list, surely. After all, he and Maurice had been at loggerheads recently over buying that other printing company. And he's never made any secret of wanting total control of Purbeck Print.' She looked away, then added quietly, 'And over the last few months, that's not the only thing he's confessed to wanting.'

I'll swear my ears must have swivelled round towards her. 'Oh. . . ?'

'Yes, oh, Mr Marklin. Malcolm has always had an eye for other women. Even his wife is well aware of that. She blames it on his stubby stature. She says all small men have something to prove. And what better way to prove it than by conquest of some poor, unsuspecting soul. . . ?' She sighed. 'Funny, he'd never shown any real interest in me, until, well, until I belatedly started to "blossom", as they say.' Laughing, she went on, 'Maybe it's the all-over tan that first excited him. Or just the thought of me disporting myself on that naughty end of Studland beach . . . anyway, he started to call round when he knew Maurice was away. Even surprised me down on the beach, one afternoon. But, thank the Lord, he soon felt so self-conscious being the only clothed person around, that he soon left. Anyway, he makes it quite plain he fancies me. And would like to carve my name too on his . . . totem pole.'

I liked her turn of phrase. But before I could comment, the door of her room opened to reveal a huge bunch of flowers, behind which lurked a diminutive nurse.

'My goodness,' Mary Maitland reacted. 'Who on earth can those be from?'

A medical digit pointed through the stems with an accompanying comment, 'Him.'

She looked round at me.

'You?'

I nodded. 'I handed them in at the sister's office before I knocked on your door. So that they could be put in water.'

The nurse placed the vase down on a small table by the window.

'Don't they look nice, Mrs Maitland?' the nurse chirped. 'Irises and carnations are two of my favourite flowers.'

'Me too,' she beamed at me. 'You really are kind. You shouldn't have.'

'I didn't know whether you liked grapes,' I blushed.

She laughed and after the nurse had gone, said, 'Can I now ask *you* a question, Mr Marklin?'

'Go ahead.'

'My husband's, sorry, I suppose I should now say "late" husband's toy collection.'

I could guess what was coming.

'You see, it was solely his interest, not mine. So, as you can imagine, I would now like to dispose of it. Perhaps you can give me some advice as to how best to go about it. I mean, would I get a better price selling them through dealers like yourself or at an auction?'

'Well, it depends a little on how quickly you want to realize some money.'

She smiled. 'By that, are you saying that waiting for the right auction might take some time?'

'Yes, partly, but also that auction houses often take some months to cough up the money after the sale. With such a large collection, it would probably be advisable not to put them all up for auction at the same sale. Even rich bidders have a limit to what they can afford at any one time.'

She frowned. 'It doesn't sound as if going to auction is quite right for me, then.'

'If you want the money quicker, then the best bet is to invite a number of dealers to inspect the collection and then see what they're willing to pay you for the items they're interested in. Having seen the collection, I'm sure you'll have no trouble in disposing of ninety-nine per cent of it that way. And you'll get your money instantly, even though the total amount may be down some twenty per cent or so compared with a good auction day. But you've also got to remember prices realized at auction vary considerably. They have bad days as well as good.'

'Could you arrange it all for me, Mr Marklin? I mean, get some dealers interested? That is, unless you might be interested in bidding for the lot yourself?'

I laughed out loud. 'Are you kidding? I could no more raise what your collection is worth than fly to the moon, but I might be interested in a small part of it, though.'

'I'll give you first refusal, then. And a handling fee for arranging the disposal of the rest.'

I did not argue.

'You must come over directly they release me from this Dettol dungeon. Which I hope against hope will be later today. The doctor is seeing me at twelve with the results of the X-rays, tests and things.'

She suddenly winced and put a hand to her head.

'Whoops. There goes that silly pain again.' She reached out for a tiny saucer, that I saw contained four pills. 'I'd better take two more of these. It's almost time for them anyway.'

I handed her a glass of water from the bedside table. As I did so, she grasped my hand.

'Married, Mr Marklin?'

I shook my head.

'Never?'

'Once. Didn't work out, I'm afraid. Divorced.'

'Children?'

'No.'

She released my hand, then washed down the two pills with a little of the water I had given her.

'So you're fancy free?'

'Not quite. I live with someone.'

She looked at me. 'Going to marry her?'

'Takes two to make that decision,' I side-stepped.

She ran her tongue round her lips. 'Is she an old-toy enthusiast too?'

'Not really. She's a reporter.'

'Oh, how interesting. On a paper?'

'Yes, right now. The *Western Gazette*.'

'What do you mean, "right now"?'

'Well, she's gone for an interview today with a television company.'

'To be a researcher or a presenter?'

'I think they've got presenting in mind.'

She grimaced. 'Damn. That means she's young and very pretty. Am I right? I'm sure I am.'

'Could be,' I admitted, then rose from the chair that had by now become rather too hot a seat for me. 'Anyway, I should be going. Let you get some rest. Thanks for seeing me.'

She took my proffered hand. 'We'll see each other again. I'll ring you, directly I'm out of here. To set up a time for you to come over . . . to appraise the collection.'

'Fine. My name's in the book. Meanwhile, if you have any new thoughts about, well, that terrible night, do let me know.'

She nodded, then remarked as I reached the door, 'I will, I promise. I wish you every luck with your enquiries, but I'm afraid your friend's friend's son may still turn out to be the guilty party. After all, he is mad about old toys and I think . . .'

She stopped abruptly.

'Go on,' I urged. 'What do you think?'

She pushed a lock of hair out of her eyes. 'The police say he's developed a . . . "thing" about me. Maybe I shouldn't ever have gone to his van *au naturel*. Anyway, I certainly shouldn't have criticized my husband's behaviour in front of him, as I remember now that I did one day when buying some drinks with Chrissie. I said that Maurice should ruddy sell some of his valuable old toys so that we could lead a decent life. Go out sometimes. Go abroad on holidays. You know, *live*.'

'So you think he overheard and because he'd got a crush on you, may have decided to free you from the husband you seemed to dislike.'

She shrugged.

'But why then go on to attack *you*? And so brutally. The very person he was trying to help?'

She shrugged again. 'I don't know. I wish I did. The Inspector says he's a rum one. And maybe, once his blood was aroused, he couldn't stop himself.'

I thought for a moment. 'May I ask a delicate question, Mrs Maitland?'

She blinked, then nodded. 'I can guess what it is. And the answer is no. The intruder didn't try to rape me. Just kept on hitting me with his gloved fists. Then I passed out.'

She suddenly closed her eyes tight. 'Oh my God, I hadn't thought of that. What . . . What he might have done . . . while I was lying there unconscious. I was only wearing a thin nightdress. He could have pulled it up and . . . hell, we know for a fact that he's a voyeur.'

She hid her face in her hands and her body started to tremble. I came forward to the bed and put my arm around her shoulders.

'Try not to think of it, Mrs Maitland,' I said softly. 'I know it's difficult. But the future is what is important now. Not the past. When you're better and back home, things will gradually look a little less black day by day . . .'

She looked up at me, her eyes now welling with tears.

'Is that a promise, Mr Marklin?' she whispered.

'I'll have a word with the powers that be, Mrs Maitland,' I smiled.

But first I had a word with the power that rested in an ante-room at the end of the corridor. A rather terrifying hundred and sixty pounds worth of ward sister of some forty-five summers and Lord knows how many winters.

'Yes?' she barked at me, as I eased open her door. 'Mrs

139

Maitland . . .' I began, but she cut me off with a, 'What about her?'

'Er . . . well, I've just been in to visit her and I was wondering how she was getting on. I mean, whether she is likely to be allowed back home soon.'

Her grey eyes lasered into mine. 'You a relative?'

'No, I'm just a . . .'

She swivelled back round in her chair to face the table at which she had been writing. The chair protested with a graunch. I didn't blame it.

'Then, I'm afraid, I'm not at liberty to disclose anything about Mrs Maitland's condition.'

I persevered. 'But she is on the mend, I hope.'

She ignored me.

I tried again. 'You see, I'm a little bit concerned, because it's been quite a time now since . . .'

The graunch returned as she swivelled once more.

'Look, Mr. . . ?'

'Marklin.'

'Mr Marklin, you are wasting both my time and yours asking any more questions. But what I can tell you with some certainty is that Mrs Maitland will not be leaving here in the immediate future, as you seem to imagine. Far from it . . .'

I frowned. 'You mean, it's more serious than . . .'

She rose irritably from her chair and started to edge me back towards the door with a nudge from her fortified breast-works.

'Make your own judgement, Mr Marklin. Now, if you'd be kind enough to leave, I can get on with my work.'

Being a generous sort of guy, I was kind enough. But as I left, I was thinking some very unkind thoughts.

I did not go straight home, but on to Corfe to see if Chrissie Cartwright was home. She was and waved to me with a pair of secateurs as I pulled up in front of her house.

'Just doing a bit of tidying up,' she grinned, as she snipped a half-dead rose off one of the many bushes that grew in a half moon around the bay window of her house. She took off her gardening gloves, then leant forward and kissed me on the cheek.

'What brings you here this morning, my sleuthing friend? I thought you were seeing Mary in hospital.'

140

'Just been. That's why I've come round.'

She grasped my arm with surprisingly firm fingers.

'Don't tell me anything's wrong. With Mary. She's not worse, is she?'

'Well, I haven't seen her before, but she doesn't seem too bad. She had to take another pill for her head pains before I left, but otherwise . . .'

'So what's the problem?'

'No problem, really. Least, I hope not. It's just that she's obviously expecting to be discharged shortly, but when I spoke to the ward sister, she denied it. Said quite bluntly that we mustn't expect her to be out for quite some time. But refused to say why, because I wasn't a relative.'

Chrissie rested back against her garden barrow. 'Oh my Lord, poor Mary. They must have found something on her X-rays.' She shook her head. 'She should have agreed to staying over in the hospital the night of the murder. It was short-sighted of her not to. But I can understand only too well why she didn't want to then. Be carted off to be mauled around and mulled over by white-coated strangers and X-rayed from top to toe, when you are still in a state of shock from a brutal attack and finding your husband battered to death. Besides, Mary's always been one of those not to give in to illness. She believes in mind over matter. Or rather, bacteria. Even when she had a temperature of a hundred and four with the 'flu last winter, she refused to stay in bed. And went on cooking meals for that selfish husband of hers, just as if she was fit as a fiddle.'

She looked at me. 'But that's not the only reason you've called round, is it? Just to tell me Mary won't be out as soon as we expected.'

'Not quite,' I admitted.

Chrissie's eyes widened. 'Did Mary tell you something new? Is that it?'

I held up my hand. 'Now don't get excited. I just wanted to check on something, that's all.'

'Check away.'

'Do you remember any occasion when Ron Ball could have overheard Mary complaining to you about her husband, say, when you were buying drinks or ice-creams or something?'

She looked out across the garden.

'Now, let me think. I can obviously see why you're asking.'

After a moment, she replied, 'I remember one time. When Mary and I had a bit of a row in front of him. But it wasn't over Maurice, but over who should go back to the car to get a wind-break, would you believe? You see, I didn't want her to go, dressed as she was. Or rather, undressed. I just felt it was asking for trouble. You know, dear old Studland is not quite St Tropez or some Greek island yet.'

Turning back to me, she then added, 'Now hang on. Yes, now you mention it. Another time, we were talking about . . . yes, holidays, I think it was. And Mary was saying that she would love to go abroad for some real sun once in a while, but Maurice wouldn't run to the cost. Yes, I remember remarking that the old toys I knew he had must be worth the odd bob. So why didn't she persuade him to part with a few of those to pay for a decent holiday? And then she said something about cost being only an excuse and that it was just another example of the way Maurice liked to keep her under his thumb, or words to that effect. And . . .' She suddenly clasped her hand to her mouth. '. . . oh my Lord, it's all coming back to me now.'

'What's coming back, Chrissie? Tell me.'

'What she said next. Just as she was paying for the drinks.'

'Which was?'

'That her beloved Maurice was more married to his old toys than he was to her. And like marriage, they could never be separated "until death do they part".'

Ten

I didn't spot it until I had turned on to the Studland road out of Corfe. Here, it had little chance to hide on the numerous straighter stretches of this quiet and most lullingly attractive of rural routes. As I saw the sun glint off its white shell, I wondered just how long it had been on my tail without my knowing it. And for that matter, why the law was wasting time and effort tracking an innocent like me anyway. (I use the word "innocent" in its widest and loosest sense, you understand.)

Its driver certainly seemed to know my destination, for as I neared the small cluster of assorted houses that constitutes Studland village, my mirror showed him pulling into the side, under the shade of some overhanging trees. Obviously, he'd decided that to continue and park right outside my shop would not exactly win him the Top Tracker's Trophy at the next Policeman's Ball.

But my tail was not the only surprise right along then. For lo and behold, when I had parked my Beetle in the lean-to that jokingly pretended to keep the weather off it, I discovered my Toy Emporium open to trade, with Gus installed behind the counter chatting to a punter.

When he saw me, he grinned like an old tom cat that had raided the dairy.

'Wotcher, old son.'

I didn't 'wotcher' back, but mouthed, 'Thought you were agin credit cards, Gus. Or did you use a tyre lever from your old Ford?'

'Whatcher mean?'

'To get in,' I said, throwing a plastic smile at the customer, whom I now sort of recognized, but couldn't yet quite place. 'I distinctly remember locking up before I left.'

Gus moved a pre-war Dinky Reconnaissance car across the

counter towards the punter to join an assortment of military vehicles that I could see he must have taken from my Diorama in the window.

Gus prodded a thick digit towards the ceiling.

I frowned. 'Got in through the roof?'

'No, you berk,' he whispered. Trouble is that Gus's whispers are often equivalent to other people's loud hails and the customer blinked his incomprehension of our behaviour.

'Your better 'alf's home.'

'Arabella?'

'You got three halves? 'Course it's Arabella. Came home after her interview, she did. So she could tell you about it.'

Now I got the picture. I pointed upwards, as he had done.

'She's upstairs, then?'

'No, she's out.'

Oh God, give me strength. Or at least, find some other way of preventing me murdering Gus.

'I thought you said she was back?'

'She is. Who do you think let me in?'

'But you said she's out.'

'So she is. Didn't you ruddy notice her car's not outside?'

Of course I ruddy had.

'So she came back, found me out but you on the doorstep. Let you in, so left again,' I observed rather unkindly.

He nodded, then turned back to the customer, who was now trying to attract our attention, silly man.

'Er . . . I think I'll just take the Light Tank, if you don't mind.'

I suddenly realized who he was.

'So you've come back for it,' I smiled. 'Makes a wonderful companion for the Medium Tank you bought. Great start, those two, for a military collection.'

'Yes, yes, I know. I would have bought it the other day, possibly, had you had one in then. Even though funds were a bit tight.'

He shelled out eight fivers. 'Will you take forty for it?'

To encourage him to come again, I agreed. A fiver docked then might be worth many a sale in the future. For once a punter has collected more than one item, as he had just done, then the collecting bug has really bitten and won't release its sharp little teeth until death, or bankruptcy, intervene. But I could see from Gus's expression that he thought I was being a sucker and not of the blood variety, either.

'Many thanks, Mr Marklin,' the punter smiled, his close-cropped moustache, as before, almost disappearing into the fold between his longish nose and over-generous upper lip.

'Not at all, Mr . . . er. . . ?

'Er . . . Moreton. Duncan Moreton.'

I picked up the tank. 'Like me to pop it in a box or is it all right as it is?'

'Fine as it is. Really. Got the car.'

I loved his use of short sentences. A mode of speech, no doubt, developed in childhood to facilitate quick communication after lights-out in the old dorm, don't you know.

I saw him to the door.

'Dinky Light Dragon tractor next, perhaps? With a trailer and eighteen-pounder gun.'

He nodded. 'Could be. Good idea. I'll drop by again. When the funds . . . you know.'

I knew. And with that, he was gone, off down the street and round the corner. Again. I never saw whether my guess as to his style of transport – a five-year-old small BMW – was on the button or not.

As I came back to the counter, Gus glowered at me.

'I'd got him to pay the full amount until you turned up. And was on the way to selling him something else into the bargain.'

'Sorry, Gus. Should have left it to you,' I placeboed.

Gus flicked a finger towards the great outdoors.

'He's not short of the odd bob, I reckon. Just kidding you to get the price down. When I saw him the other time, I said to myself, silver spoon in the old gob, if ever I saw one. Did you see his 'acking jacket? Pockets cut on the slant and all that la-de-dah.'

Gus's prejudices are about as hard to pinpoint as flaws in a politician's argument.

'You may be right, Gus. But I allow scope for a little discount, when I'm pricing everything.' I stopped abruptly and looked at him.

'Here, what do you mean, when you saw him the other time? I was alone, as I remember, when he was last here.'

Gus sniffed. 'No. Didn't see him here with you, did I? No. Over in Wareham, it was. At that flipping fancy-dress place. I told you about him. Remember? The ruddy army officer who wouldn't make up his bleeding mind what he wanted. And in the end, went out without anything. Cor, luv-a-duck.'

145

I vaguely remembered his telling me. 'Well, that would explain his interest in military vehicles. Being in the army.' I rubbed my hands together. 'That means he may be back for lots more lovely goodies, doesn't it?'

Gus smirked. 'If he can make up his ruddy mind which one he wants, that is . . .'

After that little interlude, I did at last worm out of Gus where Arabella had gone. Which was just down the road into Swanage to grab something for lunch and 'a little of what you fancy to wash it down with'. Which I took to mean a six-ring necklace of Heinekens.

'Said she can't be long,' Gus explained, ' 'cos the television bloke's ringing her here between one thirty and two to tell her the results of her test.'

'Test?'

'Yeah. Tested her in front of the cameras, didn't they? Going to have a dekko at what they shot, then get on the blower and say what they think.' Gus put a massive arm round my shoulder. 'Times is changing, old love. Soon your Arabella's going to be famous, you mark my words. She'll be as much a household name as . . . er . . . er . . .'

'Oh, at least,' I smiled. 'If not more so.'

'Yeah,' Gus sniffed. 'You must be proud.'

I turned round to face him.

'Gus. Hold your horses. It's only a little, local television station and they haven't even offered her the job yet.'

'They will, old son. They will.' He lifted his elbow. 'In not so very long from now, we'll be drinking to her new career.'

I got his subtle hint.

'Thought you might be doing a spot of sleuthing by then,' I observed, nonchalantly.

He ignored my sally and hoisted me with my own petard, whatever that may be.

'Wouldn't leave, would I, before I've had a good run-down on what you've ruddy achieved this morning. Over in Bournemouth.'

So I told him the bare facts. But not my reluctant conclusion – that things were starting to look somewhat worse for his friend's friend's poor son, rather than better.

*

Once we'd cleared the Chinese take-away that Arabella had brought back and five of the six Heinekens, there was little time for a real heart-to-heart with my budding TV star, before she had to hike it back to Bournemouth and the *Western Gazette*. Especially as Gus seemed insistent on drinking yet more toasts to her successful début before the cameras. (Yes, the station had telephoned back, as promised. And with positive news. They were working on the details of an offer which they would deliver by mid next week.)

However, we did unseat Gus eventually, by suggesting he should go into Bournemouth to where Ron Ball was being held and check on the latest. Like finding out whether they were likely to bring any more charges against him, beyond plain robbery etcetera. And if possible get permission to see him, in case his hours of incarceration had inspired any new thoughts as to who might be trying to frame him.

So off he trundled, muttering he had to go back home first, because he had a slow leak in one front tyre and hadn't his tyre pump with him. (I've seen that pump. It's of the 'saddle' variety, operated by hand, not foot. Fit only for a museum of useless artefacts of the early twentieth century. If ever one of his old Popular's seventeen-inch tyres went entirely flat, Gus would receive his telegram from the Queen before he could finish reflation.)

Thus, the following short exchange was about all Arabella and I managed. And most of this whilst she was re-fixing her make-up, then going out and getting into her Golf.

'Congratulations, darling.' (Quick buss on half-linered lips). 'You must have wowed them.'

Raised eyebrows.

'Aren't you happy?'

Sad look.

'Not sure. Ego's sort of happy. But not sure I am, really.'

'About the test? Or about the coming offer?'

'You know.'

'The offer . . .'

Ferret in shoulder bag.

'Oh hell. Where did I put the car keys?'

'But you weren't afraid of the camera, obviously.'

'No, yes, no. Oh, I remember now. I left them in the car. What's the time?'

Look at watch. 'Two twenty-two.'

'Wow. I'd better be going. They only gave me the morning off.'

Now, out at car, parked behind mine.

'Going to accept?'

'Accept? Oh, er . . . I don't know yet.'

'Wait and see the fine print.'

Wave of hand. 'No, it's not that. I'm sure that it'll be all right.'
Smiled grimace, like schoolgirl, when asked about exams.

'Bet Kate Adie felt just the same, when she was offered her first
chance.'

Glower. I mentally smacked my foot.

'I'm not Kate Adie.'

There was no answer to that. Leaned in car window and gave
her a little buss on the cheek.

'Don't have to make up your mind until next week.'

Whine of starter, roar of motor. 'Plenty of time.'

I wink. She smiles a 'sorry, but you know how it is'.

I know how it is. So I change the subject.

'How about my getting a video out for tonight?'

A nod. But the enthusiasm in her look was only at Regulo 2.

A quick wave from both and she was gone. I stood thinking for
a moment. But my contemplation was soon rudely shattered by
the most familiar sound this side of the Pecos. Gus 'Saddle-
pump' Tribble had just shuddered back into town.

'Howdy,' I saluted, reluctantly. 'Thought you were off to
Bournemouth.'

'Don't need to now, old son,' the prize wotsit responded. 'Got
a call, didn't I, before I could leave the house. From Milly.' A
smile broke across the stubble. 'They've released him, haven't
they? Ron Ball is out.'

I should have felt some sort of relief at the news, but, somehow, I
didn't. But I refrained from letting Gus know. For he now looked
like a fisherman with two tails – and both of them mermaids'.

The next move was fairly obvious to both of us. And that was
that at least one of us should peel off down to the ice-cream
fellow's place and get the run-down of exactly what the boys in
blue had said when they released him.

Gus, of course, volunteered the instant I hadn't got round to
asking him and said he would pick up his Milly on the way, so
that she could share in the delight at his release.

'Well, in all the euphoria, Gus, don't forget what you've gone round for.'

'What's that, old son?'

Would you believe it? He'd forgotten already.

He scratched the balding patch around his head's back door and saw my scowl. 'Yeah, well, all right then. I haven't forgotten really. Ask all about what old Digby and the police said, when they let him out.'

'Not just then, Gus. But before. Get a complete run-down on his interrogations, in case they tell us something we don't know.'

'Know what you mean,' he sniffed, then with a thick finger to the forelock, shuffled off back to his car. 'See you later, old son,' were his last shouted words, as he fired up the old boiler and steamed off towards his Milly and beyond.

Meanwhile, I reckoned that my mental and financial needs might as well be met by a spell on my stool in my shop. For one, Ron Ball's release had fazed my whole thinking on the Maitland affair. Having learned what he could have overheard of Mary and Chrissie's conversation when they were buying drinks at his van, I had only just come round to the idea that he might, after all, be guilty of more than just voyeurism that terrible night at the Maitlands'. And two, Friday p.m.'s are often more productive of punters than any other afternoon of the week, bar Saturdays. I guess because some end their working week early on Fridays and others have freshly packeted money in their pockets, jingling away to be spent. What's more, to put not too fine a point on it, I needed to make the odd bob. Dashing up Shit Creek to hand over the paddle that Ron Ball had omitted to take with him, had already caused my Toy Emporium to be too downright eccentric in its opening hours or, certainly, as proven again that morning, double downright eccentric in its choice of stand-in shopkeepers.

So for a couple of hours, behind the counter I sat. And mused. And watched the door. Mused again. Watched a G & T (gawper and toucher – a species of old-toy buff that is to toys what Ron Ball seemed to be to the genus 'woman'). Back to musing. Then a SALE. Only one, but one that helped out the week considerably; although I was rather sorry (emotionally) to see the gem go. Even for the marked price of two hundred and seventy-five pounds. For it was a mint tinplate racing seaplane made in the thirties by Jep (*Jouets en Paris*), clockwork driving a four-bladed propeller that actually could tug the aircraft across any patch of calm water. (Proven in my bath, much to Arabella's alarm, who had raised her long legs high in the air to give it passage, so to speak.)

But I digress. My musings, understandably, were all on the old hoary subject. Maitland's death and whodunnit. Was it poor, lonely, fixated Ron Ball, after all? At least I now had evidence from two sources, Mary and Chrissie, that he could well have known that the object of his obsession had a pretty unsatisfactory marriage. The big question, however, remained: whether he was so besotted with Mary Maitland that he would actually go to the length of murdering her husband to free her of him. And anyway, why then turn around and beat up the very person he was trying to rescue, impress or what-have-you? And what's more, beat her up so badly that she was even now back in hospital and likely to remain there for some little time.

Yes, I know there could have been a motive for beating her up. Or rather, knocking her unconscious. A seedy, unpleasant motive that had so distressed Mary Maitland, and rightly, on my visit to the hospital. For like my customers that afternoon, gawpers sometimes are tempted to touch the objects of their desire. Poor Ron Ball might well have been driven next door to crazy just seeing Mary Maitland day after day in the well-endowed flesh and full frontal, that he just had to . . . well, let us say, find out for himself whether it was all real.

But at least, whatever my suspicions, or maybe even theirs, the police had now released him. I guessed that Digby Whetstone just did not possess enough evidence, forensic or otherwise, to nail a murder charge to his door alongside the one for burglary – which I supposed would be some consideration for all the Balls and Gus's Milly.

But then if it wasn't the odd-ball ice-cream vendor, who else had a motive for killing Maurice Maitland? And upon that question most of my inter-customer afternoon was spent. The trouble was that almost everyone I could think of seemed to have some motive or other. To begin with, Maurice Maitland seemed to have been the kind of dour, mean and overbearing individual who must have inspired dislike wherever he went. Or almost wherever. And the exception, Morgan Fairchild, was almost as puzzling a phenomenon as the actual murder itself. Oh, I could see instantly what that dull and pedestrian man must have seen in her. A flash of brilliant colour and no doubt much else, in the

150

monotone of his life. But what the supercharged lady could have seen in him, I had no idea. Unless, of course, she knew of his million-pound attic. But even then, I reckoned a woman like Fairchild would want the toys translated into actual greenbacks before starting up an affair with someone so apparently drear and boring.

Somewhere, I felt, there must be a key to solving this particular riddle. Why a firefly should be attracted to a wood-louse. Without that key, any surmises as to whether the Fairchild woman really had sufficient motive for snuffing out the louse, would be tenuous in the extreme. And I could only think of two anyway. First, that he might have promised to leave his wife and set up with her and then gone back on it. Second, and this a wild one, that he might have pretended to make a will in her favour just to facilitate the removal of whatever dress, fancy or otherwise, the dear lady was wearing at any one time. What I have heard described as 'ploy meets girl'. The louse may even have shown her a copy of said will to substantiate his lie. An action that, little had he known, had instantly locked him in an embrace more deadly than loving?

Then, of course, there was someone who much more obviously stood to gain from Maitland's death. His stubby, extrovert and now revealed as lecherous, partner, Malcolm Savage. With Maitland out of the way, Savage would have – indeed, had now –the chance to buy his partner's share, Mary being willing, and at last turn the company any which way he chose. What's more, he could have imagined his partner's widow might then also be willing to be his sleeping partner – in the most literal sense of the phrase. Or his overheated brain may have imagined something even more rewarding than bed alone. Like a marriage certificate to a million-pound fortune. After all, from what Mary had told me, Savage hardly seemed to hold his current marriage in any high regard.

Then, after I had Savaged myself silly, my mind scanned over other possible dramatis personae of whom I knew. The new liberated friends of Mrs Maitland, for instance. I could discount at least one now, the Mrs Valentine, as she apparently had left for America before the murder. And perhaps also Miss Churchill, if she did actually leave for the States on the day of the murder, as she had obviously told Mary. That left the Matilda woman, up in Bristol. But as Mary had pointed out, she would hardly have left

151

her husband and motored down to dear old Dorset at dead of night just to eliminate one more chauvinist pig from the face of her feminist earth.

Besides, the trouble with the whole shebang of lining up any woman as a suspect, was that the police seemed to reckon the blow, from its force, had to have been struck by a man.

As you can see, I was getting nowhere fast that afternoon. The more I mused, the more fantastic and ludicrous became the theories. These, by the time I shut up shop, went so far as to include a lot in which jealous closet lesbians (Mary's new found friends?) gang together to contract a hit-man to remove the obnoxious pig of a husband. Hit-man surprised by wife. Panics. Beats her up, leaves her for dead. Steals some toys and . . . and . . . WHAT, in God's name? Just happens to hide them in the garden of a bloke he presumably doesn't know from Adam, who turns out to be the world's most obvious suspect for the murder?

Hey ho, you can see how far gone I was by that time. Indeed, as a corollary to the above, I had also been through several scenarios where the unfortunate Mary herself might have arranged for a hit-man to remove her husband. But every one of these foundered on one very simple premise. No one in their right minds, and certainly not, from what I had seen, Mary Maitland, would voluntarily invite such injuries to be inflicted on the person that he or she would have to be hospitalized for weeks afterwards. A token black eye and a few abrasions were one thing as a bum steer for the law, but such severe damage to the skull that blackouts occur days afterwards and ward sisters shake their heads and hint of long hospitalization, seemed to me quite another. Besides, naturism and feminism by no means a murderess make. But more importantly, nothing I had heard about Mary and the way she had behaved over many years with her husband, indicated that she had any element of the vicious, vindictive or conspiratorial in her character. Anyway, had she had such, she would hardly have left the disposal of her husband to this late date. Also there were more ways of breaking up a marriage than with a twenties motoring trophy, thank God. Otherwise, yours truly would still be trussed like a prize turkey by the bonds of a marriage that had not really worked from day two, but which, through personal pride and decency's sake (not ours, but mainly of our respective mothers') we strung out for a further one thousand six hundred and fifty-three. (I know. I counted them one by one at the time.)

So much for my incisive deductions, my dear Watson. Now back to the rest of my day. Gus had not returned by the time I turned my 'Open' sign to 'Closed', for which I was somewhat relieved. For I still had to swan into Swanage to pick up that video that I had promised Arabella for the evening. So off I beetled, this time with top down, as the sun was still shining away and I needed some refreshing breezes over my brain to cool it down.

But I was hardly out of second gear, when I spied the white patrol car, still parked under the trees. On impulse, I slammed on the anchors and pulled in behind him. As I got out and walked back to him, I smiled as I saw a pair of rather goggly eyes staring out of the rear-view mirror.

'Good afternoon, officer,' I cheerfully greeted him.

He looked at me, more surprised than suspicious, then cleared his throat, presumably to give him time to think up his devastatingly appropriate reply.

'Good afternoon, sir.'

I didn't want to make him feel lonely, so I cleared my own throat.

'Officer,' I smiled, 'I wonder if I could ask you to do me a favour.'

Another clearance. 'A favour, sir?'

'Yes, a favour. Won't take you out of your way. And in return, I'll tell you where I'm off to now, to save you all the trouble, time and petrol of turning round and following me. Okay?'

This time he swallowed hard. So, doubting the imminent arrival of a witty comeback, I went on.

'The favour is this. Tell your boss, Inspector Digby Whetstone, that I am much indebted for the care and attention he is paying to me by providing an escort,' I patted the side of the door, 'in this case, made by Ford, wherever I go.'

His eyes now goggled so much, his lids had some difficulty closing over them to blink nineteen to the dozen.

'When he has absorbed that, go on to say that I'm being quite sincere when I state I much prefer this brand new method of dealing with my activities, than his old full-frontal opposition tactic of open warfare. Indeed, tell him I'm very flattered that he thinks by following my every move, he might get a lead on who is the real culprit in the Maitland case.' I held up a cautionary finger.

153

'But then you must remember to add this, I'm afraid. Tell Digby that I have so far made as much progress as a snail on the London Marathon. Less, in fact. At least, we must assume the snail knows where he's going and what his next move will be. I don't. Right. That's the end of the message to your Inspector. Now the little reward I promised you.'

I pointed back down the road. 'Right now, you don't need to tail me, because this next move of mine is purely private. I'm off to Swanage simply to pick up a videotape to enjoy tonight. Okay?'

'Er, er . . . sir . . . er . . .'

What his words lacked in coherence, they somewhat made up for by rhyming. I saluted.

'So I'm off now. Right? And to prove that I'm not lying, if you're still here when I get back, I'll wave the videotape to you out the window. Even shout you the title. Fair?'

His expression told me little of his thoughts, but plenty about his emotions.

The video turned out to be the latest Steve Martin; a comedian whose work Arabella and I had loved ever since the days of *Dead Men Don't Wear Plaid* and the wild *Man with Two Brains*.

'You'll like that,' the pebble-glassed, peroxided assistant assured me, quite unnecessarily. 'Real laugh it is. Even though he doesn't dye his hair.'

Such a *non sequitur* boggled my mind most of the way back to where I had parked the Beetle. My usual practice in busy times to avoid parking tickets – the car-park of the nearest hotel. In this case, the quite impressive Victorian pile of the Dorset.

Whilst I was unlocking my car door, my boggle was instantly swept out of mind by a reflection. The reflection in the door window. I froze, as if any movement might destroy the image. Two people were descending the steps of the hotel behind me and each in his and her own right were pretty unmistakable. But to make certain, I shiftily and slowly glanced back across my shoulder. The reflection had not lied.

Now making their way across the tarmac from the steps were Malcolm 'Stubby' Savage and Fiona 'Morgan' Fairchild. And the latter was carrying a small suitcase.

154

Eleven

Gus raised the briary bush of an eyebrow.

'Did they see you, old love?'

'Don't think so,' I replied, 'unless either of them knows I drive a yellow peril.'

'Where were they going? Did you follow them?'

I shook my head. 'They split up the second after I saw them. No doubt to go to their respective homes. Or at least, places of work. He went off in his Vauxhall and she disappeared around the corner, presumably to where she had parked her Morgan.'

Gus scratched his stubble. 'Did you know they knew each other?'

'No. No idea. Gave me the surprise of my life.'

'Did you . . . er . . . check on them, like? I mean, in the hotel?'

'If you mean did I ask at reception if the couple who had just left were resident there, then the answer is yes, I asked, but no, I learnt nothing. The receptionist coolly informed me that it was the hotel's practice always to preserve the privacy of their guests or visitors.'

Gus sniffed. 'So they could have just dropped by for scones and ruddy clotted cream, couldn't they?'

I raised my eyes to the ceiling. 'Gus, you don't actually need a suitcase to enjoy the normal cream tea.'

'Oh yeah. S'pose you don't.' He looked at me. 'So what d'yer think they were up to, then?'

I shrugged. 'Beyond the obvious, Gus, I haven't a clue.'

He frowned. 'The obvious?'

Sighing, I began, 'Oh come on, Gus, you know. You weren't born yesterday. A married man and a sexy woman at a hotel with a suitcase, really . . .'

Then I saw his grin. When will I ever learn?

This time I frowned. 'Really, Gus. I need sending up right now

155

like a hole in the head. After all, I'm only bothering about this Maitland business because of you.'

'Thought I could let you off the hook, I did, this afternoon, when Milly rang about Ron Ball's release. Sorry, old son.'

Now I felt guilty for my petulance. 'It's all right, Gus. Don't worry. We'll keep right on to the end of the road, as my mother used to say.'

'Wasn't your mother. That was Harry Lauder.'

I waved my hand. 'Let's leave it that they both said it and get on. Tell me again, what Ron Ball said about his release. I mean the exact words Digby Whetstone used. Exact, mind, Gus, this time.'

He took a deep breath. Bing, who was on his lap savouring the piscine aroma from his sweater, looked distinctly miffed at its sudden inflation.

'Well, sort of, "Don't think we've finished with you yet over the murder" and then, "We reckon you know far more about this whole thing than you're telling. But we'll get it out of you sooner or later".' Gus shrugged. 'That's about all, old lad. Near as ruddy dammit.'

I thought for a second. 'See any signs of a police car hanging about the area round the Balls' house?'

'Didn't see one. Wasn't looking, mind.' A hand stroked Bing flat on his lap. 'Why? D'yer think that's Digby's idea? Release him, then follow him.'

'Could be.' Bing struggled, but to no avail.

Gus smirked. 'You've got follow-me-itis, you have, since they've taken to going after you. Still, thought you said yours had gone when you came back just now.' He held up a digit, giving Bing a chance to escape to the floor. 'And remember this, old son. The police've got more to do than have ruddy cars haring after everyone mixed up in a murder case. 'Sides, can't afford enough Fords.'

He grinned at his last remark. Least I think that's why he grinned. Right then we had little else to laugh about.

Then he said, ' 'Ere. If the flippin' hotel won't tell you what that fancy piece and Savage were up to, why don't you go and ask them? Direct like. Tell 'em you've ruddy well seen them.'

'I suppose it's about the only thing I can do,' I said quietly, but my mind was elsewhere – suddenly distracted by a wild and woolly image of what that afternoon's suitcase might just have contained.

Gus left soon afterwards. I did not blame him. For my responses thereafter were hardly worth staying around for. Anyway, he knew Arabella would soon be home and that we had a video to watch. So prolonged Heinekening was not in prospect – with us, at least.

My next exchange, however, was not to be with Arabella. But with a somewhat excited Chrissie Cartwright on the telephone.

'Sorry to bother you, Peter, but I thought you would like to know.'

'Know what?' I blanched.

'Mary is home.'

'Home?' I repeated like a cracked record.

'Yes. Home. I was passing her place and saw her in the drive.'

'But the sister at the hospital made out she'd need to be kept in for some little time.'

'I know. I know. Let me tell you. I naturally stopped and went in to see her. And do you know what the silly woman has done? She's gone and signed herself out. On her ownio. No consultation with doctors or anyone. Just upped and asked for her clothes and left.'

'What on earth brought this on? She didn't mention anything about leaving this morning.'

'She just said that all they were now going to do was keep her under pills and observation and she could jolly well look after herself just as efficiently back home . . .' Chrissie broke off to chuckle, '. . . and, she added, with damn sight better food into the bargain. I must say, she seemed amazingly full of beans this afternoon, considering everything. Almost like a new person. Perhaps that short enforced rest was really all she needed.'

I did not respond right away, but then asked, 'Sure she's not trying to escape from something?'

'What on earth do you mean?' Chrissie asked in a shocked tone.

'No, don't get me wrong. I mean escape from, say, a course of treatment that might be painful or even involve surgery or something.'

'Oh . . . I see . . . well, I didn't think of that. M'mmm, like the X-rays might have shown up a haemorrhage or something that needs an operation.'

'That kind of thing.'

There was a pause, then she said, 'No, no, that's not like Mary. To shirk things like that. She's never been a coward. As I told you before, Mary's a great believer in mind over . . .'

'. . . what's the matter?' I chipped in.

'Right. Right. Yes, well said, Peter. So I don't think Mary would ever run away from treatment that would make her fit again, however unpleasant or painful.'

'Know her doctor?'

'Yes. A bit. But you know as well as I do, Peter, that doctors will never divulge to anyone but the very closest of kin what's wrong with any of their patients. And not even then, sometimes. My uncle, for instance, never realized that my aunt, his wife, was dying of cancer until the very end.'

'Well, maybe we needn't have any worries. The patient often knows best how he or she really feels. And you say that Mary seems pretty buoyant.'

'Bright eyed and bushy tailed almost.'

'Well then, let's be thankful that things seem to be taking a turn for the better for her at last. It's high time something good came out of all this tragedy.'

Which statement prompted Chrissie to ask, 'How's it all going? Made any progress?'

I confessed my singular lack of anything resembling that noun, but did recount my seeing Savage and Fairchild leaving the hotel.

'Good Lord. Our Savage hasn't wasted much time taking over his late partner's interests, has he?'

I liked her turn of phrase. 'Think that's what it is?'

'Don't you? I reckon he thought that if that Fairchild woman could go for a staid and boring man like Maurice, then she would be bound to fall for a bouncy, bombastic bas . . . bloke like himself. And now he's proved himself right on the button. Or on something.'

'Might explain it,' I admitted. 'But it all depends on that little assumption we and everyone else made right at the start.'

'What's that?'

'That Fiona Fairchild ever actually fell for anybody.'

Steve Martin came as a welcome relief for both of us that evening. And his latest proved, hurrah, hurrah, quite the equal of his classic early work masterminded by the great Carl Reiner. After we had finished quoting and re-quoting the best scenes and one-liners to each other, however, our dilemmas surfaced once more; but this time, we were both relaxed enough to stand back and give them more balanced consideration. Indeed, Arabella now seemed much more at ease with the television station's offer and even admitted that now, she was rather pleased that a trigger had been applied for a total review of where her professional life was heading.

'After all,' she said, 'I have no wish to be a provincial journalist for ever and a day, cushy and comfortable though the life may be.'

'So you think, by the middle of next week, you might give them a "Yes"?' I probed.

'Maybe. But I don't have to make up my mind tonight, do I? They've given me the time, so I might as well use it to make sure it's the . . .' She hesitated.

So I supplied, '. . . the *real* Arabella Trench who is saying "Yes" or "No".'

She came over and sat close to me on the settee.

'Hello, real you,' I smiled, wrapping an arm around her.

'Hello.' She looked up at me. 'You must think I'm being silly. I'm not, you know.'

I kissed her lightly on the forehead. 'No, I know you're not. It's what I should have done before jumping at a chance to get into advertising years ago. Sit and think as to whether it was all really me. I never really liked the job. Ever. Or that kind of world, those kind of operators. Just was fooled by the money, the myth of the glamour, which was only ever glitz, when it glinted at all. I used to sit through expense account lunches sometimes, listening to myself and others buttering and boozing up boringly pedestrian and often boorish clients and thinking, "What on earth am I doing here? What the hell is all this sickening sycophancy about?" And then the cash register in my mind would go ting, deafening me to the rest of my mutinous musings . . .' I squeezed her shoulder. '. . . So another day went by, another week, another year . . .'

'. . . until you stood up straight and strong and cried, "Enough",' Arabella grinned. ' "Bring me back to a world of sanity. Sincerity. Sensitivity . . ." ' She paused.

'You're running out of "S"s, aren't you?' I observed.

'No matter. I'll go on to the next letter. "T". Er . . . tolerance, trust, . . . truth . . .'

'Toys,' I laughed. 'A world of toys.'

'A world of innocence.'

My lips lingered on hers for a delicious moment.

'Not that innocent,' I smiled.

'I meant without guile, dreamboat. Not without sex,' she mimicked a Mae West. Then, back as Arabella, she said, 'So you agree with me. No one should ever act out of character. For character is one thing in this life no one can ever really change.'

I nodded. 'I guess so.'

'So next Wednesday I must be true to me. Deep down me.'

'Forsaking every other. For they are but cardboard cut-out Arabella Trenches.'

'Otherwise, I'll be like you were. Ruing every day . . .'

I held up a finger.

'Be true. Don't rue.'

'Don't laugh.'

'I'm not.'

Lips lingered a little, then Arabella suddenly switched direction and asked, 'So if your theory about the fancy-dress lady is true, how do you think it might fit in with the murder? I don't quite see.'

'Nor do I really, at the moment,' I admitted. 'But say, for instance, Maurice Maitland had threatened to expose what Fiona Fairchild was up to.'

'Not very likely, is it, if he was actually one of the players, anyway.'

I sighed. 'Okay. Let's try the other way round. Say, she in the end threatened to expose his role in the affair, unless he paid up.'

'Blackmail?'

'Could be. Maybe that's really her racket. Blackmail. Once she's involved anyone deeply enough, then, wham, she springs the threat of exposure.'

'But why might she want to have him murdered, then? It would be cutting off the source of the loot.'

'Maybe the blackmail was something Maitland regarded as worse than exposure. Remember how tight-fisted he was all his life. Never went on holiday or took poor Mary out.'

Arabella absorbed the thought, but I could see she was none too convinced.

'So what do you plan to do now, darling? Whip over to the fancy-dress shop. . . ?'

I winced. 'Don't use that word. The time I was there, the first thing the dear lady showed me was a rack of canes!'

Arabella's eyes popped. 'Oooh! Lucky man. So is that what you are going to do?'

'I guess so.'

She saw my frown. 'What's the trouble?'

'Well, whichever I see first – fancy Fiona or stubby Savage – will, no doubt, then go and warn the other that I'm on the warpath.' I chuckled. 'Ideally, therefore, I'd like to see them both at the same time. But that's obviously impossible.'

Arabella thought for a second. 'Hey, wait a minute. Maybe it isn't.'

'How do you mean?'

'Well, I have no appointments as far as I know, before twelve tomorrow morning. So if you could get over to Wareham by, say, ten or so, I could arrange to be at Savage's office at the same time. You know, spin some story that my paper has heard he has great expansion plans for his printing firm and I would like to hear about them for my paper. A man like Savage is bound to fall for any chance of publicity and that's without my fluttering my . . .'

'Leave it at eyelids.'

'One or both?' she grinned. 'And once I've got him really going, I'll drop in that I saw him coming out of that hotel with Fancy job. And see what ripples that causes.'

'Let's hope it's not a tidal wave that sweeps you away.'

She gripped my arm. 'Great idea, right? Come on, say "Yes". Otherwise I'll . . .'

'You'll what?'

'I'll . . . er . . . not.'

'You'll not what?'

The rest of this conversation, I'm afraid, is subject to the laws of censorship, decency and what-have-you.

I did not espy a spy the whole way over to Wareham. I assumed my little message to the patrolman of the day before had got through to Digby Whetstone, who had either called off my tail or had, at least, demanded that he become a little more adept at concealment. My fear was that the dear Inspector might have arranged a switch to a plain-clothes driver and a bog-ordinary, unmarked car. In which case, almost everyone in my rear-view mirror could be a tail and that was just too much to worry over.

There was no camouflaged Morgan outside the shop when I arrived. But to my relief, I could see signs of activity through the windows. So I parked in the pub car-park, almost opposite, and then, taking a deep breath, strode across the road to her shop.

As luck would have it, the customer whom I'd spotted through the window, decided at that moment to leave, almost bumping into me as I went in. As I closed the door behind me, I got the feeling of eyes lasering into my head. I wasn't wrong. When I looked around, there was Fiona Fairchild staring at me.

'*You* again,' was the kindly greeting.

'Surprised?' was my cool reply.

Her eyes narrowed. 'Not really. From what I've heard about you, you are always sticking your nose in where it's not wanted.'

I decided not to beat around the bush. For the warmth of my reception did not exactly hint of a long sojourn in her shop.

'Like at the Dorset Hotel.'

She froze.

'Yesterday p.m.'

She unfroze just enough to blink. It was an attempt at a look of disdain, but it didn't come off. Her poise had been knocked too off balance.

'Mr Marklin, I don't know or care what you are talking about, but would you kindly . . .'

I cut in. 'I'm talking about the racket you're running.'

'Racket?' she blinked again.

'Yes. And I don't mean tennis. Though a sport may be connected with it, come to think of it.'

She recovered somewhat. 'Really, Mr Marklin, whatever anyone may think about running a fancy-dress shop, no one has ever called it a racket.'

'I'm not referring to the shop and you know it, Mrs Fairchild.'

She attempted a smile. It could have still frozen Studland Bay. 'Miss. Not Mrs. After my divorce, I went back to my maiden name.'

'But went on to unmaidenly activities,' I tried, as a last throw to pierce her armour. For I knew that if I didn't succeed pretty damn fast, she'd have every right to have me on the street before I could learn anything. Trouble was I had nothing more than a hunch to go on and I just prayed she wouldn't notice it.

'A divorced woman is free to do what she likes, Mr Marklin.' She took a move towards me. 'And what I want to do right now is throw you out.'

I held up a hand and tried, 'Even a divorced woman is not free to break the law.'

'Break the law?' she frowned. 'Since when have I broken the law?'

I shrugged. 'For quite some time I would think. I doubt if Maurice Maitland was the first of your . . . clients.'

Suddenly hearing a fumble at the shop door, I whipped across and turned the key. 'Sorry. Closed,' I mouthed to a henna head with a two-year-old freckle in a pram.

'Now look here, Mr Marklin, I've put up with your tomfoolery quite long enough. I must ask you to leave.'

'Cane me if I don't?' I teased. 'That's one of your little cameos, now isn't it? What are the others? Now let me guess.' I pointed to a rack on which hung two or three nurses' uniforms. 'Nursie, nursie, could be another, now couldn't it? The possibilities are endless with a shop like this. There's cruel Nazi kalafactresses, schoolgirls, headmistresses; then there's all the stiletto, silk stockings and suspender stuff. Oh dear, oh dear, there's no end to it all. Dressing up as a schoolboy or slave girl or an air hostess, any old male fantasy – or female for that matter – that's hot off their little fevered minds . . .'

But the reaction that all this evoked was hardly what I had been expecting. For suddenly her expression softened and she limply took a step or two forward and would have collapsed, had I not held out my arms.

'I'm sorry, I'm sorry,' she gasped. 'How silly I've been.'

Her own arms were now around me and I could feel the hardness of her nipples against my chest, her blouse being about as robust – and concealing – as your average gossamer.

'I don't know . . . since my divorce, I suppose, I've been too . . . well, free, I suppose you'd call it.'

'Are you sure you don't mean "expensive"?'

She looked up at me, as if butter, or an equivalent, would not melt in her overripe mouth.

'Mr Marklin, I assure you, all your suspicions are wildly wrong. How can I convince you?'

I instantly pleaded the fourth amendment to that one.

The eyelids now worked overtime. And not with disdain.

'I can see now how you came to the kind of conclusion you did. You must have been asking yourself how I could possibly have fallen for a dull man like poor Maurice or even now, his partner,

Malcolm Savage. You no doubt recognized him as the man I was with at the Dorset Hotel.'

I nodded.

'Those thoughts did cross my mind, yes.' I tried to disentangle myself, but to no avail. She was like a limpet, only a rather more sexy shape.

'Well, the answer is much more simple than yours.' Flutter, flutter. 'You see, for some time now I've been a bit of a mess emotionally. The divorce was very messy and seemed to go on for ever. It left me completely drained. Empty. And I'm afraid, ever since, I've been grabbing at almost every chance of, well, let us say, companionship that I can. Relationships really that I can be sure will never touch me emotionally. For right now, I'm not ready for that. Not ready by a long shot.'

Had I a violin with me, I'd have played it. She went on, musical accompaniment being there none. 'Yet I have need of, well, men, I suppose.' Her clasp tightened. 'You can understand that, surely, Mr Marklin? Woman needing man.' She looked up. 'Man needing woman.'

Whilst I've nothing against nipples, right then I'd got too much against them. So, as they say in the comic books, 'with a mighty leap, I was free'. Well, next best thing. I gave her the push off. Literally. But I was gentlemanly enough to reach out with one hand and prevent an actual fall to the floor.

'And man needing to play-act with woman too. And vice versa,' I countered. 'Especially vice.'

This time, I realized, I had gone just too far – even in her fancy book of Do's and Don't's and Try Me's. And maybe, even for my own good.

'GET OUT,' she spat. 'Get out right now or I'll call the police. I'll have you for forcing your way in, locking out my customers, slandering my good name . . .'

'Slander?' I smiled, as I made to unlock the door. 'I doubt you'd succeed on that last, "Miss" Fairchild. You see, you might have to unbutton too much of your life to prove I was wrong, now wouldn't you?'

The glass door missed my nose by the hair on a gnat's testicle. As the old lyric almost goes, 'It was getting to be a habit with me.'

Outside, of course, it had decided to rain. (So much for the TV weatherman who had said it wouldn't, poor fish.) By the time I got to my Beetle in the pub car-park, it was of the mixed pets variety. And where was my hood? Neatly folded down for the fair weather, as promised on the box, wasn't it? Now, in addition to feeling distinctly pissed off for having failed to scare Morgan Fairchild sufficiently to come clean (or dirty) over anything worth a damn, I was now being literally pissed on by the elements.

Thus it was a great deal less than merry Marklin who journeyed back through Corfe and then cross country along the lane to Studland. My main hope now lay in what Arabella might have been able to prise, or flutter or flatter out of Malcolm Savage. I just prayed she would have time to ring me before her twelve o'clock appointment in the office.

The rain, now scudding across the landscape like arrows from some giant unseen army, seemed to have frightened most of the traffic off the road. So much so that over the last couple of miles, there was no one in my rear-view mirror – save for a body-less head staring back at me, that is. And I was just finding a crumb of comfort in the morning, in that, at least, I had no tail, when around the bend ahead roared a white wonder, blue lamp a'flashing and sending up sheets of spray from its speeding wheels.

As it passed, the driver seemed to peer across at me, as if I were some freak in a sideshow; which behaviour I put down to bright yellow Volkswagen convertibles being not an everyday sight in any part of Britain these days, let alone sleepy old Dorset. How wrong can you be?

In well under a minute, he was right on my tail, headlights flashing into my mirror. Even above the noise of motor, wipers and the smack of water hitting the wheel-arches, there was no mistaking now the 'dee-dahing' that every motorist born has nightmares about.

Like a dutiful citizen (but an inwardly cursing one), I pulled into the nearest farm gateway that would give us both room to park without blocking the road. The patrolman was at my window before I even had time to wind it down. I decided to get all his options over at one go.

'What's the trouble, officer? I was only doing fifty. My licence is up to date. My insurance only just renewed. My car was MOT'd only a month ago. My eyesight is such that I can read the bottom line of the chart better than the optician. And my alcohol intake today rests at zero.'

The right arm of the law was raised. I stopped. Then he said quite simply these thrilling and cheering words.

'Your shop's been burgled, Mr Marklin. I just thought you'd like to know.'

Twelve

It was Arabella who had discovered the break-in when she had dropped by after her meeting with Savage to share notes with me over mine with Morgan Fairchild. And she had instantly called the police and had told them I had gone to Wareham.

It was the back door of the actual house that had been forced. It was not hard to see why that means of entry had been used, rather than the door of the shop. It was hidden from direct view from the street and its window, once broken, nullified the locks and chain.

The police were still there when I got back. But not the Bournemouth brigade. Just a couple of local constables from Swanage. And they stayed around until I had a chance to give them as detailed a list as I could manage of the items that had been taken.

Luckily – if you can call anything to do with a burglary luck –the thief had been a tidy one and not one of the vandal variety that one reads about and dreads. Those who seem to get more kicks out of the destruction of what they leave behind, than out of the loot they take with them. So, at least, the scene that met my eyes was not one of desolation. The still fairly neat arrangement of my stock around the shop made spotting the gaps comparatively simple. The snag was, sometimes, to remember what exactly had filled the gap, say, between a Minic Streamline tourer and the same manufacturer's neat little caravan, or between a Schuco 3000 Telesteering car and a Gnom sports model, and so on and so on.

Anyway, as every toy buff will have guessed from the small selection quoted above, the gaps were all amongst clockwork and wind-up toys. For the far more numerous ranks of the die-cast items seemed to be still complete and totally undisturbed.

Well, to cut the sad story short, by the time I had finished my inspection, my tally came to some twenty-five items, all clock-work, all mint, but not by any means all of them boxed. My morning marauder was either not like most collectors – a box freak – or he had not boxed as clever as he might have done. For boxes can add up to half as much again to the value of any one toy. In my view, ludicrous, but there it is. And talking of value, my tally totalled some seventeen hundred pounds.

The beetroot-faced constable whistled through his moustache, when I announced the figure. Then licking his pencil, he remarked, 'Your thief certainly knew what he was about, Mr Marklin.'

I felt a rat disagreeing. 'Not exactly, constable.'

His eyebrows lifted into his helmet. 'Oh, really, sir?'

'Yes, really. Given that the thief was selective enough to differentiate between clockwork and non-clockwork items, I am surprised he didn't also go for the more exotic toys that are worth considerably more than any he took.' I pointed to a rather beautiful twenty-two-inch-long model of the Sunbeam Silver Bullet record car. Made around 1930 by the renowned German manufacturer, Gunthermann.

'That little job is marked at three hundred and fifty pounds, but could well fetch up to five hundred pounds at a good auction.'

I swung my finger across to a metallic red Phantom futuristic dream car made by Tipp of West Germany in the fifties. 'Why, even that post-war item there regularly makes a hundred and fifty or so at auction. Even I have it marked at a hundred and thirty.' I turned back to the pencil-licking lawman. 'So you can see, constable, why I'm not so sure he really knew what he was about, when he broke in.'

He looked at me. 'So what are you saying, sir?'

I thought it had been perfectly plain, but nevertheless, elaborated. 'That the whole thing seems a little curious to me, that's all. Someone breaking in who was presumably a toy buff and then not taking the most valuable items of the particular type he seems to be after.'

'Clockwork?'

'Right,' I said, disguising my admiration of the brilliance and incisiveness of his mind. 'Doesn't it seem a bit strange to you, too?'

He sniffed. At least it made a change from licking. 'Yes, now you mention it, I suppose it does.' He looked again at the items I had picked out. 'Unless, sir . . .' he hesitated.

'Unless what?'

'It's like this here. Those expensive cars are fairly large, aren't they, sir?'

'I suppose so.'

'Tell me, how large, in comparison, are the ones he's made off with?'

'Since you ask, yes, they are all considerably smaller. But . . .'

A knowing smile broke across the beetroot. 'Well, there you are, sir. He must have reckoned they were easier to carry. Or conceal.'

I prayed for strength from whomsoever.

'Constable, he took twenty-five different ruddy items. He need only have taken three or four of the others to make up the same value.'

Another smile. Hell, what was coming now?

'Ah, sir. But think of this.' He held up his pencil. 'One, size isn't everything in life. Small is beautiful, sometimes. Miniatures often have great appeal.'

I refrained from pointing out that the theory fell down the instant it got to brains.

A finger now joined the pencil in prodding the ether. 'Two, wouldn't you, as a professional toy man, so to speak, agree that were a thief stealing, not for himself so much, but perhaps to sell again, then cheaper smaller items might pass unnoticed; whereas more, as you term it, exotic toys might raise an eyebrow or two and thus a query as to where they originated?'

I reluctantly agreed that might be so, but instantly stated that my gut told me that was not the reason for that morning's particular selection.

He patted his stomach at my comment. 'Gut, sir? Oh dear, I know what you mean. But I'm afraid if we police just relied on guts, we wouldn't get very far. Today it's up here what counts.' He transferred his hand to his helmet and tapped it. 'Got to try to get into the criminal's mind. Try and be him, if you like. Now I remember a case when . . .'

I cut short his trip down memory lane.

'I'm sorry, constable, but if you don't mind, I've got one or two things I must do now. Like notify my insurance company for one, ring round the list of stolen items to some of the other vintage toy-dealers, for two . . .' I stopped there, as I had no intention of revealing what was in my mind for three, four and five. But they were quite as urgent as calls to insurance companies and dealers. If not more so. For stolen toys, however valuable or beloved, are hardly a matter of life or death.

But it still took a further quarter of an hour to finally shift the boys in blue. As Arabella and I watched their white wonder pull away from the shop, she turned to me and said, 'You seemed in a hell of a hurry to get rid of them. Why? They were only doing their job. Trying to help you. And if you're worried about my appointment, don't be. I rang up and cancelled it, once I had discovered the break-in.'

I gripped her shoulder. 'Arabella, tell me about Savage first, then I'll explain.'

'Potted version?'

'For now. I can hear the rest later.'

'Okay. Well, at first he wouldn't admit a damn thing . . .'

'Ditto Fairchild.'

'. . . then, when I persisted, he said, yes, he had met her at the Dorset Hotel, but only for a meal. He said he had invited her to lunch purely out of curiosity as to what his dead partner's mistress was like.'

'Is that the limit of his admission?'

'More or less.' She smiled. 'How about your fancy woman?'

'Thanks for calling her that, my love. Well, she did at least admit that their appetites had been fed with rather more than a meal. Clung to my shoulder and wept that, since her divorce, she'd been, perhaps, too free with her favours and that the reason she puts up with men like Maitland and Savage is that they provide her with, well, sex without any complications or committal of any kind.'

Arabella's face showed her scant respect for that little line.

'Did you comfort her with your theory as to what she's really up to?'

I nodded. 'Briefly. That's what prompted the sex without committal bit, in the first place. But I couldn't pursue it any further, as she then threw me out of the shop.'

Arabella looked up at me. 'So we are both only further forward by . . .'

'. . . one adultery,' I smiled. 'But enough of those two. Right now, you and I – that is if you can spare any further time . . .'

'I did warn the office that the burglary might mean my not being able to come in for the rest of the day.'

'Thank the Lord for that. For you and I have work to do, if what's going through my mind right now is even half on the ball.'

'About the burglary?'

'About the burglary. And maybe, about Maitland's murder.'

Her eyes quizzed me. 'Don't tell me you've already worked out who broke in.' She suddenly clasped her hand to her mouth. 'Of course. Why didn't I think of it, for goodness' sake? You think it's Ron Ball, don't you?'

She caught my expression. 'No, maybe not. Though the stolen toys were all wind-ups, weren't they? And that's his thing.'

I did not interrupt, as I wanted to hear if she would eventually work her way round to what I was thinking. If she did, it would give me a little more confidence that the theory might just hold water.

'. . .but then,' she continued, 'it's pretty common knowledge, I guess, by now, what Ron Ball collects, so . . . well, so someone could have . . .' She looked at me, as if to discover whether she was right so far. '. . . decided to arrange a robbery, so that it looked as if he had done it. If that is correct, then it would have to be someone who knows Ron Ball has been released.' She paused and pursed her lips. A purse I would be raiding very soon, if she eventually ended up at the same conclusion as myself.

'But I guess quite a bunch might be aware of that. There's Ron's mum, Milly and, no doubt, friends of theirs we know not of.' She looked at me. 'I wonder if Chrissie Cartwright has heard the news.'

'Probably. She seems to know most things that are going on round this neck of the woods. Anyway, I dare say Digby Whetstone would have to let people like Mary Maitland know he was releasing his chief suspect. And if Mary had learnt it, then I don't suppose it was long before she told Chrissie.'

'On that score, then, Digby might have felt he ought to tell Maitland's inamorata as well. And if Fiona knows . . .'

'. . . then the whole ruddy world probably knows by now, I dare say.' I grimaced. 'So that little bit of reasoning has hardly narrowed down our list of suspects, has it?'

Arabella thought for a moment. 'Let's approach it from a different angle. Whoever broke in here, must have known about you and your shop, mustn't they?'

I nodded. 'I don't quite see how that narrows things down. After all, nearly everyone concerned with the case must know who I am by now and what I run.'

We sighed in unison.

'Okay,' Arabella went on, 'let's try this one. Who of all of them actually knows this place? Has actually been here?'

'I don't think any of them have.'

Arabella raised a finger. 'Hang on. Chrissie Cartwright's been here.'

I raised my eyebrows. 'You're now including Chrissie in the list of suspects?'

'Why not? She's the person who freely admits to having probably started Mary Maitland off on her feminist kick. So, maybe, she decided the only way her friend Mary would ever be able to gain her real freedom was to remove the chauvinist pig of her husband.' Then she added quietly, 'Who knows how Chrissie's own husband died? We've never delved into that, have we?'

I had to admit she was right on the last point, but disputed the accuracy of her overall proposition.

'There are one or two problems with that theory, my darling. One, the police say that the blow that killed Maitland was most likely to have been delivered by a man . . .'

'Chrissie is not exactly a fragile feeble little flower of English womanhood.'

'Maybe not. But she's no female Stallone, either. And secondly, when she's talked about her late husband, it's been with the greatest affection – and I don't think she was putting it on. And thirdly, I don't reckon she's feigning her desire to help find Maurice Maitland's real murderer. I do believe that she is genuinely on our side and not a dastardly clever murderess getting in with the amateur sleuth to find out what's going on in his head so that she can throw him off the scent.'

Arabella smiled. 'You like Chrissie Cartwright, don't you?'

'I like her spirit. She's got guts, that lady.'

'And your gut feeling is that this gutful lady hasn't used her guts to murder and pillage?'

I nodded. 'Your intestines disagree?'

'Not really. Not with that one. Now if it were baked beans and bad curry . . .' She put an affectionate arm round my shoulder. 'You know what we should be doing right now, instead of getting nowhere fast with our deductions?'

172

I Groucho'd my eyebrows up and down.

'Really, Mrs Teasdale, at a time like this? Have you no shame?'

She scowled and said with mock severity, 'Prime Minister Firefly, I wasn't referring to you-know-what, upstairs. But to we-know-what, downstairs. Like a forced back-door lock and ugly gaps in your toy display.'

She was right, bless her cotton socks. (She looks absolutely devastating in them in the summer months. She should carry a health warning for those with already high blood pressure.) But before we got down to repairing the damage, I made a quick call to Gus. For something had just hit me, that made a little trip in his Ford Popular very desirable. Just for him, that is.

Gus, when he came round, was horrified at the break-in and instantly raised an admonishing digit.

'There you are, see. Comes of not inviting me round to open up shop, while you were gone. Not only would that have saved you from ruddy burglars but I might well have made you a bit of money into the bargain.'

'Could be spot on, Gus, but right now there are more urgent things to do than conduct post-mortems.'

'Post what?' he grinned.

'Forget it, Gus. I want you to do something for me. Or rather, for you, for your Milly and for the Ball family.'

'What's that then?' His eyes glowed. 'Bit of sleuthing?'

'Might call it that.'

He rubbed his great hands together. Sounded like a sander. 'Fire away then. What you want me to do?'

'Get in your car and go straight over to Ron Ball's.'

He frowned. 'What's the good of that, old son? That's not ruddy sleuthing.'

'Yes, it is, Gus. Because I want you to stay there. Watch over the place, and see that Ron Ball doesn't go out.'

His furrows deepened. 'Why not? He's hardly going to like me imprisoning him in his own flippin' home the second after he's got out of a police cell, now is he?'

'Maybe not. But tell him it's for his own good.'

'Going to tell me why, then?'

'I could be wrong, Gus, but there's just a chance this burglary and Ron Ball's release might be connected.'

Gus's mouth fell open and I was privileged to glimpse a dentist's worst nightmare.

'You mean . . . you mean . . . *he* pinched yer stuff?'

I waved my hand. 'I don't know quite what I mean, Gus. But if he didn't, then someone, I reckon, might be trying to make it look as if he did. You see, only wind-up items were taken and we and many others know that's his particular bag.'

Gus scratched his stubble. 'I still don't quite see why I've got to go over and stop him going out.'

'One, you're going to watch the place and see no one tries to dump the stuff anywhere on the Ball property. Two, you're going to see that no harm can come to Ron Ball.'

'What kind of harm?'

'Not sure. But it could be, if someone is trying to frame him again for Maitland's murder, that he might be in some kind of personal danger. Don't know quite what but, for instance, there's no better way of incriminating anybody than a body being found alongside the loot. You know the kind of thing. Faked suicide. Drop off a cliff or hose-pipe from the ice-cream van's exhaust. Drowning in the Blue Pool or anywhere. If that happened, dear Digby would jump at the opportunity of declaring the Maitland murder solved. "Guilt, in the end, got too much for the poor, lonely, deranged lad." I can hear him now and see the headlines in the papers.'

'Want me to tell him all that, old son?' Gus asked, after a moment or two's reflection.

'Only if he won't do what you say without it. I don't want to scare him unduly. After all, I could be so terribly wrong about the whole thing. And maybe this break-in has got nothing to do with the Maitland murder at all.'

Gus sniffed. 'Better be safe than sorry, though, eh? All right, I'll go. But I can't hang around for ever, you know. Got things to do.'

'Pick up Milly on your way. She can keep you company,' I smiled.

'Not just Milly . . .' he began.

'Well, pick up some Heineken as well,' I grinned.

And on that thought, he strode off, with a half-hearted wave of his hand.

'Ring me if you have any trouble,' I shouted after him. But all I got by way of reply was a, 'Not staying the ruddy night, you know.'

I had only just fixed the back door, a little cack-handedly, I'm afraid, as I'm no carpenter, locksmith or DIY merchant, when the telephone rang. Arabella went to answer it and within seconds, was shouting for me.

'Ron Ball was already out, when Gus arrived,' she whispered, then handed over the receiver. Gus repeated the same message.

'Know where he's gone?' I enquired anxiously.

'His mum doesn't rightly know. Seems someone rang him, then he said he had to go out, but wouldn't be long.'

'Does his mother know who might have rung or where he might have gone?'

'Nope. Seems he answered the phone. She was dusting upstairs. Didn't hear nothing of what he said. And he didn't ruddy say where he was off to. Just said he wouldn't be long and not to worry.'

'Great,' I sighed. 'That's all we needed.'

'What shall I do now, then? Stick around until he comes back or . . .' His voice trailed away, as he realized an 'or' didn't really exist. For he could hardly go searching for him. Dorset may be small, but it's not that small.

'Did he take the van?' was my next question.

'No. It's still in the drive. Went off on foot, he did, so he can't have gone that far.'

'Used to travel quite a way at night on foot,' I reminded Gus.

'Oh, yeah. Forgotten that. 'Ere, that's given me a thought. Think he's gone round to Mrs Maitland's place? I mean, he might have, mightn't he, seeing as how he's a bit dotty about her, like. Want me to drop by her house and see. . . ?'

'No, Gus. You stay where you are and ring me again the second Ron Ball returns.'

'Yeah,' he mumbled. 'So you do think he'll be coming back, then?'

'I don't know, Gus.' I closed my eyes. 'I really don't know.'

The second I put down the receiver, I picked it up again. To ring Chrissie Cartwright. To ask her to ring Mary Maitland on the pretext of seeing how she was getting on, but really, to check whether she had seen anything of Ron Ball. For I was somewhat hesitant to ring her myself direct, in case I put the fear of God in a woman who was obviously still not fully recovered from the shock of her terrible ordeal. But, sod's law, Chrissie was out, for answer came there none. I hesitated before ringing Mary

Maitland's number, but then had visions of her at the mercy of a Ron Ball about whom I might prove to have been so tragically wrong. If even the slightest harm came to her, I would never be able to forgive myself.

So I dialled. The dring-drings seemed to go on for ever, but just as I was giving up hope, I heard a click and her hesitant voice say, 'Yes, this is Corfe 759632.'

'Mary?'

'Er, yes. Who's that?' ·

'Peter Marklin. You know, the toy . . .'

'Yes, yes, yes,' she cut in hastily. 'I remember. Is that what you're ringing about? The old toys? Want to make the date to go through my collection, is that it?'

'Yes, I do some time, certainly. But that's not the prime reason I'm phoning.'

'Got a new lead on Maurice's death? Is that it, Mr Marklin? If so, please let me know. Or even ring the police. Now that they've released that ice-cream fellow, they probably need all the help they can get.'

'So you know about Ron Ball?'

'Yes, yes. Chrissie Cartwright told me. She heard it on the local radio.'

'Well, I'm sorry to disappoint you, but I haven't really got any solid news about anything. I was just phoning to check if you knew Ron Ball had been released, that's all.'

There was silence for a moment, then she said, 'What, are you worried about me or something? Is that it? Worried I might be . . . well . . . in some kind of danger, now he's out and about?'

I cleared my throat. 'Yes, well, I don't want to panic you or anything, because I still feel Ron Ball is probably innocent of your husband's murder, but nevertheless, knowing that he seems to have some kind of crush on you . . .'

I heard a quiet laugh. '. . . he might come round again in the hope of catching me in the altogether, is that your worry, Mr Marklin?'

'I suppose so, yes.'

'Don't worry. I'll stay indoors, if you like, fully dressed – even though I was considering doing a little topless sunbathing this afternoon, now that the rain has stopped and it's warm again. My whole body somehow feels in need of the injection of something stimulating. The sun's rays would be as good a start as any, don't you agree?'

Before I had time to comment any which way, she concluded, 'Come to think of it, why don't you do your toy evaluation this afternoon? Then you could kill two birds with one stone. Be around to protect me, while I get in a tan in the garden *and* advise me on the value of the toys and how best to dispose of them.'

Had I been wearing a collar, I would have felt a little hot under it, right then.

'Thanks all the same, but there are a few things I have to get on with this afternoon, I'm afraid.'

But she seemed reluctant to give up the idea.

'Like what, Mr Marklin? The sun's come out again. I could make a jug of cooling Pimms. And I'm sure you needn't be long in the attic and then . . .'

'Another time, I'd love it, but really this afternoon . . .'

'I'm disappointed in you, Mr Marklin. I thought a man like you would jump at the idea of combining business with pleasure.'

I decided I had better tell her. 'On a normal day, I might. But this morning someone burgled my shop and I have to stick around in case the police might want to see me again.'

'Oh, my goodness. How dreadful. Anything valuable stolen?'

'Could have been worse. Whoever it was missed all the best stuff, I'm glad to say.'

There was a moment's silence, then Mary Maitland said hesitantly, 'You don't think that . . . Oh Lord, it could be, couldn't it?'

'Could be what?'

'Well, the ice-cream fellow has been released. And we know he's not above stealing toys, is he?'

I didn't answer directly. 'It could be anybody who did it, I'm afraid. There are a lot of old toy collectors around these days and a lot of them with more enthusiasm than money to indulge it.'

'How dreadful. I'm so sorry, Mr Marklin. Still, I'm sure the police will want to include this Ball chap in their list of suspects and who knows, you might get your toys back in no time.'

And on that uplifting note, I tactfully tried to draw the exchange to a close, with a last admonition to keep a wary eye open for anyone lurking around her house or garden.

'I will, Mr Marklin, don't you worry. By the way, do you want me to call you if I spot anything untoward?'

'If you would. But only after you've called the police first.'

'Yes. I see the sense in that. Well, goodbye for now. Don't forget to ring again soon about coming over.'

As I was about to bid her goodbye, I suddenly heard the sound of breaking glass in the background.

'Mrs Maitland? Are you all right? What's that noise?'

She laughed. 'Oh, don't worry. It's not someone breaking into the house or anything. It's just me. I seem to be getting so clumsy recently. I just dropped a glass of wine I was drinking when you phoned. Shattered on the tiles, that's all.'

I was, needless to say, immensely relieved and told her so.

'That's nice, Mr Marklin,' she said affectionately. 'I mean, nice to have a man concerned about my well-being. You see, after donkey's years of dear Maurice, I'm afraid I'm a bit of a sucker for anyone who shows me an ounce of care and sympathy.' Then she added, very quietly, 'Especially right now.'

After a quick lunch, there was little that Arabella and I could do but hang around anxiously for Gus to ring with, hopefully, news that Ron Ball had returned from his walk-about. Everything else would really have to await that. So, as it was Saturday afternoon and normally one of the better selling times of the week, I opened up shop. And lo and behold, I almost immediately started having customers. And what's more, real punters rather than G & T's.

Within half an hour of opening, I had sold over two hundred and fifty pounds' worth of goodies, ranging from fifties Dinky and Corgi cars to a Bayko house constructor set and a chipped Dinky 'Queen Mary' liner. Which turnover slightly lifted my troubled and anxious spirits and somewhat lessened the affront of the burglary.

But the telephone did not ring for a further twenty minutes. Arabella was first to it, but then shook her head and mouthed, as I caught up with her, 'Not Gus.' I sighed and bent my head to catch who it was, but I needn't have bothered. Arabella instantly supplied the answer.

'Yes, he's here, Inspector. Would you like to speak to him?'

A second later, she handed me the receiver.

'Yes, Digby, what can I do for you?'

'Two things, Mr Marklin,' he answered firmly. 'One, tell me where you are hiding Ron Ball. And two, leave that Fiona Fairchild well alone. You've muddied the water on that one far too much already. Now let's get back to Ron Ball. What have you done with him? His mother tells me he had a telephone call and then went out. When we went round there, who do we find but your fisherman friend, Mr Gus Tribble? It wasn't hard to put two and two together, since we've known for yonks that you've been up to your ears trying to protect Ball from his just desserts.'

'Inspector,' I protested, 'I'm afraid your arithmetic is well out. Two and two do not make nine hundred and forty-eight. Okay, I admit I'm involved in the Maitland affair, but only to try and see justice done, I assure you. But Gus Tribble only went to the Ball house to check things out after my burglary this morning. You have, no doubt, heard by now that I've had a break-in.'

'Yes, we've heard. And that only wind-up toys were taken, Mr Marklin. That's why I sent my boys round to see Ron Ball this morning. But he isn't there, no one will admit to knowing where he is and so far he has not returned. Now I warn you, Marklin, if you've had anything to do with spiriting him away to protect him from the law, then you're in serious trouble. I have been very accommodating of your antics on this case so far, but now . . .'

I could not let him get away with that last remark.

'Really, Digby, don't give me all that "accommodating" garbage. You've only not interfered with my so-called antics so far on this case, because you thought I might be able to lead you to the real murderer faster than any of your own force – including your good self. That's why you've had me tailed.'

Digby laughed scornfully. 'My dear Mr Marklin, do you realize that if you hadn't thought yourself so ruddy clever delivering that message to me the other day, your burglary might never have happened. You see, because then I might still have had a patrolman keeping watch over your shop. A real case of being too clever by half on your part, I think you'll admit.'

I ignored his barb, even though it did have a modicum of relevance. 'Digby, just listen to me for a minute. I promise you I haven't spirited Ron Ball away anywhere and that Gus is only there to see that no one makes an attempt to frame him for my burglary this morning.'

'So you don't think he did it, is that it? Even though the toys were all clockwork. Would you mind telling me what divine insight has given you that idea?'

'Nothing divine about it. Just the nature of the toys taken and the unlikelihood of anyone, let alone Ball, committing a burglary so soon after release from a police cell.' I went on to expand on both and Digby, for once, did exhibit the courtesy of listening. His reaction at the end was fairly vintage Whetstone, though.

'Don't think the same thoughts have not passed through our minds, Mr Marklin, but nevertheless, we wish to interview Ron Ball right away. Now would you mind telling me where you think he might be.'

I took a deep breath. 'I hope I'm very wrong, Inspector, but since you ask, I think if he does not turn up very soon, he may be in serious danger.'

'Danger? Really, Mr Marklin, what kind of danger?'

There was only one reply to that.

'The mortal kind, Inspector, the mortal kind.'

Gus rang only seconds after I had put the receiver down on Digby. But, curses, all he had to report was what we knew already. That the police had been and indeed, were still at the Balls' house and that they had given him a really hard time and only then allowed him to make a quick telephone call.

He ended by asking if I wanted him to stay all the time or would it be all right if he dropped out for a bit and left Milly there. He knew what my answer would be, before he asked. But you have to admit, he's always a trier, especially if he feels he's losing out on an hour or two of opening time.

As I wandered sadly back into the shop, now distinctly rattled by the possible ramifications of the Ball disappearance, a customer blew in, full of the joys of . . . well, spring, I guess.

'Hello, sir, hello,' he beamed heartily.

I nodded a greeting. 'Can I do anything for you, sir?'

'Not sure, really. That's why I thought I ought to come in.'

'Come in?'

'Yes. Into the shop, you see.' He swung the barrel of his body around and pointed to the window. 'Saw your military stuff displayed on that . . .' he hunted for the right word.

I helped him out. 'Diorama. Otherwise known as a plastic hill with ditto hedgerows.'

He guffawed. 'Oh yes. Very good. Splendid. Makes a nice display.' Coming up to the counter, dispensing the unmistakable aroma of whisky over me and my stock, he went on, 'That's what caught my eye. You know, might have missed the old tanks and stuff, if they'd just been stacked like those other toys.'

Bully for my Diorama. 'So it's military vehicles you're interested in, is it? Do you collect them?'

He shook his head and his dewlap wobbled like a cow's at milking time. 'Not really. But used to be in the Tank Corps. During the war, you know.'

He looked me up and down. 'Long time ago now. Bit before your time.'

At least I wasn't looking as old as I felt, right then.

'So, how can I help you?'

'Oh, yes. Sorry. Of course. How can you help me? Well, I saw the Chieftain tank and the German Leopard – quite an enemy, that one, I can tell you – and the Daimler Armoured Car and so on in your window, which set me wondering if you have any models of the actual tanks I commanded over the war years. Might like to buy one or two if you have, you see.'

'Well, give me the names of the types you're interested in and I'll let you know if any manufacturers produced them and whether I have any in stock.'

'How kind,' he gushed. 'Now then, let me see. I started off with a rather effective little infantry tank – used at Alamein amongst other places – called curiously the "Matilda". Finest British tank of the early war years, by far.'

I shook my head. 'No, I'm sorry. No one has ever made a model of that one. Let's hope we have better luck with your next.'

'Next up would, I suppose, be another infantry tank used at Alamein – the Valentine. Not at all bad when it had an American engine fitted, but a bit noisy and unreliable when it didn't.'

He looked at me hopefully. But again I had to disappoint him. 'No, drawn another blank, I'm afraid.'

'Oh, dear, oh dear,' he grimaced. 'Only got two more to go.'

'Try me,' I smiled.

'Well, let's try the one with which I finished the war. Splendid tank in almost every way. Trust it to be American. The Sherman.'

He detected my smile instantly.

'You have one? Or could get one? That right?'

I came out from behind the counter and went over to a stack of 'Solido' die-casts, amongst which I knew was the model he wanted. I took it and handed it to him.

'Sorry the box is a bit battered. But I bought it in with some other "Solidos" the other day.'

He carefully took the khaki tank out of its box and appraised it.

'Yes, this looks to be pretty accurate, as far as I can remember the original. How much?'

'Well, it's not really a vintage toy. This one was made in the seventies. So let's say fifteen pounds.'

He looked somewhat relieved. 'Well, I'll take that one then. Splendid.'

'And your last?' I enquired.

'Ah, my last. Yes. Well that would be a rather big and clumsy monster. But jolly useful on D-Day and all through Normandy. Named after our great wartime leader.'

'Churchill.'

'Yes, Churchill.'

I hated to shake my head yet again. 'No, sorry. No one has made one of those either. In die-cast, anyway. Had you said the American Lee or the German Tiger, I could have obliged. Or a bren-gun carrier.'

'No, it's the Churchill I would have liked.'

He reached for his wallet and from it extracted three crisp five pound notes. 'Well, here is for the old Sherman. I guess no one is likely to bring out the Matilda, Valentine and Churchill at this late stage, are they?'

Suddenly at least a thousand light-bulbs flashed above my head and I held on to the counter, as I had visions of what they might be illuminating.

'No, no, no,' I stuttered. 'I doubt it, in die-cast.'

But my brain was saying it reckoned it might well know someone who *had* trotted those very vehicles out recently, but for a very different purpose.

Thirteen

My mind was in such a turmoil that directly my 'tanks for the memory' man had vamoosed, I just had to shut up shop for the day.

Arabella caught me slipping the bolts and consulted her watch.

'Early yet,' she observed, then added with a knowing wink, 'Oh. I can guess what you're planning to be up to, now, my darling.'

'No, you can't,' I smiled back.

'Yes, I can.'

'No, you can't.'

'Yes, I can.'

'One more time. No, you can't.'

'You're off to join Gus at the Balls'.'

'Balls. I'm not.'

'Balls to you too. Then if you're not on the Ball, then you'll be going to Wareham to your fancy piece.'

'No fancy piece.'

'Savage?'

'No Savage.'

'I give up.'

'Told you you couldn't guess.'

'All right. So I was wrong.'

I took her hand, and led her quickly into the house.

'Look. The reason you couldn't guess, my sweet, is that I've only just had it.'

She screwed up her face. 'Had what?'

'That guy who's just been in the shop . . .'

'You've had that guy who's just been in the shop. Really?'

I play-smacked her hand. 'No, don't fool about. We may have to act fast. You see, something he said, I've heard before. But in a different context.'

183

Now, I could see she was listening. So I explained my theory. By the time I had finished, her beautiful mouth had dropped quite open enough for even the most inquisitive and probing of dentists.

'What do you think? Could be, couldn't it?' I asked, hope against hope.

She put a hand to her brow. 'Wow! I suppose so. But it could still be a giant coincidence. After all, tanks are named after people and not usually the other way round.'

'Granted.'

She thought for a bit. 'So you think the code might be covering three different people or just one?'

'Don't know. But if it is a code, then it would be quite a clever twist to use three different names for the one person, wouldn't it? I mean, if you're trying to cover your tracks and make out you're innocent as the day is long, then using three names enables you to have three times the number of assignations with . . .' I hesitated. Arabella looked at me.

'Yes. There lies the rub, doesn't it? Assignations with whom?'

I held up a hand. 'Hang on a minute. Let's think. Now, if those are code-names, I don't reckon it's just a coincidence they happen to be the names of tanks, do you?'

'Maybe not.'

'So . . . whoever thought of using them must know a little about military machines, history and tanks in particular.'

'Could be.'

'So . . . I therefore doubt that a woman is likely to have dreamt up their use.'

'So the lover or lovers or whatever might have.'

'Exactly.'

'So . . .' she imitated me, 'said person or persons must have that knowledge.'

'So . . .' I grinned, 'said person or persons might just have some connection with the military.'

Arabella's eyes suddenly burned bright enough to indicate a thousand bulbs were now illuminating her brain.

'Oh, my Lord, I've just had a thought.'

I looked behind my shoulder. 'Addressing me?'

'No, idiot. Look. It's staring us in the face. What's just up from Wareham and Wool?'

I frowned. 'Blandford Forum?'

184

'Not as far as that. Between Wool and Bere Regis.'

'Countryside. And a bit spoilt at that.'

She held up a finger. 'And what is it a bit spoilt by?'

'Why, like a lot of land round here. By the military.' Then suddenly it hit me, and now my eyes must have flared a thousand watts, for Arabella said, 'Get it?'

'Got it.'

'Good.'

'Tanks.'

'Don't mention it,' she smiled.

'And the tank museum is on that road.'

'Right.'

'Anyone who has anything to do with that museum or the division of the armoured corps that's stationed round here, will know all about the history of Matildas, Valentines and Churchills.'

She saluted. 'Exactly, sir.'

'So . . .'

'So . . .' she mimicked. But she could get no further, for she was interrupted by one of the juiciest kisses ever this side of Florida and Hollywood.

Fourteen

But our elation was somewhat short-lived. For it speedily dawned on us that finding a possible assignee amongst the hundreds of men that must be stationed at Bovington camp, was like looking for the proverbial needle etcetera.

So we plonked ourselves down in the sitting-room for, as Arabella termed it, 'further deliberation, your worship'.

Neither of us spoke for a while, each, no doubt, scurrying up possible mental avenues, only to find they're cul-de-sacs. I think it was Arabella who broke the silence first, with something like, 'Where could they have met, I wonder?'

'Met?'

'Yes. If it's just one chap the code-names stand for, she must have met him somewhere.'

'If it is a chap.'

Arabella looked askance. 'But just now, you said you doubted that a woman would think up a code based on tank names.'

I nodded. 'Yes. That's true. Thanks for reminding me. Besides, a woman would hardly need a code to cover meeting another woman or women, would she? If the code was invented for the poor husband, then I doubt he was the type who would suspect anything naughty in a female relationship.'

'Okay. So let's go back to it being a male. And a male who may have something to do with Bovington Museum or the military camp. Where could they have met?'

I shrugged. 'Almost anywhere, I suppose.'

'But from what Chrissie says, Mary Maitland hardly went out when her husband was alive. Except, I suppose, for shopping or to Chrissie's or whatever.'

'That is until she met the code-names.'

'Right.'

'Well, she did go one place alone, come to think of it. At least over recent months.'

'Where?'

'The beach. What's more, we know she went frequently. Her tan shows that.'

Arabella curled her legs up underneath her on the settee. 'Good. So she could have met him on the beach.'

'The naturist end, remember.'

'Ah. So there's just a chance he might be a naturist too.'

'Or just a wobbly-bit watcher.'

'Either.'

'Or both,' I grinned.

'So, we have a tank type, who might just be a Health and Efficiency fan. Any other place they might have originally met?'

I racked my brains and came up with, 'How about that fancy-dress ball that Mary dragged her husband off to. Remember? That's how he apparently met the fancy piece. So it might be where Mary first met . . .'

'. . . her fancy piece. Could be.' She smiled to herself. 'A touch ironic, if true, don't you think?'

I nodded. 'Wonder if your conjectured assignee actually went to Fiona's to choose *his* costume.'

Arabella looked distinctly dubious. 'Can't see a military type hanging round in that poncey place to . . .'

I suddenly reached across and grabbed her arm. 'Hang on, darling, I've just remembered something.' I sat up straight, nearer her. 'Something Gus said the other day. That he had seen an officer type hanging around Fiona's place the day he did his first piece of sleuthing on the Maitland case. And he mentioned that it was the same guy he served in my shop some days later. The guy collected . . .', I spelled it out like a lip-reading teacher, 'T.A.N.K.S.'

'Tanks?'

'Yes. Lovely green, camouflaged tanks. And what's more, he's been in once before that, when I served him.'

'How long ago?'

I could see the drift of her question and I searched my memory bank. 'Not too long. Since Maitland was murdered, I'm sure.'

'H'mmm,' was Arabella's guarded response.

I h'mmmed alongside her.

Then she offered, 'It may all be stretching things a bit far, but now we could have a tank-type with an all-over tan, who goes to fancy-dress parties . . .'

'Only one we know of,' I cautioned.

'Correction . . . went to a fancy-dress party and who collects vintage military toys.'

'Further corrections. If it is the same man who came into my shop, and he spoke the truth, he has only recently taken up toy-collecting and what's more, he's not into toys in general, but just die-cast tanks.'

'So he's a recent collector . . .'

I gripped her arm once more. 'Hell, he might not even be that. Or a collector at all. Don't you see? He might have come to the shop, not for toys, but to check me out. Discover what this amateur sleuthing guy he's been told about is really like.'

Another 'H'mmm', then she added, 'So what's *he* really like? He didn't by any chance give you his name, did he?'

'Well, he's around thirty-five or so, I suppose. Not too bad looking in an old-fashioned, "anyone for tennis?" kind of way.'

' "Anyone for volley-ball?" more like it, if our guesswork is correct.'

'Or "anyone for murder?" maybe,' I grimaced.

'Name?'

'Ah, now he did give me it, I'm sure. I sort of recall it had something about it that made it easy to remember.'

'And you've forgotten?'

'Ah. Now not so fast . . . it was something to do with . . . yes, that's it. This area. He had the name of a place round here.'

'Wouldn't be Bovington, by any chance?' she twitted.

I scowled back. 'No, don't throw me. It was . . . it was . . . MORETON. That's it, Moreton. You know, up Owermoigne way. And his Christian name was . . . Duncan, that's it. Reminded me of my great uncle Marklin. He was a Duncan.'

'Duncan Moreton,' Arabella toyed with the name. 'Sure it's his real name? I mean, it sounds a bit too much of a coincidence to have a guy stationed down here whose monicker is the same as a local village.'

'You're right,' I mused. 'Anyway, if this guy is who we think he might be, he might well not use his real name. Blast. Blast. Blast.'

We were silent for a moment, then Arabella asked, 'Think we might just be being silly about Valentine, Matilda and Churchill being code-names for a lover or lovers?'

'Could be. But it would explain quite a few of the little mysteries, when you come to think of it. One, why Mary has never introduced her so-called feminist friends to the very woman who started her on the liberation road – Chrissie Cartwright. Two, why no one else seems to have met them either. Three, why, when I ask Mary about them, she doesn't proffer their addresses or any real information about them. Just fobs me off with "one lives miles away in Bristol". And the other two are incommunicado across the Atlantic.'

'Four,' Arabella added, 'it might explain why Mary suddenly developed a passion for naturism. Like, he might have introduced her to it in the first place.'

'And what better place to meet than in the dunes behind that end of the beach? You could lose yourself there in no time.'

'Or find yourself,' Arabella observed wryly.

'Even if you were observed by someone, nudity is so commonplace round there, that a necking couple with no clothes on wouldn't raise a . . .'

'Never mind what it wouldn't raise,' she smiled. 'So where have we got to now? That Mary Maitland may have had a lover or lovers over the last few months – which also, Peter, might help explain her seeming change of character from church mouse to liberated lady. But Mary having a lover or lovers doesn't really get us any nearer to discovering who murdered her husband . . . or does it?'

'Exactly,' I smiled. 'It might. Think of it this way. First of all, I'd better say, I doubt if it's lovers in the plural. Mary doesn't strike me as quite that type. So, say it's a lover in the singular. She's attracted to him, imagine, for the moment, at that fancy-dress ball. They begin meeting secretly. He introduces her to nudism and so on and gradually learns more and more about her. But not only about her. Also about her husband.'

Arabella's eyes brightened. 'I'm ahead of you. He quickly learns about his extremely valuable toy collection . . .'

'. . . officers in the army don't earn a fortune and if Mary left her husband for him, she'd have to bid goodbye to the million pounds' worth of toys . . .'

'. . . so gradually, an idea occurs to him or maybe to both of them, that if the husband died before their affair became public . . .'

'. . . they could both live happily ever after in the lap of comparative luxury.'

'Providing their consciences let them.'

'The army doesn't have much time for consciences. Don't forget a soldier is trained to kill and not to think too much about the why's and wherefore's or the ethics of his whole calling.'

'But Mary's track record is hardly heartless. Look how she's looked after her husband's every need over all those years.'

I had to agree with her. Our scenario was not all that impossible until you came to Mary's character. There it did certainly falter. For, as Arabella had pointed out, when discussing her own personality in relation to the television offer, people just can't make themselves into something they fundamentally are not. Unless . . . and it was this 'unless' I offered up.

'Mary was dominated by her husband, right?'

'Right.'

'So, she has exhibited a character trait of subservience.'

'Maybe.'

'So, it's just possible that she is playing the same subservient role with this lover. He thinks up dastardly plan and so dominates her that her natural instincts are overridden and she agrees to go along with it.'

But Arabella rapidly side-stepped that one and went on to major flaw number two in our latest scenario. A flaw of which I was only too well aware.

'Okay. So the lover, I suppose, just could have browbeaten someone like Mary into going along with such a heinous plan, but it still leaves us with the fact that she was very badly beaten up herself that night. Now, I'm just about willing to concede mental browbeating could have occurred, but *physical* browbeating on *that scale*, just to throw the police off their scent? I can't see any woman or anybody, for that matter, agreeing to that. Anyway, a token beating up would have been quite sufficient. There was no need for one that is still hospitalizing the poor woman yonks later. And don't forget, she'd still be there, if the doctors and nurses had had any say in the matter and she hadn't signed herself out.'

'Touché,' I sighed.

'Yeah.'

I turned round to her. 'But supposing they hired a contract killer and he just overdid it. Went way beyond his instructions. Remember, anyone who is into the contract killing business is hardly a squeamish sort of soul who fights shy of violence and blood.'

'Some sadist who enjoys beating up women?'

We both looked at each other. Then I got up instantly from the settee and took her by the hand.

'We're wasting time sitting here. If we think there is even a shred of possibility in this theory, we should begin checking it out right now.'

'Where do you suggest we start?'

'We'll finish at the Tank Museum. But as Wareham is on the way, it might be worth, say you – she won't let me again, I wouldn't imagine – popping into Fiona Fairchild's shop first, and trying to discover whether she might know the name and identity of that army officer Gus saw in her place. I'm sure, on the way, we'll be able to invent some plausible story to explain why you need to know.'

A moment later and we were in Arabella's Golf – my yellow Beetle being a trifle too conspicuous – and heading for Swanage and Wareham.

We were half-way through Plausible Story number three, when we heard it. I saw Arabella peer into the rear-view mirror to check which of the services it was. I looked over my shoulder and the expanse of shiny red told me instantly. Arabella slowed and pulled in as far as possible to the side, without actually ripping the door handle off her car.

The fire-engine roared past us. Still a stirring sight for the likes of me – and for anyone who has not exchanged that last whit of childish wonder for one hundred per cent stolid adulthood.

'Wonder whose wiring is faulty today?' I grimaced.

'Or who is trying to pull a fast and fiery one on an insurance company,' Arabella nodded.

'Or who's careless with cigarette ends.'

'Or who's trying to burn his wife to a crisp.'

I frowned across at her. 'Arabella, how is it that all your conjectures are criminally orientated, whilst mine are so innocent and accidental?'

She laughed. 'Must be the Maitland case. Getting to me.' Looking across at me, she added, 'Or maybe it's just living with a guy who's perpetually getting himself up to his armpits in murder and mayhem.'

'Good word, "mayhem". Must be one of the most all embracing words in the criminal dictionary,' I mused.

191

'Never mind about that, my darling,' Arabella reminded me, 'let's get back to what I'm to say to your fancy piece. We're almost there.'

I looked back through the windscreen. We were, indeed, almost there. But by the look of the queue of traffic ahead of us, a snail could make it to the fancy-dress shop quicker than we would.

'Must be the fire,' Arabella observed.

I pointed ahead. 'Yes, look, you can see the lights flashing up at the far end of the High Street. They've probably got half the street blocked off. Or maybe, the whole of it by now.'

As we inched forward, it became clear that we were right and very soon we saw the smoke billowing up from the roof tops.

'A shop, most like,' Arabella mumbled.

'Shop? Yeah . . .' My heart suddenly missed a beat. 'SHOP,' I shouted. 'Hell, you don't think. . . ?'

Arabella obviously did think, because she instantly ran the Golf up the nearest piece of pavement free of driveways. A second later and we had abandoned the car and were running like scalded cats past the stationary vehicles ahead of us.

We were just in time to witness the horror of the glass window, with the words 'Make-Believe' in fancy gilt script, explode with the searing heat and scatter shards left, right and centre over the pavement.

No one was hurt by the flying fragments, as the police and firemen were keeping everyone well back from the now fiercely burning shop. Arabella suddenly left my side and disappeared towards an ambulance pulled up two shops away. I stayed where I was and tried to get some sense out of the police officer standing next to me, keeping the considerable gathering of gawpers away from the scene.

'Anybody inside?' I shouted over the crackle and roar of the flames.

'Not any more,' he bellowed back. 'Unless there was more than one person in the shop, when it went up.'

'Who got out?' I persisted. 'Was it the owner?'

The officer firmly took hold of a spotty youth who was trying to dodge around him.

'Back you go, sonny, unless you want to end up as a bit of toast.'

He raised his eyes to the heavens. 'God! Some people.'

'Who got out?' I repeated, then coughed as the wind directed smoke our way.

'A woman. Don't know who she was.' More waving of arms, accompanied by a load of 'Get back, will you's and 'Please give the firemen room to breathe's.

'Was she around thirty and. . . ?'

He turned round to me, his eyes now no longer obeying rule number whatever in the police manual of Good Public Relations. 'Really, sir, don't bother me now. I don't know, anyway. Her face was so blackened, she could have been young or old as Methuselah.'

The officer moved a little away from me, I assume to advise a lady with a pram that the smoke and fumes might not be the best diet for a growing one-year-old. I tried to scan the crowd for any sign of Arabella. But no sooner had I started, than I felt a tap on my shoulder. It was the subject of my quest.

'She's alive, anyway,' she shouted rather breathlessly, above the noise of the flames and the ambulance sirening away up the street. 'Managed to have a word with the driver.'

I leaned close to her ear. 'Fiona?'

She nodded. 'Yes. He said she was the shop owner, anyway.'

I took Arabella's arm and led her back through the rapidly growing crowd and down the High Street to where you did not have to compete with all hell let loose to converse.

We stopped outside a newsagents. 'How bad is she? Could you find out?'

'All the driver would say is that she's suffered considerable burns, but that she was conscious and he didn't think her condition was critical. Oh, and he added that luckily her face was not too affected. Apparently, she had protected it with her hands.'

'God,' I sighed. 'I suppose no one said anything about how the fire might have started, did they?'

'Not directly, no.' Arabella took my hand. 'But listen to this, Peter. On my way back to you, I overheard one of the firemen saying that there was a distinct smell of petrol when they first arrived.'

I let it ring, and ring and ring, and ring. But not a dicky bird. I looked at Arabella.

'I think we ought to get over to the Tank Museum,' she sighed.

I waited another twenty or so drings, then put down the receiver.

'Okay. But it would have been nice if she'd answered, wouldn't it?'

Arabella nodded. 'She could be out shopping. At Chrissie's. Or on the beach. It's a lovely day for it. Or just lazing in the garden and not able to hear the telephone.'

We both left the call-box and got back in the car.

'Still, it would have been a relief, if she'd said, "Hello",' I reiterated, as Arabella slipped into gear and headed away from Wool.

'Pardon, sir?'

I showed the attendant again the page of the thirties Dinky toy catalogue that I'd brought with me.

'I was saying that I recently sold these two toy tanks here,' I pointed to the small black and white pictures of the Vickers Medium and Light tanks, 'to a gentleman I believe may work here at the museum or be stationed at the camp.'

He peered short-sightedly at the catalogue. 'Oh, very old, are they, sir?'

'Late thirties,' I said. 'Like the real things.'

'Ah,' he sniffed, 'that Vickers Medium. We have one of those here in the museum, you know. Lucky to have it. Only one left in the world, I believe. That what you've come to see?'

'Not exactly, no.' I glanced at Arabella, who gave a slow blink. 'No, as I was explaining, I sold these old toys to this gentleman the other day and now I've managed to find two very much better examples of their kind. And thus I'm trying to trace him to let him know. He didn't leave me a phone number or anything, you see.'

At last the attendant seemed to be roughly on the right wave length. 'But you think he may have something to do with Bovington, right?'

Arabella took over. By the hardly disguised leer she received, I could see the questioning had passed into more promising hands.

'Let me try and help,' she smiled sweetly. 'The man we are looking for is certainly in the army, an officer around thirty-five or so, fairly good looking in a conservative kind of way.' She looked at me. 'Moustache?'

194

'Yes, as I recall,' I replied. 'Close-clipped, military style. But biggish mouth.'

'Yes, largish mouth. And he did give a name but we can't quite remember it. We think his Christian name might have been Duncan. And his surname something like Moreton. But we really aren't sure of either.'

The attendant rubbed his blue chin. 'No, I know most of the officers stationed in the camp. I can't say I know any Duncan Moreton. And you must understand, there are quite a few with moustaches around the age you mention. Isn't there anything else you remember that might. . . ?'

Arabella raised a delicious digit. 'Ah, yes, now thanks so much for reminding me.' (Oh, bully for you, my darling. That's the way to do it. Creep.) 'Now you mention it, there are one or two other things he mentioned that might help. He said he attended a fancy-dress party not so long ago and that he was a bit of a naturist. That's why he said he comes over to Studland – that's where we both live – so often.'

A broad smile now spread across the British blue. And he, in turn, now raised his own (not a happy contrast) finger.

'Why didn't you say so in the first place?'

'You mean, you might be able to help us?' Arabella gasped, with breathless anticipation like a *Girl's Own* heroine. By golly, the girl was playing well that day.

The attendant blushed. Least I think he did. The blue seemed to turn purple anyway.

'Well, I won't promise anything, but I do happen to know one of the officers over at the camp is, well, a bit of a lad.' He cleared his throat. 'The others rag him a bit about his goings-on. One of the things I know they twit him about is his, well, going to that . . . er . . . nudist beach of yours.'

'It's not ours,' I muttered, but he did not seem to hear. Which was just as well, I suppose.

'Some time ago now, I also heard that he dressed up as, would you believe, the Duke of Wellington for some fancy-dress do or other. He gets around, does our Captain Railton.'

'Railton? Arabella queried.

'Yes, that's his name. Railton. Captain Spencer Railton. Not Moreton, I'm afraid. Nor Duncan.'

We both thought for a moment, then I asked, 'You don't happen to know his full initials, do you?'

195

Now it was his turn to ruminate. 'Well, I think he's an S. D. Railton. But to be sure, I'd have to check over at the camp.'

'D for Duncan, perhaps?' Arabella fluttered at him.

'Perhaps, Miss, but as I say, to be sure, I'd have to . . .'

I cut him short. 'What does he look like, this Captain Railton? I mean, would our description fit?' •

'Yes, I suppose it does. He certainly has a moustache and is in his thirties. But whether he's good looking or not, I wouldn't know. Men don't ever know things like that about other men. Now if you were to ask me about good-looking girls or women . . .'

But alas, we hadn't waited to pose that conundrum and were making it out of the building and back to our car, as fast as my nylon and her cotton socks, respectively, would carry us.

Enquiries at Bovington Camp itself, however, got us nowhere. Oh yes, the powers that be eventually confirmed that a Captain Spencer Railton was stationed there, but without an official letter of authority or a pass, we were not allowed any further information – especially concerning his present whereabouts.

It was only as we were dejectedly leaving the camp that we learnt any more. And that was strictly unofficially – from a young officer in an old, open MGB who happened to be spluttering (on no more than two and a half cylinders, by the sound of the engine) towards the camp gates. From the battered suitcase stacked on the passenger seat, I took it he was returning from leave.

So, nothing ventured, etcetera, I stopped him and explained, with Arabella's seductive help, our supposed dilemma vis-à-vis the Dinky toy tanks and how we would like to meet up with Captain Railton to inform him of my new finds.

'Oh yes, old boy, matter of fact I've seen the ones you sold him. He showed them round the mess one night. Didn't look too bad to me considering their age.'

I assured him the fresh discoveries were quite superior.

'So you'd like to meet up with Spence, that it?' He tipped his lieutenant's cap back off his forehead. It left a red line. 'You've come at rather the wrong time, old boy. Old Spence is on leave right now. Don't know quite where he's hiding himself. Never do with Spence.' He winked. 'But knowing him, I wouldn't be surprised if he wasn't with some lady friend or other.'

I upped eyebrows at Arabella. Her eyes flashed the rude version of, 'Oh, tut, tut.'

'When do you expect him back?'

He looked at his watch. Presumably for the date, considering his reply. 'Another four days. No, I tell a lie. Five actually. Due back five days from this morning.' He waved a hand and revved what was left of his engine. 'Better get going now. Do you want me to give old Spence a message or anything?'

I waved my own hand. 'No, no. Don't worry. We'll catch up with him . . . or somebody will . . .'

Seated back in the Golf, Arabella sighed and looked at me.

'So what now, Ercool Parrot?'

I shut my eyes in thought. 'We'd better get back. Gus may have been trying to get hold of us. Besides . . .'

'Besides what?' She started up the engine, and performed a masterly reverse through two closely parked ranks of cars. Then we were off at a rate of knots, back towards Wool and home.

'Besides, I think I ought to contact Chrissie.'

'Chrissie? Why?'

'To tell her what's going through our minds.'

'Re, who we think the Misses Churchill, Valentine and Matilda may be?'

'Yep. Funnily, it may not come as such a huge surprise to her as it did to us.'

'Why?'

'Well, I've had the feeling all along that Chrissie's been a bit suspicious of these so-called new-found feminist friends of Mary's. She's nobody's fool, you know.'

'I could see that. But why do you think she hasn't said anything about it to you?'

'Mary is one of her best friends, don't forget. I'm still a comparative stranger. Thing called loyalty. Besides, whilst she may have had suspicions, she may not have realized the women may be men.'

'Or a man.'

'Anyway, she probably doesn't connect her suspicions, if I'm right and she has any, with the husband's murder. Two different things, maybe, in her mind.'

Arabella flashed me a knowing look, as she braked for a tank transporter that was turning off to the left.

'Two different things. Like that poor Fairchild woman and Maitland's murder.'

'Now don't let's go running ahead of ourselves,' I cautioned. 'We don't have any proof yet of any of our suspicions.'

'So how the blazes . . . whoops, I shouldn't use that word, after what we witnessed in Wareham, should I? . . . are we going to get any proof? This Railton fellow is not expected back for five days and . . .'

'That's what I'm going to discuss with Chrissie.'

She reached across and gripped my knee.

'Why? Have you got a plan?'

'Sort of.'

She squeezed harder.

'Aren't you going to tell me?'

'Won't need to, will I?' I smiled. 'You'll be with me when I'm trying to set it up.'

Fifteen

Chrissie Cartwright looked from me to Arabella and then down at her lap. A sigh seemed to be her only response. And we hadn't told her all our suspicions by a long chalk.

'I'm sorry, Chrissie,' I went on quietly, 'but we ought to check. If only, as the law says, to eliminate it from our enquiries.'

She rose from her chair and went over to the window.

'I was with her only half an hour ago. I popped over to ask if she would like to go into Dorchester with me. She said she would rather stay home. The headaches, apparently, are no better. I told her she should never have signed herself out of the hospital . . . too soon, by half.'

She turned back to us. 'Know what she said? "Too late, by half". I didn't like to ask what she meant. She seemed, I don't know, as if she was in a different world, somehow, this morning. She spoke almost as if I wasn't there, if you know what I mean.'

'As if to herself?' Arabella commented.

'Yes, you might say that. Maybe it was just the drink. By the looks of the bottle, she had got through a few glasses of wine by the time I called. Poured me one, but then dropped it handing it to me.'

She returned to her chair. 'Oh, I'm not sure, Peter, that today is quite the right time to bring up . . .'

I looked at Arabella. She nodded.

'I still think we ought to, Chrissie. Look, if you like, you handle the call. Then, perhaps, if she is really feeling too rough to respond, then she will tell you. Whereas she might not feel she could tell me.'

Chrissie forced a slight smile. 'All right. If you think we ought to. Now what do you want me to say?'

'Just that I have rung you and said that I've discovered something out at Bovington Camp that might have a bearing on her husband's death. And could she come out to meet me at the Tank Museum in, say, an hour or so.'

'And if she says she can't or won't?'

'Then we will have to think again. But anyway, it's very important to try and read her reaction accurately. Like, is it one of shock and surprise? Or merely dismissive and uninterested? Or the whole notion laughable, or what?'

'The "what" being does her response sound genuine, whatever it is?' Arabella added. 'Or is it a bluff?'

Chrissie rested her head in her hand. 'You want me to ring right away?'

I nodded. 'Better get it over with.'

She reluctantly got up and started to walk towards the door into the hall. 'I pray you're wrong, Peter.'

There was no reaction I could really give.

Then she added, 'But if you're right, it will have been all his doing, you know. Not Mary's. She would never, ever, ever do . . .' Then she turned and went out of the room. A second later, we heard the ding of the receiver being taken off the hook.

We were back at the Tank Museum within fifty minutes. I asked Arabella to stand guard in her Golf in the car-park to give me warning of any lone woman either driving in or being dropped at the entrance.

'All right,' Arabella shrugged, 'but I don't know why we're doing this at all, really. Mary told Chrissie she did not feel well enough to go anywhere today.'

'But remember Chrissie's comment,' I cautioned, 'after she had put down the phone? She said . . .'

'. . . that Mary just sounded like she did earlier. In a sort of daze. That's not a sign of guilt or anything. That's just a sign of how ill she still must be.'

'All right,' I conceded. 'So we may be wrong, and on a wild goose chase. And if after a while, she doesn't turn up, then we'll pack it in and go home. But we ought to give it a couple of hours.'

I got out of the car, but Arabella wound down the window.

'It may not be Mary who turns up, don't forget. So watch your step, my darling. Just remember what soldiers are trained to do.'

I boy-scouted a promise. 'You be careful too. If anyone approaches the car, who bears the slightest resemblance to Railton's description, start up instantly and get the hell out of here.'

200

'And leave you?'

'What can he do in a museum?' I wishfully thought. 'And anyway, if he starts anything, I'll just jump in a tank and shut the lid.'

'You do that,' Arabella scowled, as she waved a farewell.

To kill time, I wandered down the memory lanes between the giant, iron-clad exhibits, their guns pointing directly forward, as if aimed at ghostly enemies that still rumbled across plains and pastures of long ago. There were few people about to admire their now silent, stationary power and brutal majesty; due, I supposed, to the brilliance of the afternoon that beckoned beaches rather than beachheads, to the enjoyment of a peaceful present, rather than a wartime past.

I stopped eventually by the tall, upright silhouette of the Vickers Medium tank about which the attendant had told me on my earlier visit. And rivet by rivet, armourplate by armourplate, compared it with its miniature replica made by Dinky. The accuracy of the toy manufacturer had been quite outstanding, for not only was the detailing precise and correct, but the 'feel' of the vehicle had been totally captured. It is this elusive 'feel' that always marks out the greater from the lesser toy designers. For this quality, alas, is not just the sum of accurate details, but a look, an aura, a presence that almost exists outside the world of physical dimensions.

It was whilst I was losing myself and my worries in this particular form of escapism, that I was awoken by a car horn from outside, repeated four times – the signal Arabella and I had pre-arranged.

It took me a little time to make my way back through the massed ranks of armour to the museum's entrance and I cursed my stupidity in having strayed so far from the doors.

By the time I got to the ticket office, there was no sign of either Mary Maitland or the man I assumed now to be Spencer Railton and not a Duncan Moreton. Somewhat embarrassed now, I enquired of the collector whether a woman had just paid to enter. He confirmed that one had just gone in and pointed to the right. But there was no sign of anyone there, the tanks obscuring most lines of sight.

Cursing, I ran off in the direction he had indicated, but rounding the first rank of tanks produced not a dicky bird. And certainly not a Mary Maitland. I retraced my steps and ran on to the next opening between the iron dinosaurs, but again, no luck. Just a child on his father's shoulders peering into the open hatch of a gun turret.

I now knew I might just as well have been in Hampton Court maze. The only difference was that the hedges were made of armourplate. For the tanks were crowded into a building, in essence too small for them. So that gaps between vehicles were minuscule and certainly did not give broad views of the next narrow alleyway between the rows.

My silent swearing reached new heights (or is it depths?) and I could feel myself trembling with both frustration and anger at my own easy seduction by the Vickers Medium and its Dinky toy connection. After a second's hesitation, I ran on to the next alley, but only two elderly gentlemen with clipped moustaches frowned back at me. No doubt, in their old boys' brigade book, 'twasn't form to run around like a Dervish in such a hallowed hall of remembrance.

However, I did explain my actions a little by asking them if they had seen a lady of Mary's description anywhere around. But their reply was interrupted by a sudden sharp clang of iron on iron that reverberated to the very rafters.

'No, can't say I . . . Oh, my goodness, Carstairs, what's that? Someone meddling with one of the exhibits, I'll be bound. If things go on like this, I'm afraid we'll have to shut museums to the general public and just keep them open for special . . .'

But I didn't wait to hear any more. For I had suddenly realized what might well have caused those rafters to ring.

The clang had seemed to me to come from one of the two ranks just in from the entrance. So I belted back to the nearest of the two and slowly went down the completely deserted aisle, my ears peeled (maybe you can't peel ears, only eyes) for the slightest hint of a sound from any of the tanks. But other than the hushed sound of voices elsewhere in the museum, I could hear nothing.

Reaching the end of that aisle, I was just turning round the worn tracks of a tank to go back up the next one, when I bumped into something far softer than the leviathans. For a split second, I thought it might be my quarry, but it turned out to be Arabella looking for both of us.

'God, you gave me a shock,' I gasped, but all Arabella would say was, 'Where is she? Didn't you hear my horn?'

A speed-of-sound explanation then ensued, which seemed to leave her speechless.

'So,' I concluded, 'it just could be that she may have got into one of these monsters for some reason known only to herself.' I took her hand. 'Anyway, I'm sorry, but that's all I can think of right now to explain her disappearance and it would fit with the clanging noise.'

Arabella exhaled, as if letting her tyres down, then we both started up the second aisle.

'But most of them seem to be well battened down,' she pointed out. 'How on earth do you get in them anyway?'

'Through their turrets. You must have seen them in war movies. Richard Burton popping up with binoculars and then popping down again and shutting the lid.'

'That means we'd have to clamber up on every tank and open its lid. I can't see the attendants letting us do that for very long. Besides, while we were busy clanging away, she might hear all the kerfuffle and get out from wherever she's gone and escape.'

I sighed. 'She doesn't want to escape, Arabella . . .'

She closed her eyes. 'Oh, no, no. Hell, I see what you mean.' Then suddenly her eyes opened wide and she exclaimed, 'Peter, do you know where the Valentine is? Or a Churchill? Or a Matilda?'

I pointed across the museum. 'The Churchill is way over there. I passed it just now.'

'The Valentine?'

'I don't know if they've got a Valentine. Haven't seen one yet.'

'And the Matilda?'

'Just over there, Miss.'

We both whipped round to see an attendant pointing to the end of the row we were in. We had not heard him come up behind us.

'Here, I'll walk up with you,' he offered. 'Heard a noise just now that seemed to be coming from somewhere in that area, so I thought I'd better investigate.'

We started walking with him, only too willingly.

'Always have to be on the look-out. Kids, you know. Only last month, we had one lock himself in a Sherman. Took us over three hours to get him out. Turret hatches lock on the inside.'

He chuckled. 'Have to, you see, otherwise only too easy for any enemy to leap up and lob a grenade inside.'

We at last stopped by the Matilda. A smaller vehicle than I had been expecting. Almost innocent looking beside some of its neighbours, with heavy guards over its bogie wheels that Arabella later described as making it look like a schoolboy with his trousers falling down.

'There you are, Miss. The Matilda,' the attendant proudly announced. 'Not a great tank, ever. But a real saviour for the Tank Corps in the early stages of the war . . .'

I cut him short. 'Look. Can I ask you a favour?'

He blinked. 'What's that then, sir? I'll do whatever I can.'

I pointed up to the turret. 'It may sound silly to you, but would you climb up and see if anyone has got inside it?'

He frowned. 'Inside it, sir? What makes you think anyone might have done that?'

'A lady I know came in here and has disappeared. When I heard the same noise just now that you heard . . .'

'You put two and two together,' he smiled, then tapped the side of the Matilda with his knuckles. 'Well, sir, if there is a lady inside here, it'll be the first time in the museum's history . . .'

Again I cut him off. 'Please would you hurry? It could be a matter of life and death.'

A thought he dismissed instantly. 'No, no, sir, there's no need to worry. These things are not air-tight, you know. Weren't when they were new. Certainly aren't now they're old and broken and rusting through in a few places.'

He put a foot into the indentation in the bogie guard and was about to mount up, when we heard it. Not a clang this time, but a dull, muted thud. Coming from inside the thick, iron skin. Then another thud. Then another. Then another and another.

'Oh my Lord, sir,' the attendant panicked. 'There *is* someone inside. And God knows what damage they'll be doing.' He started up towards the turret with an agility his stolid appearance belied.

God knew, indeed. A moment later, he announced what Arabella and I had been dreading all along.

'It's locked, sir. Whoever it is has locked themselves in.'

The thuds, though continuing, were now less intense. Then, abruptly, they stopped, to be followed by a longer, softer, less regulated noise. Then nothing. Nothing. From *inside* the tank, that is.

For very soon, the attendant's fists started to pound on the turret, accompanied by shouted warnings as to the penalties that could be incurred for damaging museum property.

But response came there none. And after a while, I stopped even looking at his efforts up at the hatch.

Dejectedly, I stood in front of the tank and stared at the floor, Arabella holding firmly on to my hand. It was then that we both saw the first drop. A tiny stain, darkened almost purple by the hulk of the chassis. Then one more, and another, like tears shed for the evil this Matilda had once lived through, for wars long since over, lost or won. And maybe, who knows, for conflicts and violence yet to come. Tears for man and womankind, without whose aggression and cupidity Matilda and her like would never have emerged from the darkness to stalk the sunny uplands of our fragile world.

It took nearly two hours to get Mary Maitland out. And I still shudder when I remember the limp body being raised from the turret, her forehead an unrecognizable bloody wound of pulped flesh, streaked with wire-thick strands of hair, stiffened by the gore that welded them. Even the army personnel aiding the police and ambulance crew seemed to go groggy at the awful sight. The inside of the tank, they told me later, was almost as gruesome. Flesh stuck to levers and projections, where she had deliberately struck her head time and time again until she had at last and mercifully slumped senseless across one of the seats, her head dangling downwards to drain the last of its life-blood through a hole in the floor.

Digby Whetstone had arrived in time to witness the last horrifying moments of the recovery of her body and the instant it was stowed aboard the ambulance, had me and Arabella closeted in the museum's office.

I had been expecting him to be furious at the revelation of my activities and the suspicions that had led me and, via me, Mary Maitland to Bovington Camp Museum. But if he was, for once in his life he made a reasonable job of disguising it. And even kept quiet to the very end of Arabella's and my admissions, when he said with a certain amount of accuracy, 'Well, at least you didn't go haring after this man you now reckon might be the murderer. That's one relief.' He held up a freckled sausage. 'Not that I'm agreeing with any of your conclusions, mind. Not by a long shot, yet. But I will go along with you this far. We need to talk to this, what did you say his name is. . .? '

'Captain Spencer D. Railton.'

'. . . this Railton fellow, as soon as possible. If only to see if he can throw any light on why Mrs Maitland reacted as she so tragically did to your . . . pardon, your friend, Mrs Cartwright's phone call.'

Ah, at last, the traditional Digby dig. But I didn't resent it. After all, it certainly seemed as if Mary Maitland would still be alive, if I hadn't asked my 'friend' to lift her receiver. Right then both Arabella and I felt a deep sense of guilt about the result of our stratagem, if not the stratagem itself.

'You say he's on leave?' Digby continued.

I nodded. 'Due back in about five days, according to a fellow officer we talked to. But he had no idea where he'd gone for his leave.'

'No matter,' Digby grunted. 'We'll soon track him down. Anyway, when he sees about all this on television or in the Sunday papers, he will probably contact us. That is, if he has any connection at all with poor Mrs Maitland.'

'But only if he's innocent, Inspector, don't forget that.'

His eyes went to the ceiling. 'Please, Mr Marklin, please . . . I've bent over backwards to be forbearing over your continued interference in this case, now don't try my patience any further. We know what we're doing far better than you.' He sat back in the only chair in the meagre office and smiled thinly. Least, I think it was a smile.

'Your harrying of Mrs Fiona Fairchild is a fine example of how very wrong you can be. Do you realize that you nearly jeopardized a police operation that I had been conducting for months now? That lady, whatever her other faults, certainly is no murderess. It wasn't in her interests to kill Maitland. I can't tell you all the details now and certainly not while Mrs Fairchild is in hospital, but . . .'

I looked at him.

'You mean she wouldn't have murdered Maitland because he was one of the golden geese.'

He frowned. 'Geese?'

'Yes, Inspector. A goose that lays golden eggs, but only if it gets laid itself. Mrs Fairchild's fancy-dress business is not her main form of income, is it? But sexual fantasy is, right? Arranging for

206

her so-called customers to act out their fantasies and perversions, all dressed up as who they would most like to be. Headmasters, schoolboys, slave girls, Roman emperors, Nazis, schoolgirls, headmistresses . . .'

I did not need him to reply directly. I could see from his eyes that I had hit the right button.

I went on, 'Maitland was never her lover. I should have seen that from the start, I admit. He was always her client. God knows what his kink was, or what costumes he chose for himself and her to wear for their little fantasy dramas. No doubt Fiona will tell you, if and when . . .'

'By the way, Inspector,' Arabella cut in, 'what's the latest on her? Is she going to be all right?'

Digby nodded. 'From what we hear she should make a complete recovery. The burns she suffered are nearly all first degree.'

'Know who started the fire?' I asked.

He pursed his over-red lips. 'Oh, so you reckon the fire was arson and not accidental, do you, Mr Marklin? Now what little bird has told you that?'

'A rather tall bird, holding a hose and wearing a brass helmet.'

Arabella shouldn't have said that, for Digby now exploded.

'For God's sake, you two, don't get involved in the slightest ruddy way with any aspect of the Fairchild business. We are well on top of it and need your interference like a hole in the head. Got it?'

I raised my hand like a schoolchild in class.

'Can I ask one last question? I promise it's the last.'

He sighed like a bull walrus that had just finished mating. 'All right. What on earth is it?'

'If it was arson, have you any idea who might have done it?'

He first looked at me and then at Arabella.

'Why ask me? You profess to know all about that Make-Believe shop and who its real customers are. Ask one of them. If they're as kinky as you say, any one of them might have done it, wouldn't you say?'

I shot a glance at Arabella. Her eyes said, 'Cool it,' which fitted my thoughts to a tee. So I changed the subject.

'No word on Ron Ball, I suppose?'

'Oh Lord, you're not banging away about him again, are you? I suppose you're worried now about those toys of yours that were stolen. No. For your information, there's no word on him yet, but like I said about this Spencer Railton of yours, we'll find him sooner or later, don't you worry.'

This time, I sighed. But not like a walrus who'd just wotsit-ed. 'Let's just pray it's sooner, Inspector, don't you think?'

A moment later and we were on the road back, not to Studland and home, but to Corfe and Chrissie.

She took the news in sad silence. And did not speak for quite some time after we had finished. Then she said generously, 'It's not your fault, Peter. Nor yours, Arabella. Please don't think it is. Or that I feel that way. I don't.'

I quarter-smiled our appreciation.

She continued, 'Though Mary is . . . was, I suppose, my best friend, she had really changed quite a good deal over the last months from the Mary I used to know. And since poor Maurice's murder and her injuries, she has been hardly well enough, either mentally or physically, to be anybody, really. Let alone her old self. But even so . . .'

'. . . you can't believe she was involved with her husband's death.'

She looked away. 'No, I can't. For though she had certainly changed, as I've said, people don't alter their characters totally, now do they? And the Mary I knew all these years would certainly not have conspired with anybody to kill a jack-rabbit, let alone a human being.'

'All we can think,' Arabella said quietly, 'is that Mary may have been the kind of person who was fairly easily dominated by men. And that, if we're right, this Railton may have been the evil genius behind it all. Or even, for that matter, he may have done it all on his own, without her knowledge. Then after an appropriate time, he could marry the wealthy widow.'

Chrissie turned back to us. 'It's a more comforting thought, but it doesn't quite fit with Mary's suicide today, now does it? I can hardly credit that she would take her own life, just because someone had discovered she'd lied about having feminist friends and actually had a lover.'

'She was hardly herself,' Arabella pointed out. 'You've said so. Maybe her brain . . .'

A thought suddenly hit me like a thunderbolt and I shot up out of my seat. Both Arabella and Chrissie stared up at me as if I were mad.

'What on earth's the matter, darling?'

I struck my head with the flat of my hand.

'My brain. That's what's the matter. Or rather, not mine. Hers.'

'Mary's?' Chrissie frowned.

I forced myself to sit down again and leaning forward, went on, 'Chrissie, you said the other day that you know Mary's doctor.'

'Yes, I do. But as I said then, he won't tell me . . .'

'He probably will now,' I stopped her. 'Once he's heard of his patient's death. He will know he'll be called at the inquest, anyway. Then everything about Mary's health will become public.'

'All right,' she sighed. 'I'll give it a try. But I still don't see how knowing about her injuries at this stage will help us.'

'That's the point, Chrissie,' I said excitedly. 'We have been assuming all along that it was her injuries that were the cause of her being hospitalized.'

'Well, of course we did, Peter. What else could it have been?'

I got up and took Chrissie's hand to lead her out to the hall phone. 'That's exactly what you are going to try to find out right now.'

'Did you know him?' Arabella asked on the way home.

'No. He was dead before I was born. But Mother used to talk about him occasionally. I suppose because, not only was he her brother, but his last days were so bizarre.'

'Not quite as bizarre as . . .' Arabella began, then stopped.

'Well, it might have been. If he'd been married to a mean and dour mate, who browbeat him and was worth a fortune. And then met someone he really fell in love with and wanted to marry. Especially if this someone put the idea into his head.'

Neither of us spoke for a while. We just watched the Purbeck countryside paint the car's windows with the quiet and idyllic peace our souls cried out for that day. Then just before joining the Swanage–Studland road, Arabella said, 'From what you say about how it affected your uncle, it could have changed Mary's character completely, couldn't it?'

'A frontal lobe tumour doesn't exactly change your character. But as Mary's doctor confirmed just now, it makes you behave as if it had.'

'By freeing the person of all inhibitions.'

'Well, a lot of them, certainly. More in some people than others, he said. My uncle turned from a quiet, kind, loving sort of guy into a heavy-drinking, womanizing lout, according to my mother. And no one knew why, until he finally collapsed.'

'Without inhibitions, we entertain thoughts and actions that normally we would suppress or recoil from. In Mary's case, like being unfaithful or . . .'

'Murder. What a freedom,' I grimaced. 'If only Mary Maitland had stopped at naturism or fancy-dress parties.'

'Perhaps she did,' Arabella muttered, with very little conviction.

'No wonder that gorgon of a nursing sister would not reveal anything but that Mary would be kept in hospital for quite some time.'

'And no wonder Mary released herself from hospital the instant she'd been told she had only a short time to live.'

'Well, wouldn't you? The last hours are too precious to spend cooped up in bed or curtailed to carbolic corridors.'

Arabella looked at me. 'Especially if you've still a few things to do. Uninhibited things. Like taking revenge on the woman who you think seduced your husband . . .'

That thought finally put paid to further conversation, until we were safely locked away in our little home in the west and refreshing and fortifying our souls with the fire of that other demon – alcohol.

Sixteen

There was very little Arabella and I could do now but wait. For the finding of Ron Ball and Spencer Railton was way beyond our limited resources and had to be the first priority now for Digby Whetstone, his boys, his banks of inter-force computers and his power over the media. As regards the latter, we were disappointed. For nowhere on that Saturday evening's TV news did we see an appeal for a Captain Spencer Railton, believed on leave in the west country, to come forward to help the police with their enquiries, etcetera, etcetera.

Gus, naturally, was hardly chuffed about Ron Ball's continuing absence from home, but at least thankful that I had relieved him of his vigil over at the mother's house. When he at last dropped by on his way down to his cottage, he also expressed his appreciation for the fact that the ice-cream vendor seemed now to be absolved from suspicion of murder, if not yet of burglary.

'But that'll come too, old bean. Don't you worry. Them toys were planted all right. Said so right from the start now, didn't I? I reckon that there officer chap got that poor Maitland woman to work on young Ron, so that he'd get a thing about her. Hang around the house, like, on the off chance. What d'yer think?'

I thought he could be right and said so. 'He or she might have heard or read that he had been had up before for being a peeping Tom. So then, they would estimate that with a little encouragement from her, he might put himself in a nice compromising position, suitable for framing, as they say.'

Gus sniffed, then having drained his second Heineken, commented, 'Doesn't help us find him right now, though, does it?'

Impeccable logic, as always, if hardly a sequitur. Still, you have to be thankful for small mercies with Gus.

'No,' I said, quite unnecessarily.

211

'Where d'yer think he is, then?'

I didn't want to worry him, so I left out the most deadly of options. 'Depends whether he's been kidnapped or has gone off of his own accord. If someone has taken him, it's most likely to be this Railton fellow, if our guesses are right. The police didn't find any trace of him at Mary Maitland's house. I've rung the Bournemouth police and checked.'

'And if he's not been kidnapped?' Gus asked, displaying his now empty glass in his usual subtle fashion. Arabella obliged. With a fresh Heineken, that is.

'He could be hiding away almost anywhere, terrified that the police are going to slap a murder warrant round his neck at any moment.'

'Which they're not,' Gus hoped.

'Well, we hope they're not. But he probably doesn't know that yet.'

'Poor bugger,' Gus muttered. 'Wish we could think of where he's ruddy gone to. Or been taken to.' He took a long draught of his lager, as if to lubricate his grey cells, then suddenly looked up at us both.

' 'Ere, if that army bloke took him, where would he be most likely to hide him? I mean where he wouldn't be likely to be found in a hurry.'

I shrugged, deliberately not mentioning my first vision of a trench some six foot under, or my second vision of a considerably deeper, liquid grave.

Gus, now a-quiver with brainwaves, shuffled his body around in his chair. Bing, who had been on his lap, took exception to his sweater tremors and flopped down on to the floor with nary a backward glance.

'Well, 'ccurs to me that the army, like, have got plenty of empty buildings about the place nowadays, seeing as how they're cutting back. He might be held in one of them.'

'Might be,' Arabella concurred, then looked at me. 'Perhaps we ought to suggest it to Digby . . . or perhaps not.'

I thought for a minute. 'This army property idea of yours, Gus, . . .'

'Yeah,' he looked up expectantly.

'. . . well, they own more than empty Nissen huts round here.'

'You can say that again,' he muttered. 'For donkey's years nearly all the land round Lulworth has been closed off for their

212

sodding war games and manoeuvres. Can't hear yourself break wind round there sometimes, for the bangs and thumps and crumps, and the whoosh of bloody shells and rockets. Cor, if they ever return that land to its rightful owners, they'll spend the next ruddy century sorting out the unexploded mines, shells, rockets; you name it, they'll be digging it up.'

During this homily, Arabella had been looking at me and directly Gus had run out of steam, she said to me, 'I know what you're thinking.'

'Well, a restricted firing range has to be one of the better bets to search, I would have thought.'

'Yeah,' Gus added, 'and there are still old buildings on that land, you know Bit knocked about now, I should think, after all these years, but you can still see some of them from the road. Barns and stuff.'

'Perhaps you should contact Digby after all,' Arabella urged. 'He may not have thought of the firing ranges.'

I gave a sort of non-committal nod. Not because I disagreed, but because I had just thought of an additional person who I reckoned should be fed the information.

'What's the problem?' Arabella frowned.

'No problem,' I countered and then went on to explain my thinking. When I had finished, Arabella looked a little sceptical.

'I don't know them that well yet, you know,' she explained. 'They might not do it.'

'Worth a try though,' I encouraged, 'isn't it?'

'Okay. I'm willing to give them a ring. But I've got nothing to bend their arm with.'

I got up and went over to her. 'Think of it this way. If the idea works, you'll be a super-newswoman . . .'

'Girl,' she smiled.

'. . .super-newsgirl in their eyes.'

'And if it doesn't?'

'I'll still give you a kiss for trying,' Gus cut in, with a king-size leer.

Naturally, with that kind of inducement, Arabella could hardly refuse. And she didn't.

Arabella straightened her arms. Her breasts, up to then squashed against my contrastingly flat chest, swung free.

'I guess we ought to get some sleep now,' she yawned. 'Can't make a sandwich of you all day. Sorry, all night.'

'And just as I was thinking we might stick together forever,' I grinned, reaching out and switching off the bedside lamp.

'Quite literally, if we're not careful,' she joked, as she rolled off to her side of the bed.

It was some time after our respective 'Goodnights. Sleep tights. Snug as a bug in a rugs' routine, that Arabella suddenly remarked, 'If this fellow Railton was her lover, it must have been awful for them, mustn't it?'

'Awful?' I queried, my mind by then half-mesmerized by the sandman.

'Yes, awful. The secrecy, I mean. Not being able to go freely together anywhere they wanted, always furtive little assignations. Think of it. You and I having to meet just in cars or remote sand-dunes or . . .'

'. . . motels in Bristol.'

'. . . wherever. It must have been horrible, degrading even. And having to stoop to inventing code-names to explain her absences.'

'But necessary,' I pointed out. 'That is, for the murder to come off without suspicion and Mary Maitland to inherit the million that the old toys will fetch.'

Arabella snuggled into my side. 'Doesn't bear thinking about, does it?'

'Nope. So don't let's.'

'Deal. Goodnight.'

'Goodnight.'

But 'good' was not exactly the most apposite adjective for the night that ensued.

At first I thought it was Bing prowling about downstairs. I am often woken in the dead of night by paws toppling ornaments, wobbling saucers on quarry tiles or claws sharpening themselves on chair legs, door-jambs or even curtains. But somehow, the noise that night, to my ear, did not seem to fit with Bing's usual repertoire. So, carefully so as not to wake the sleeping beauty, I eased myself upright in bed, all ears, as they say.

I heard nothing for around half a minute and was just about to mouth a silent curse and settle down under the covers again, when a creak re-awoke all my senses. It was quickly followed by another. Which was immediately followed by my swinging out of bed, my heart now thudding like the guns Gus had described around Lulworth.

The creaks continued and they were getting louder. No Bing, no cat outside a tiger, could exert that pressure on my old stair treads. Good as Whiskas claims itself to be, I doubted if it built bodies that fast. My hand instinctively felt around in the darkness for something to wield or throw, or anything. But in reality, I knew there was nothing of the slightest use in the bedroom. After all, I didn't collect motoring trophies, bronze or otherwise.

As my only last resort, I flattened myself against the wall beside the bedroom door in the hope that at least I could surprise the intruder, should he decide to try to come in.

The creaks I could hear now were of a different quality. And nearer. So whoever it was, was now on the landing. I braced myself further up against the wall. God knows why, but I guess it was fear that governed my actions rather than brain and cunning planning. Anyway, tense as a bow string, I waited. And waited. And the more I waited, the more terrified I became that Arabella would sense my absence from the common-law style conjugal bed or hear the intruder's movements and shout out or . . . My mind boggled.

The footfalls suddenly stopped right outside and a second later, I heard the faint rattle of a hand on the old brass doorknob. I raised my right hand above my head, like I had seen Karate Kings do in movies and, for that matter, perhaps more appropriately, Inspector Clouseau.

In a thin shaft of moonlight, I could just see the knob slowly turning. I was poised. I was primed . . . The door slowly opened. And I froze, right hand already a third of the way down its karate chop. For in the intruder's hand – but sod's law, the one furthest from me – glinted the cold muzzle of a gun. And it was pointed directly at the bed and Arabella.

All I could do then was to reach for the switch next to me and flash on the main light in the room. For any false move on my part might well have caused the gun to go off and I didn't dare risk a bullet going anywhere near Arabella.

My eyes blinked against the sudden glare. But so did the intruder's. I reckoned I had one advantage. I knew what I was going to do and he didn't. Shouting 'Arabella, keep down' to

215

attract attention away from the bed, I threw myself at his legs in the nearest I could muster to a rugby tackle.

He certainly stumbled, but that was about all. And as I continued my struggle to bring him down, he must have got impatient. For in next to no time, I felt a blow to the head that . . . well, ended my little story for a good fifteen minutes, according to Arabella's smart, slim-style tick-tock.

I came to on the bed. Next to Arabella, who had the bedclothes pulled up to her chin. At first, I couldn't quite make out what I was doing. Waking up and finding the light on was somethng Arabella and I had only ever done once. And that was right at the hectic start of our relationship, for reasons that should be plain to even the most unsophisticated of us.

'Arabella . . .' I grunted and blinked.

She lowered the clothes enough to lean over me and ask, 'Peter, are you all right?'

I raised myself on one elbow. 'Yes, I think . . .' but then, suddenly the pain at the back of my head took all the words out of my mouth. And no sooner had I put a hand to the lump, than I saw our visitor. Sitting opposite us by the window and holding his little friend that had put paid to my new rugby career.

The sight, luckily, brought me instantly to my senses.

'Railton,' I gasped.

'That's right, Mr Marklin.'

I sat up straight and looked at him. Curiously, even with the gun, he did not look too menacing. Much as I remembered him, in fact, from his two visits to my shop. Not a man to set the world alight, exactly. And yet . . .

'He's told me a little about it,' Arabella whispered. 'Now he wants to tell you.'

'Go ahead,' I winced, as my head throbbed with pain. 'But first, tell me why you've come to *me*?'

'The television,' he replied quietly.

I would have frowned, had I not guessed it would hurt too much.

'But they didn't mention me on the late-night local news round-up.'

He gave a thin smile. 'But really, Mr Marklin, who else could it have been?' Mimicking a news announcer, he went on, ' "We've had a call from a listener who believes he knows where the missing Ron Ball may be. Somewhere on army property on the firing ranges around Lulworth . . . recommends the police should get over there as soon as possible." Dear, oh dear, did you expect I was so dumb I wouldn't work it out?'

I shook my head. Big mistake. Lump took exceptional exception. 'I didn't much mind. You see, I only asked them to transmit that report in the hope that both you and the police would hear it. If our guess was anywhere near the truth and you'd heard it yourself, you would realize the game was now up and there was little to do but surrender to the proper authorities.' I winced yet again. 'And I'm hardly the proper authorities, Captain Railton.'

'And I'm not surrendering, Mr Marklin.'

'Maybe not,' I rejoined, now starting to get my senses and courage more together. 'But the net is closing fast. You see, by just coming here, you've more or less given away where Ron Ball may be and what's more, that you must have been his kidnapper.'

'Untrue,' he scowled. 'It was Mary's idea to phone him. Mary picked him up in her car.'

'But you must have spirited him away on to army property. No one else would have or, for that matter, could have.'

His eyes flicked round the room, as if his brain was at a loss as to where to land.

'All right, I confess that I took Ball on to the range.'

I looked at Arabella. She shut her eyes. I swallowed hard, then asked. 'So where have you hidden him? In one of those ruins that your army guns have deigned to leave standing?'

'Maybe.' He looked away.

'Look at me,' I ordered, in as stern a voice as I could manage. Surprisingly, he glanced back at me. 'Is he still alive? He'd better be, you know.'

There was no instant reply, then he said, 'He was when I left him.'

'What do you mean by that? That now he could be. . . ?'

'That was Mary's idea too, you see,' Railton said quickly. 'Everything's been her idea right from the start. You must believe me.'

'The idea being, no doubt, that with any luck, he would be found killed by a mine or a shell or a rocket or, at least, later, you'd see that you faked it that way. No doubt, somewhere nearby would be found the toys you yourself stole from the shop,

217

thus pointing the final incriminating finger at Ball as the man who burgled and killed Maitland that night. That's right, isn't it?'

He didn't reply.

I tried to get out of bed, but Arabella, bless her, reminded me I had no clothes on. Marvellous, isn't it, how modesty prevails in even the most dramatic and tragic of circumstances? I can see lovers sleeping on the *Titanic* being more concerned with donning their Sunday bests than life-jackets. Hey, ho.

Resignedly, I stayed where I was and rapped, 'When was the last firing practice out there, Railton?'

He hesitated, then said, almost in a whisper, 'Still on . . .'

This time I did get up and I was painfully aware, not of my nudity, but of his gun pointing at my vitals.

'It's all right, I'm . . . only . . . dressing,' I said falteringly, waves of dizziness sweeping over me as I reached for my clothes off the bedside chair.

'You've no need to dress, Mr Marklin. You are not going anywhere.'

'Oh, yes I am. And so are you. Downstairs to the phone first and then . . .'

I had only got to trousers and socks, when he rose from his chair and came over to me. I had never realized how cold muzzles of fire-arms can be on naked flesh. If you run out of ammunition, you can literally freeze someone to death.

'Stay where you are, Marklin. I haven't finished yet.'

I glowered. 'Finished *what*, Railton?'

'I think he wants to convince us,' Arabella intervened discreetly, 'that it wasn't his idea to kill Maitland.'

I lifted mine eyes to the heavens. 'Oh God, here we go, here we go, here we go. Don't tell me that you are going to plead that poor Mary Maitland bullied you into all this, are you? You, a macho officer of Her Majesty's Tanks Corps . . .'

His eyes flickered. 'I know it must sound crazy to you, but it's true. All true. I didn't realize it at the beginning when we first met on the beach. She seemed all soft and loving and desperate for help. But really, all along, she was playing with me. Working me up so that, when she at last came up with the idea, I'd be so besotted and sorry for her, I would agree to almost anything.'

'My other foot has bells on,' I said, contemptuously.

'No, it's true, you must believe me. Don't you see, she'd

218

obviously nursed this hatred and resentment of her husband for so many years, that it just had to explode in the end.'

'You know she's dead? Killed herself at the Tank Museum?'

He moved back from me. I could now see the moisture welling in his eyes.

'I . . . I know,' he stammered. 'I saw it reported on television.'

'Whose TV?' Arabella asked. I'd quite forgotten we still had no idea where Railton had been hiding away.

'The motel I've been staying in.' He anticipated the next question. 'Near Bridport.' He jabbed the gun towards me again, but now I reckoned the gesture was much more defensive than offensive, a means of making a point rather than causing a death.

'Anyway,' he went on, 'surely that's proof of what I'm saying. She committed suicide because her guilt got too much for her.'

'Mary Maitland had a terminal brain tumour,' I interrupted. 'They found out when she had to go into hospital. News like that could be enough to make the most balanced of us wish to end it all.'

Railton seemed not to take it in at first, but then moved slowly backwards to resume his seat on the chair.

'Oh God . . . how . . . terrible . . . terrible . . .'

For the first time, he relaxed the arm of his gun, which now would do more damage to my floorboards and carpet than to Arabella and me. But I made no move. I was starting to feel, in time, I just might not have to.

'. . . hell, I knew I hadn't hit her that hard . . . just enough to make it look like she'd been attacked . . . that's all . . .'

'No, you may not have hit Mary that hard,' I sighed, 'but the blow you struck Maitland was in a different league altogether.'

He looked up and now the glint was on his cheeks. 'I was only trying to help . . .'

I lost my patience. 'Help yourself to a million pounds, you mean.'

'No, no, no. I fell for Mary *before* she told me about the toys. You must believe me . . . PLEASE . . .'

I moved cautiously over towards him, despite Arabella's cry of 'Peter, for God's sake, don't.'

He remained seated, staring up at me.

'Please. Please. It was all Mary. Not me. Not me.' His grip on the gun relaxed even further. 'Can't you see? She worked that Ball fellow up so much he didn't even know left from right. And she did the same to me. The same bloody thing. No difference. Only Ball was to be the fall guy and me the . . .'

I moved even closer. 'Murderer,' I said in measured tones. Neither of us spoke for a second, then I asked, 'Why did you come here, Railton? Because you thought I'd prove a more likely sucker for your sob story than the police? So that if and when you decided to turn yourself in, I'd be batting on your side like you obviously know I have been doing for that unfortunate Ron Ball?'

He shook his head. I envied him his ability so to do. Right then, the hot hammers in my brain were starting to give me double vision.

'No, no, no. I know you're not a sucker . . . I just wanted someone to know my side of things before . . .'

'Before *what*?'

He suddenly re-aimed the gun at my vitals. Or rather, I suppose, the singular vital.

'I'm going now.' He rose from the chair. 'Get back, Marklin.'

'You have nowhere to go,' I said quietly. 'It's all over, Railton. They will track you down wherever you hide. Here. In another county. In another country.'

I decided my time had now come. I offered my hand and said firmly, 'Give me the gun, Railton. Give it to me. We may still have time to prevent another death, if you surrender right now.'

He hesitated, then trembling, turned the gun around and proffered it to me, butt first. I took it and Captain Spencer D. Railton collapsed on to his knees and grasped my legs in supplication. Above his desperate cries for God's or, I guess, anyone's help, I said, 'Now you are going to ring Bovington and call off that bombardment.'

I prodded him with his own weapon and he slowly got to his feet. I led him like a lamb to the door and held his hand all the way downstairs. It was then I realized that there might be more than a germ of truth in Railton's version of the Maitland murder. And that a hand more delicate but more deadly than mine might well also have had no trouble in leading him to places he had no real desire to go.

Ron Ball was found bound and gagged in the ruins of an outbuilding on the firing range. Much to my insurance company's relief, beside him was a large Gladstone bag, full of my toys. Whilst just about alive, he was to spend months in hospitals and nursing homes recovering from the sheer terror of his ordeal on those shell-swept Lulworth hills and the strains and stresses of the whole Maitland affair. He and his mother have now moved away, much to Gus's Milly's friend's disappointment, but even the beauty of our Purbeck countryside cannot heal every wound.

At Railton's trial for murder, the judge, in his summing up, seemed to have been considerably influenced by the officer's service record and character references. For it appeared that he was never considered to have been a 'real leader of men', but a man too easily influenced by others and over-subject to emotional responses to a crisis, rather than rational ones. As a result, further promotion from his rank of captain was considered by his superiors to be unlikely and even his current rank was questioned on more than one occasion.

These influences, together with the medical evidence of the effects of frontal lobe tumours in often freeing the individual from normal inhibitions, thus led the judge to ask, 'How many of us here in the courtroom today have not had murderous thoughts about someone or other we know or of whom we have heard? But our thoughts are not normally translated into actions, because over thousands of civilizing years, the human animal has developed inhibitions about his aggressive instincts and thus controls them. But by the same coin, how many of us here today can say, hand on heart, that were some dread providence to blank out these civilizing control factors, that we would not be tempted, as you may consider the poor, tragic Mary Maitland to have been, to give in to . . . etcetera, etcetera, etcetera.' You can imagine the rest.

This line of reasoning, together with the oft repeated in different forms at the trial, 'Mary Maitland's long years of subjugation, denial, indifference and at times, even humiliation at the hands of her husband, must have gradually generated a heat of resentment that, at some time, just had to boil over . . .' led the jury and indeed, most people in the courtroom it would seem, to temper their condemnation of the murderer with more than a little sympathy for him, as well as, of course, for Mary Maitland. Railton saluted the court in strict military style after his life sentence had been delivered.

The boys at our local TV station, as might be expected, enjoyed and exploited to the full the scoop of their lifetimes. And they now have a regular late-night programme for phone-ins giving possible leads on local crime, burglaries, muggings and the like. It's called 'CrimeBusters'. No prizes for guessing who is now chief researcher on following up those leads, and co-producer of the whole shebang. I said 'researcher', not 'presenter', notice. Arabella ultimately decided that there is no real way a leopard can change his spots (bar one, that is. And heaven forbid) and that her particular cat preferred the dark jungle of the backroom to the blinding glare of the presenter savannah.